W9-CZH-655

Hard, Hard City

Hard, Hard City

Jim Fusilli

Property Of
Bayport-Blue Point
Public Library

LARGE PRINT

This large print edition published in 2004 by
RB Large Print
A division of Recorded Books
A Haights Cross Communications Company
270 Skipjack Road
Prince Frederick, MD 20678

Published by arrangement with Penguin Books Limited

Copyright © 2004 by Jim Fusilli

All rights reserved. No part of this book may be reproduced in any form or by
any electronic or mechanical means, including information storage
and retrieval systems, without permission in writing from the publisher, except by
a reviewer who may quote brief passages in a review.

This book is a work of fiction. Names, characters, places and incidents
either are products of the author's imagination or are used fictitiously.
Any resemblance to actual events or locales or persons, living or dead,
is entirely coincidental.

Publisher's Cataloging In Publication Data
(Prepared by Donohue Group, Inc.)

Fusilli, Jim.
  Hard, hard city / Jim Fusilli.

  ISBN: 1-4025-8501-2

1. Orr, Terry (Fictitious character)—Fiction. 2. Private investigators—New York
(State)—New York—Fiction. 3. Large type books. 4. New York (N.Y.)—Fiction.
5. Mystery fiction. I. Title.

PS3606.U85 H37 2004b
813/.6

Printed in the United States of America

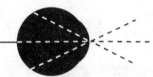

**This Large Print Book carries the
Seal of Approval of N.A.V.H.**

To my brother Greg

Whoever can be trusted with very little can also be trusted with much, and whoever is dishonest with very little will also be dishonest with much. So if you have not been trustworthy in handling worldly wealth, who will trust you with true riches?

— LUKE 16:10–12

PROLOGUE

I take it whenever I can find it. Time, I mean; specifically, time in the present, the now. This moment, before it dies. I take it and I hold on to it, I try to hold on to it; try, but it's a slinky thing, an ethereal thing. Here, gone. Now. You know, *now*, as opposed to *then*, the past. Stay here, be now. Be here now. Be here now so I no longer daydream of the past, about what was. Fantasize about what I wish had been. Living now is the antidote for fantasy and, sometimes, for fear.

(Oh. You knew that already? Sorry.)

Anyway, anyway, I try to live now, not then, not whenever else. I fail often. (Like, what? About every 30 seconds or so?) But I don't bruise myself over this failure, this repeated failure, this repeated . . . I mean, I'd spent much of the past five, six years daydreaming, fantasizing about Marina and our son, about Marina, mostly, and the wonderful years we spent together, all sun and stars, as she created the art that brought her world-wide acclaim, dabs of autumn orange on her olive fingers, a smudge of cerulean blue above her

1

eyebrow; later, I'd find the tiniest dot of wheat green below her navel, as I descended to kiss the inside of her thigh.

And then there's me: in the back of the house, writing my book, articles; and in the playpen, Davy, rattling his plastic keys, grasping at a chiming ball. Cooing, gurgling, laughing: Christ, that toothless smile. "Yah, yah, yah, yah, yah!" says Davy Orr. "Yah!"

Marina adoring me, the American man who shared a family and fulfillment with this beautiful Italian artist. And me, I . . . As for me . . .

She created me too. Made a cocky jock from small-town Jersey into a man who dared write, explore, think, feel. Love. What I was before, and what I was with her: Solar systems could fit easily in the gap between the two. Eternities.

(Forgive me if I've told you this before. It helps me, sometimes, to remember why I fail.)

The stroller rolled off the platform, she tried to grab it—

In fact—time to rebut a fantasy now—she did not try to grab it. She was not there.

She was with another man, kissing him fervently. A man who was "cosmopolitan, elegant, European. Everything you're not."

Or so I've been told. By a woman who had been shot. By me. (Actually, I didn't shoot her, but I decided it would be best if we said I did, D and me. A little less messy.)

But Marina left that man's embrace, and she

ran around the rusted girder, and then she dove onto the tracks to retrieve our boy.

But the express train, rumbling—

And so there you have it. She did not adore me. I had been deceived.

Perhaps I'd always known.

She did not adore me, yet she tried to save our son.

Dismiss her, Terry Orr, send her back to the stars, to the corner of the cosmos reserved for women who betrayed their vows, for a woman whose passion for another man would allow her to ignore her child as he tumbled to his death.

Or deliver her to a magnificent place among the angels, satin pillows, Bach, the smell of azaleas, the skin of a peach, always a warm, soothing breeze, where women who surrendered their lives for their children are rightfully exalted.

"Terry. Listen, man. Don't go off on me or nothing," Diddio said, as we pulled linoleum in the Tilt, sweat dripping off our noses, dirt caked under our nails. "But this guy Loretta mentioned . . . the guy Marina . . . I mean, are you going to, you know, kill him or something? Kill him dead?"

And so I try to live now, not then, not whenever else. Wherever else.

D and I, we went three layers down, slicing away the years, tearing through what had once been new, a source of pride, and we found scraps of old wallpaper under the tiles. Faded orange and dull cerulean blue. Wheat green.

"'Cause, you know, T, you do and they know it's you," Diddio went on, when I failed to reply. "And then what's going to happen to Gabby? Right? I mean, you go to jail, man, and what happens to Gabriella?"

I'd already had this conversation with myself.

I was on my knees, and I looked up, wiped my brow with my forearm. "D, are we working here or what?"

He stuck out his bottom lip. Dejected, he muttered, "Working." Rebuffed, he tugged on his long, stringy black hair.

A minute later, maybe less, I said, "Sorry, D."

"Yeah, yeah," he sighed, as he gathered chunks of linoleum, "I know."

Yesterday, we tossed them toward the barrel like Frisbees, laughing as Diddio played some old Airplane, psychedelic guitars, on Leo's jukebox. Today, no laughs.

"Put on some music, D," I said. "Cheer me up. Like you do."

Diddio liked that: Put on some music and change the mood. Share the joy.

He dusted his dirty hands on his equally dirty jeans.

"And I'm not going to kill him," I added.

"Good, man," he nodded as he stepped gingerly around patches of old glue. "Because of Gabby, right?"

4

No.

Because I don't want to know him, don't want
to see him.

I don't want to know what else I'm not.

You know what?" she asked, as we crossed Canal,
heading back to TriBeCa, a $200 pair of Nike
high-tech b-ballers in the red sack at the end of
her arm. "You're lazy."

"Out of nowhere, Bella," I replied, turning west
on Beach, moving toward the river. I had to bribe
her with new shoes to get her to go for a walk
with me.

"It's a month since you saved Weisz or whatever, and you haven't done anything. *Niente.*"

A month since she took my P.I. license and hid
it in her room, and I've done nothing?

I began an outline for a bio of Weisz; resumed
researching the life of George Jones, publisher of
the *Times* during the breakup of the Tweed Ring;
and worked some of my agent's suggestions into
Bella's Mordecai Foxx manuscript.

Didn't go five minutes, though, three minutes,
without drifting away.

At the request of its principal, Everett Langhorne,
I turned out a couple of Wall Street deadbeats who
bounced checks to the Zora Neale Hurston School
up in Harlem. That last job gave me a chance to
revisit Mabry Reynolds, the school's tough yet kind-
hearted head of security, a man I'd come to respect.

5

That took my mind off, you know, things for a couple of days.

"I'll try to stay busy," I said as we reached Greenwich.

"Busy isn't working. Writing: That's working."

"How about if I go look for a few archcriminals?"

She turned up her pretty nose. "You go to hell for wasting your talent, you know."

To our right, a fat red sun hung above the Jersey palisades. It was early October then, three months ago, but it felt like mid-August, and dumb-ass stories about global warming speckled the tabloids and local TV news. The summery scent of sticky tar was still in the air.

"You'll have to give me a little more on your doctrine," I said. "A hell full of lazy writers, ventriloquists, lethargic shamans . . ."

"You laugh now," my daughter said. "But we'll see in a thousand years who's laughing."

Running now on the riverside, the slap of icy water against the rocks below me, the rattling of the floes, darkness, the Empire State Building in the distance, the George Washington Bridge. Sidewalks thatched with black ice. Running on West Street, and I was thinking of Bella and Julie, thinking hard now, the two of them back at home on Harrison, now, my daughter and my girlfriend, the fluttery lightness of their conversations, their

6

laughter ringing like a song, and maybe they did get along as well as it seemed, and maybe they were laughing now as they tried to whip up a beef Stroganoff from memory, Beagle staring up at them, eager for scraps. Julie, clad in a mulberry cardigan over black cords, black stockings; Bella, who dressed as if she had raced through a thrift shop and wore whatever stuck. Julie, shoes off, three, four inches shorter than Bella. Bella, no baby fat now; all gone.

Maybe they did look a little bit alike, these two Italian-Americans with their brown hair, brown eyes. Diddio said that. Leo too.

Bella certainly didn't look like me, and it wasn't just my nose, broken twice, that defined the difference.

Bella had Marina's lips, the way they curled at the corners, and her—

Like her mother, Bella could be prickly, more so with time, though never with Julie, rarely with Beagle or her friend Daniel Wu. Julie, as even-tempered as a monk; Julie, always hopeful. Though circumspect, as in thoughtful, astute.

Circumspect. That can't be the right word for a woman as sexy, as, you know, when the door is shut and the lights are down low.

Those black stockings. Thigh-high, rose lace. Black bikini panties. For me.

Of Bella, Julie said, "Terry, I'm sure you know this, but Gabriella is amazing."

"Well, I don't think I can take much credit for

that," I said, as we strolled past a Beaux-Arts townhouse not far from her apartment in Kips Bay. "She was amazing from day one."

There's amazing Bella, age nine or so, with Marina and Mrs. Maoli, our stout housekeeper in her *schmatte* and perpetual apron, on the small patch of grass in our backyard, the summer sun bathing them as they watched Davy struggle to walk on stout, rubbery baby legs.

"Go, Davy!" Bella shouted as he tottered toward us. "You're doing it!"

Look at him smile. Listen to that laugh. Pure joy: a boy surrounded by love, acceptance.

Running now, pushing it, a good, crisp pace, and I could see out of the corner of my eye the jagged cliffs, headlights over on River Road.

I heard the water rush and roil, heard the ice groan.

I looked at the concrete beneath me, a blur as I ran, my legs churning, my pulse climbing, and I heard the rustle of my nylon sweats. I saw patches of ice, rock salt cast far from where water had trickled, a few old dried leaves, a discarded ballpoint pen, a wrapper from a Chunky bar.

They're good with a tawny port or Madeira, reports *Wine Spectator*. The nuts, raisins, the not-too-sweet chocolate . . .

★ ★ ★

I was walking home from Sunday mass, by myself, coming up Buchanan Avenue, and I was thinking of what I usually thought about when I was nine years old, amusing myself with reflections on, what, comic books, John Tunis novels, the college basketball season that had ended months earlier, stuff on TV, homework, the bullies and jerk-offs in my fourth-grade class. It was late March, and certainly cold, for I had on my winter jacket and earmuffs to buffer myself against the winds off the Hudson that rushed past Adams Street and assaulted at each intersection, the main thoroughfare in Narrow's Gate.

I had chosen to give up candy for Lent, a modest sacrifice since it wasn't my weakness as much as were Wise potato chips, Cheez Doodles and the like. But it was a popular offering among the students at St. Matthew the Apostle Elementary School, one sanctioned by Sister Mary Thomas, the stern principal who insisted we put aside our candy money for so-called mission babies in Africa and elsewhere.

My sole duty on the way home from nine-o'clock mass was to pick up the Sunday *News* for my parents, and when I stopped in Kaessmann's, there was a crowd at the newsstand, jostling at the register, a layer of blue cigarette smoke near the tin ceiling, and, surrounded by grown-ups, I slipped into a corner, near the candy rack, to wait my turn, and I looked down, saw a Chunky bar in the rack and, without giving it a second's thought, I reached out, grabbed it, slipped it into my pocket. Moments later, I paid for the newspaper, made no mention of the candy, and I left the store.

With the Sunday *News* tucked under my arm, I slithered over to Eighth Street, off Buchanan, closer to Cleveland Street, and I ripped off the silver wrapping and ate the thick Chunky in three bites. From impulse to theft to devouring the fruit of the crime took maybe 60 seconds, during which I went from a boy pure of heart and soul to someone who had violated a commandment and, thus, committed a mortal sin.

Guilt consumed me, and I felt my face flush with shame.

After four and a half years of indoctrination, I knew full well that were I to die between now and my next confession, I would go directly to hell.

And rightly so, for I was a common thief.

I was still trembling when I put the newspaper on the kitchen table.

"What?" my mother said, as she came toward me. "What did you do?"

She was in her housecoat, and her ever-present Winston sat in the black lacquered ashtray that had once been in the Elks Club. Dark-brown Chock Full o' Nuts coffee lingered in her cup.

"I—"

Some Jack Jones schmaltz wafted from the radio on the counter.

I brought my fist from my coat pocket, opened it and revealed the Chunky wrapper.

She gasped. "You ate candy?" Her socks allowed her to glide on the yellow linoleum.

I am sure that, at this point, she was teasing: My mother didn't gasp when she was upset, and things like Lent or noble sacrifice didn't mean much to her.

But I had done a terrible wrong.

"Ma, I st— I stole it from Kaessmann's," I stammered, my throat catching. "I—"

I didn't see her hand, didn't see the blow.

She smacked me across the face with as much force as she could muster, and my head snapped back.

As I reached for my stinging cheek, she shoved me.

"Get out of my sight," she spit. "You miserable little *thing* you. Get— Go to your room."

I scurried off and she chased me.

"I'm going to tell Eddie," she charged, her finger jabbing the air, "and they'll throw you in jail, you thief. You're nothing but a common thief!"

When she was angry, and irrational, my mother's voice was a hideous screech.

I knew my uncle wouldn't have me put in jail. They'd been threatening that for years for crimes as minor as waking up from a nightmare while they watched TV, Schaefer beer and Seagram's 7 flowing, generic lemon-lime soda, pretzel sticks, A&P-brand peanuts, my mother and uncle, my

11

grandmother too, with my reticent father on his side of the sofa, dull eyes fixed on the screen.

But hell was something else, and I cried in my room, and I prayed until my father came home from visiting his sister down on Second and Garfield, in the Italian section of town, and he was assaulted by my mother's voice, her harangue. I was his son now, and I was his problem, and what was he going to do about it? And my poor gullible father, who spent all week, save Wednesdays and Sundays, on his feet for 10 hours a day in Anthony's Barber Shop, and who, to my knowledge, never wronged anyone, had never stolen anything, came to get me and, taking my hand, he brought me to Kaessmann's and I paid for the Chunky, sliding a dime across the counter toward Helga, and we went home, and I stayed in my room until the following morning when my mother sent my sister Regina to see if I was ready for school.

(Of course I was. I was sitting on my bed in my blue uniform pants, white short-sleeved shirt and blue clip-on tie. Hands folded, I'd been ready since 5:30 a.m.)

CHAPTER 1

"**B**ella, I'm right-handed. Bo's right-handed,"
I said, as I went to retrieve the ball. "Throw
it to my right. High, real high."
She'd snapped it toward my belt, just as I posted
up to the left of the lane. Not a bad pass, but I'd
have to stop, catch it and bring it up before I could
take a shot. Unless I went left, under and up,
jabbing an elbow into my man's kidney.

"Let's do it again." Monday night, and we were
alone at the far end of the gym at the Carmine
Rec Center, the dull scent of sweat clinging to the
dry air. Bella worked summers here, and after the
games ended for the Wall Street gang, scurrying
since the Downtown Athletic Club closed, they
let us in, let us be, the father and daughter running
drills in an empty gym, sneakers squealing, 10:15
p.m.

She said not a word, gestured for the ball, tucked
it under her left arm, used the bottom of her blue
Whitman High T-shirt to wipe her red face.

"Go to half-court," I said as I strolled to the top
of the key.

It wasn't going well for my daughter, no. Coach

Guidry insisted she join the varsity squad, making her and Bo the only sophomores on the team, and yet Bella barely got five minutes' playing time per game. If she dropped any lower on the roster, they'd use her to give fouls.

Bella wasn't accustomed to failure. She didn't like it, not at all.

"Ready?"

My right knee was throbbing. Last night, I went at it too hard, ran north on West Street, then 11th Avenue, like a stand-in racing to Broadway before the curtain went up. I must've had something on my mind.

"Let's go," she said, determined.

She dribbled to the key as I slid down the lane to the post. Drifting to her left, she looked around, looked at me, stopped the dribble. And she threw the ball maybe eight feet above my outstretched arms, way, way above my open palm.

"Shit," she said, slamming down her sneaker in disgust.

"Be easy," I told her as I went after the ball. "You'll get it."

I wasn't sure she'd get it; she had little instinct for the game. But she'd die trying. We had that in common: both stubborn, thick as bricks.

I lifted the ball with one hand, put it on my hip as I went toward her.

"What are you doing here?" she said, her voice raw with frustration.

"Me?"

"What?" asked Daniel Wu, as he came up behind me. "I'm banned?"

"Daniel," I said, nodding a greeting.

"It's not going very well, is it?" he whispered.

"*Daniel . . .*" Bella said, impatiently.

They'd spent the late afternoon together, working in our living room on a project they called Operation Tip-Top, which, I was told, was none of my business. ("Dad, butt out. Please.") Also none of my business was Daniel's whereabouts on Saturday night; he stuttered, opened his eyes wide, when I asked him where he'd been. But I had it figured, at least the Saturday part: When Bella and Daniel were apart, she was with Marcus, the boyfriend I wasn't supposed to know about. Her friend Glo-Bug was the beard.

"We're kind of busy here," Bella said.

Pudgy Daniel had the collar of his fat black coat up over his ears. Undeterred, he tugged it down to have his say.

"In fact, I am here to speak to your father." His eyes were moist, his stout cheeks red, from the cold wind that bullied Varick Street.

"Really?" Bella and I said it at the same time. The Orr choir, voices now down to two.

"Yes. If nobody minds."

I tousled his hair. "Mind? Not me, Daniel. You know that."

"What?" Bella asked as she walked toward us. "Tell me first."

15

"Ha," he replied, smiling triumphantly. "I'm not such a bother now, am I?"

"I'll tell you what, Daniel," I said as I handed Bella the ball. "Give us 10 minutes to nail this move and we'll talk."

Daniel agreed, unzipped his down coat, withdrew *Slaughterhouse-Five* from an inner pocket, went toward a plastic chair that had been tucked haphazardly under the scorer's table.

"I've never heard of this kid," Bella said.

She and I were sitting on the gym floor, sweating still, and Daniel was up in the chair, which now wore his coat. He had the ball in his lap; he had traded it for the dog-eared Vonnegut, the subject of a Lit class at Whitman called, appropriately, Vonnegut.

"I don't see how you could have," he replied. "You're not friendly with Elixa."

"She's a follower, Dad. Tats, the nose ring, the constant hoody, old Doc Martens," she explained. "Her protest is conventional, if you know what I mean. Like long hair in the sixties."

"She's a little weak, is that what you're saying?"

"She yearns for approval," she added, with a definitive nod.

"Be that as it may," Daniel said. "Her friend is missing and she's concerned."

Seems a Whitman student named Elizabeth Oostenbrugge, better known as Elixa, also takes

classes up at the Fashion Institute of Technology. An FIT classmate, one Allie Powell, hasn't been seen, hasn't contacted anyone, nobody knows where he is. Elixa told Daniel she called the kid's home in Silver Haven, New Jersey, and a maid dismissed her without reply. An uncle who lives on the Upper East Side wasn't much help either.

With Daniel at her elbow, Elixa called Silver Haven High School, pretending to be an intern in Admissions at FIT. Alexander Powell was absent, and had been for several days.

"Maybe he just cut class," Bella said as she toyed with the rainbow of rubber bands on her wrists, liberated now from the dark-blue sweatbands she wore over them.

"Never," Daniel replied. "He loves FIT. Elixa says he lives for it."

"Elixa says . . ." Bella mumbled.

"Apparently, this boy has problems," he continued.

"Shouldn't somebody just contact his parents?" I asked.

"They are the problem."

Bella nodded knowingly, and kept doing so, despite my frown. Finally, she smiled wryly.

"What?" I said. "They took away his Benz?"

"He's 14, Mr. Orr . . ."

"They beat him?"

"They may," Daniel said. "That may be why he's staying with his uncle."

"So what do you want me to do?" I asked.

"Perhaps you could make a few inquiries. Maybe you could create a sense that this boy has friends."

"Daniel, this young man has a family, right?"

"Perhaps in name only."

I looked at Bella, who, shrugging, silently repeated her claim that Elixa was unreliable.

Maybe this Allie Powell was sick of his parents' shit and took off for a few days, trying to throw everybody into a panic. Nothing more than that, and me stepping in makes it a soap opera.

She said, "You could talk to the uncle."

"Yeah, I suppose . . ."

"I have the address." Pleased, Daniel spun the ball in his chubby hands. "Would tomorrow be too soon?"

"I have to be in court tomorrow, Daniel. To see Julie—"

"Julie's not up until the afternoon, Dad."

I turned toward Bella. "You'll have to give me back my license."

She grimaced. "Dad, don't make this into a soap opera, all right?"

The following morning, after a short, shivering run over to SoHo and back, a shave and a hot shower, I called John McPorter, introduced myself and asked if I could drop in on him at his home on East 64th. An amiable man with a

soft, accommodating voice, he told me he needed an hour or so to make his place neat enough for company. He never asked why I wanted to see him.

By the time I dressed in a navy-blue V-neck sweater over a faded blue T-shirt, jeans and old running shoes, walked to Lafayette at Canal, took the Lex line up to 59th and pushed through the crosstown wind and made my way to 64th and Park, my hands over my ears, the hour had passed.

Dodging traffic that raced north and, on the other side of the snow-flecked island, stuttered and lurched toward the gold-topped Helmsley building, I scooted across Park, went down 64th and found McPorter's place. The red-brick building, on the south side of the street, was set back from the line of brownstones that stretched along the block, and resilient weeds poked through the cracked concrete behind its shoulder-high cast-iron fence. High above me, an engraved stone cornice, which preceded the arrival of the bland brick face by perhaps 75 years, was chipped and tattered, and it tilted awkwardly, as if the building's foundation had shifted and one side sunk into sediment. Black cast-iron guards, which looked like small, rounded fences, protected the lower half of each window, even those of the top floor.

As I ran my eye down the three-story front, I saw that the top-floor apartment lacked the storm windows the other two apartments had, and its blinds were arranged to form an unbending line. McPorter's place, I wagered silently; that flimsy window, and the care he'd taken to make it look its best, offered a glimpse into the home of an accommodating, and perhaps undemanding, man who had prepared for a visitor.

I got no reply when I first rang his buzzer, but when I pressed the black nip again, I heard a window open. Peering again into the silver sky, I saw a key, floating miraculously as it descended toward me. When it reached me, I removed it from the fishing line, opened the door and headed up stairs that seemed to sway under each step.

McPorter was in his mid-to-late 60s, bald except for the white hair above his ears, with a paunch under his brown corduroy shirt and burgundy sweater-vest. He wore khakis and his slippers almost matched his shirt.

"Come in, my son," he said as he shook my icy hand. "My goodness, you must be chilled to the bone."

As I handed him his key, he stepped aside and let me enter the narrow corridor of his apartment. I could see a tiny kitchen behind him. His collection of spices sat on a lazy Susan at the center of a small table set for one.

As I unzipped my jacket, he said, "A cup of tea will do wonders. Warm the bones. Warm the—"

The tea kettle beckoned.

He smiled as he threw a thumb over his shoulder. "The Lord provides."

I was going to tell him the Lord had provided the 12-degree weather outside too, and the howling wind, but I didn't. No sense antagonizing a contented man.

"Please," he said, "find your way to the living room and I'll join you."

"Mr. McPorter, don't you think you ought to be sure you know who I am?"

"Why, you're Terry Orr," he replied. "The private investigator."

The kettle whistled furiously behind him.

"How do you know?" I asked.

"Ho, ho," he laughed. "A test? Fine, fine." He patted me on the leather sleeve. "For one, I recognized your voice from your telephone call."

I looked down at him. "I don't believe my voice is all that distinct—"

"But more to it, you have been sent to me to recover my belongings," he smiled.

"Your belong—"

"Now, you go sit. Sit and gather yourself. I'll be right back."

As he went toward the kitchen, I turned and moved toward the living room, which was meticulously kept, with an old sofa and matching love seat arranged to face the TV or the framed reproduction of a Warner Sallman painting of Jesus above it. McPorter had a bird in a cage, a green canary with a bit of orange above its beak, and the little bird flitted back and forth along its thin, wooden stand.

"You like it in there?" I whispered softly to the bird. It looked askance at me, then jumped away to cling to the other side.

On the nest of tables, he had several framed snapshots: McPorter in Vatican Square, McPorter in Paris, near Notre Dame. McPorter in front of Marie-Reine-du-Monde in Montreal.

In one of the frames was a photo of a man about my age, maybe a few years older, with sad eyes, a pleasant if forced smile, and a good solid body under a Chelsea Fitness T-shirt, standing in front of the Empire Diner on 10th and 22nd, a phalanx of yellow cabs rolling by. He looked like a younger version of McPorter, but the minivan taxis said the shot was recent, maybe taken in the past year or so.

Behind the sofa was a rollaway bed, done up and secured, as if McPorter had recently had a guest who left but might return. Young Allie, maybe. Probably, if Elixa had her facts right.

"Have you met Penelope?" McPorter asked as he entered, carrying a tray with a green porcelain teapot, matching cups and saucers, a pitcher of milk, a sugar bowl and two spoons. He set it on the table next to a candy dish filled with peppermints.

The cuff of his brown shirt had pulled back, and I saw he was wearing a WWJD bracelet. I knew the initials stood for "What Would Jesus Do?"

"The bird? Yes," I said, as he placed the tray on the table. "Very lively."

"I let her fly around when there's no one home," he said as he gestured for me to sit on the sofa that faced the TV, and Jesus.

"You'd better keep the windows closed."

"Oh, I trust Penelope will fly right back to me, Mr. Orr."

And I trust she'd be a light snack for the scruffy cats that prowled the alleys behind the row of brownstones.

"Is this your son?" I tapped the glass in the frame.

He smiled proudly. "Yes. Yes it is."

"There's a resemblance."

"I think so." He sat in the love seat and poured me a cup of hot tea.

"English breakfast," I said, as I went to the sofa.

"Indeed. Are you an expert on tea, Mr. Orr?"

I told him about Diddio's venture, the tea bar on Hudson.

"Well, God bless him then," he said as he lifted his delicate cup as if to toast D and the Tea Water Pump.

I pretended to take a sip, pausing to let the steam rise into my face. I loved D, but hated tea, especially now that I'd drunk several gallons in the past two months or so.

"Mr. McPorter, I'm interested in your nephew Allie," I began.

"Oh, he had nothing to do with it."

I shook my head in confusion. "With what?"

23

"My belongings," he replied as he eased back on his soft seat. "I imagine the police have told you most of what you need to know."

I could tell him I hadn't been sent by the police, but that might prevent him from opening up about the missing boy.

"Maybe you should go over it again. So I can hear it in your own words."

"My pleasure," he smiled.

He had gone uptown on Madison to do his food shopping, and when he returned, his wall safe was open and empty. Gone were $471 and a few manila envelopes his son Buddy had stored with him. No sign of forced entry, he said. And no, he hadn't left the back window to the fire escape open, nor did he believe that his neighbors had inadvertently buzzed in a burglar—the couple downstairs, dancers who entertained on cruise ships, were away, and the old woman and her matronly daughter who owned the building guarded it with irrational zeal. Besides, if someone had gotten in, McPorter said, they'd still have had to bypass his two deadbolts.

"So no one came into your apartment while you were out," I said, "but your stuff is gone."

"Yes," he replied.

"Let's see. . . . Did anyone ever run off with your key when you hung it out on the fishing line?"

"Oh no," he said heartily.

"You lend your keys to anyone?"

He sipped his tea and shook his head. "Except for my nephew, no one. No."

Here we go. "Allie," I said. "Tell me about him."

"Well, speaking technically, I suppose, he's not my nephew," he said, as he returned his cup to the tray. "He's the son of a family friend, actually, and he was staying with me for a while. To ease the commute."

From Silver Haven, New Jersey.

He said, "He attends FIT—Fashion Institute of Technology?"

"Yes, I know FIT."

"He's a good boy," he continued. "Young for his age. A little shy, if you know what I mean. But a good boy."

I scratched my forehead. "Did Allie have the keys on the day your safe was broken into?"

"Yes," he replied.

"Your keys or copies?"

"Copies."

"Mr. McPorter," I said as I edged forward on the sofa, "does Allie know the combination of your safe?"

"I don't believe— Mr. Orr, are you suggesting Allie stole from me? No, no, I can assure you."

He waved at me and let out a jovial laugh.

"Why not?" I asked.

"He's not that kind of boy," he said. "My goodness, we knew him in the womb, Buddy and I. His mother, Alexandra, is our dear, dear friend.

Besides," he added, "the police found out that Allie was in class that afternoon. Witnesses, Mr. Orr. Didn't they tell you?"

I dropped a sugar cube into tea and watched it dissolve. "Mr. McPorter, do you think Allie might have lent his key to someone? A friend? Someone he thought of as a friend who turned out to be . . . disreputable?"

"I asked him not to."

"And he always did what you asked?"

He nodded, shutting the lids over his kindly blue eyes.

"That's a remarkable boy," I said.

"Allie is a good boy. A good boy. Perhaps he could use a little bit of the rebel in him, if you were to ask me. Too mild, too amenable. Buddy agrees."

I looked at McPorter. I couldn't get my mind around him. He was an odd combination of naïveté and common sense, of childlike trust and stark practicality. John McPorter, whimsical pragmatist.

"Can you show me the safe?" I asked.

He stood. "Follow me."

We entered his bedroom, which was decorated with the same simple, down-home touch as was the rest of the place. An embroidered comforter, all pale blues and yellows, was spread across his double bed, and his two pillows were fluffed and stacked near the headboard. On the wall that faced the front of the house, a framed, hand-stitched sampler hung between the two windows. It read, SURELY GOODNESS AND MERCY SHALL FOLLOW ME ALL THE DAYS OF MY LIFE; AND I WILL DWELL IN THE HOUSE OF THE LORD FOR EVER."

"It is so," McPorter said, nodding solemnly, as he caught me reading.

He had a Bible on his nightstand, and on the wall opposite the foot of the bed, above a bare mantle, a large, vertical photo of a sunset on what appeared to be a cold, cold winter day. A huge, shimmering orange orb disappeared behind a proud lighthouse and the ocean's edge.

"God's work," he said softly.

"It's good," I said, as I stepped closer to it. "Who's the photographer?"

"It's Allie's mother," he replied. "Alexandra Powell."

On the black lacquer frame around the photo was a hinge, and behind the cold sun was the safe.

The Palmer unit had a five-button mechanical keypad on its face.

"Could you open it?"

As I held up the frame, McPorter stepped in and tapped out 2-3-6.

"Mr. McPorter, you just gave me the combination to your safe."

"Yes, but it's empty."

There was nothing on either shelf.

"Did Allie ever see you open it?"

"No," he said as he shut the door.

I nudged the photo back into place.

"I should say I don't *think* he saw me," he added.

"So only you and Buddy know the combination?"

He nodded. "I'd say that's right."

I saw the framed sampler out of the corner of my eye, and I pointed to it. "Twenty-third psalm. Sixth verse," I said. "Your combination—two, three, six."

"Well done," he smiled and once again tapped my arm. "You know your Scripture. Good for you, Mr. Orr."

I turned. "That crucifix over there," I said. "It's gold-plated, isn't it?"

"Why, yes," he said.

"And that portable radio near your Bible, the Grundig. It's a short-wave, right?"

"You can receive broadcasts from all over the world. Vatican Radio, for instance. Or the Church of England. "

I walked toward his chest of drawers. "What's this?"

Two coins sat on a small red-velvet throw.

"Those are my Judas Coins," he replied as he came up behind me.

"Do you mind . . ."

"No, please. Go right ahead."

I looked at the silver coins. They were battered and worn from age, and the images on the front and rear were barely discernible.

"I bought those in Italy," he said, laying his hand on my shoulder. "Near the Vatican."

"What period—"

"They are my Judas Coins," he repeated. "I believe they are two of the thirty the Pharisees gave to Judas to betray Christ."

"I see." I eased the coins onto the red velvet.

He stepped away as I turned, and he edged past his bed, toward the mantle. "You doubt?"

"Well, it doesn't seem likely," I said, "but what I'm thinking is that no one stole them, or the cross, or the radio. Or your wallet next to the coins."

"Well, the wallet was in my pocket when I went to the butcher's, but I see your point." He shrugged. "I suppose they wanted the $471."

"Yes, but the coins, whether they are or aren't two of the Judas coins, are surely worth more than $471, no?"

He smiled benignly and gestured for me to return to his living room.

Penelope chirped happily when he entered behind me, and he gently tapped her cage in response.

He sat next to me on the sofa.

"Mr. Orr, I have accepted the Lord Jesus Christ into my life," he said patiently. "I have given a great deal of thought to it, especially as I recovered from my bypass surgery, and I tell you with all openness that I have freely chosen to live as I do, and I have never been happier or more contented."

"No, Mr. McPorter, you don't under—"

He placed his hand on the knee of my jeans. "If I choose to accept that my two silver tetradrachms came from the hand of Judas Iscariot, one of the

29

twelve, a man who communed with Jesus, what is the harm? Can you tell me?"

I hesitated, and I turned to face him. "Mr. McPorter, I'm not questioning your faith. Please, and I apologize if I came across as if I had. But I'm here, you know, on more worldly matters. What we have here is a missing—"

"Mr. Orr, many coins minted in Tyre have lasted 2,000 years. That in itself is incredible. Given the devotion of the early Christians, isn't it possible they made sure that these particular 30 coins would survive? And that I could acquire two?"

I took a breath and held up my hand. "You know, Mr. McPorter . . ."

"Perhaps it's providence that no one took them."

"I'm sure you're right."

Penelope continued to flit in her cage. She pecked at a dried cornstalk McPorter had provided for her.

I gestured to the folding bed stowed behind the sofa. "Tell me more about Allie."

"Well, he was supposed to return to his parents' house, but he didn't."

"Mr. McPorter," I said, "the money's gone, the safe is empty, the boy is missing and it doesn't add up for you?"

"I wouldn't say he's missing," McPorter said. "He was in class on Friday when the theft occurred, and he went to class on Monday. But he didn't come back here the following Thursday evening. When I called his mother, Alexandra, she said he wasn't at home."

"So he had class on Fridays and Mondays and he'd spend the weekends here?"

"Normally, yes."

"What did he do the rest of the time?" I asked.

"Why, he went to Silver Haven High, of course."

"And it's been several weeks since you've seen him?"

"Let's see. . . . Two weeks today, if I'm right. Two weeks today. But he's with friends, I'm certain."

"What friends?"

He shrugged.

"Here or in Silver Haven?"

"His mother didn't seem particularly concerned . . ."

I reached into my back pocket, lifted out my wallet and handed McPorter one of my business cards.

"If you hear from him," I said, "call me at that number. I'd like to talk to him."

"But I'm sure he has nothing to do with the missing $471, Mr. Orr."

"You may be right." I grabbed my jacket from the sofa's stout arm and slung it over my shoulder. "But I'd feel better if I knew where he was."

He followed me as I edged toward the corridor and his front door.

The door was open. McPorter had failed to shut it when I entered.

"Thanks for the tea, Mr. McPorter," I said as I shook his hand.

As I reached the stairwell, he shouted, "May goodness and mercy follow you, Mr. Orr."

They'd be welcome, I thought, as I zipped up my coat and headed into the cold.

CHAPTER 2

"Yeah, except it's impossible," said Fred. Arnold, proprietor of Fred Arnold's Emporium, one of three coin dealers with a stall at the Manhattan Art & Antique Center, a long, flat storefront on Second, off 56th.

I had my numb hands wrapped around a cup of coffee I'd bought at a Korean greengrocer's across the street, along with an everything bagel, schmear of scallion cream cheese, that I'd eaten in seconds, shivering through every bite.

I would've bought their space-heater if it'd been portable. It was goddamned cold out there. Mike Royko might rise from the grave to strike me down, but Wacker Drive in Chicago's got nothing on the east side of Manhattan when the wind starts to howl.

"Firstly," he said from behind his waist-high glass case, "they would be the stuff of legend. Of *legend.*"

Gruff and ill-tempered, Arnold, who might've been in his late 50s, had the unearthly pallor of a man who abhorred sunlight. His mop of salt-and-pepper hair was too wild to be called merely unkempt, and he had more gray fuzz in his ears than many men his age had on their heads.

I said, "Even if there are only two? You know, somebody broke up the set?"

"Thirty, fifteen, two, one. A half of one. *Dust* from one. Fuckin' *legend,* pal. Come on."

"Look, I didn't say *I* believed it." I was wondering how much McPorter would've had to shell out to buy the coins, which might suggest how much he kept in the safe and pockets. If he had more cash than his apartment showed, young Allie might've made off with better than four Cs and change.

Arnold's stall was one story below street level, across the carpeted lane from Sadeed International Antiques Ltd., another shop that sold other people's stuff. Sadeed didn't have much to distinguish it from the other antique dealers in the center— except for the young woman behind the counter. Almond-shaped eyes, arresting features framed by glowing dark hair she brushed away from her face, a tall and shapely body beneath her forest-green turtleneck sweater.

She noticed me, paused, then smiled.

Christ, that smile could melt—

"Hey," Arnold snapped, "are we talking here or are we talking?"

I turned back to the coin dealer.

"Yeah, all right. Saleha, from Afghanistan too," he moaned. "She's a beauty. I ought to get me one of them for my old age."

"Sorry," I said.

"Secondly," Arnold continued abruptly, "these

coins are going to be in the hands of somebody you and me could know?"

"No." Outside of a small circle of like-minded cranks, no one knows the kind of people who go in for hoarding famous works that had been stolen from museum walls or private collections, for example. When they find the guy who has the Degas, Klee and Monet paintings that once belonged to Ferdinand and Imelda Marcos, he'll be a stranger to *People* magazine, a recluse, a nine-figure cave dweller. "Besides, if these coins existed—"

"You would've heard," Arnold said, "and nobody would've been selling them out of a briefcase or some gift shop in Rome or no place else."

I put the coffee cup on the countertop and looked down at the dozens of coins, multicolored paper money, military medals and memorabilia Arnold had spread on black velvet. Behind him, in his ceiling-to-floor cases, coins sat on little white pillows in tiny boxes.

"The good stuff?" I gestured toward the display case.

"Everything is good," he replied. He started to walk away.

"You wouldn't have any silver tetradrachms, would you?"

He stopped, draping his forearm on a rotating display case of vintage fountain pens—Parker 51s seemed to be his specialty.

"Why? You buying or selling?"

"I'm asking," I replied.

He came back toward me. "I thought maybe you were soaping me up, try to sell me some coins you lifted, say they were from Judas."

"Do I look like a thief to you?"

"Hey, you tell me," he said. "What's a thief look like these days?"

He had a point. None of these corporate executives who dipped into the pension fund and gave themselves interest-free loans while they laid off 5,000 factory workers looked like Chester Gould had drawn them for *Dick Tracy*. That enticing Afghan girl across the lane could be Ma Barker for all I knew.

Arnold turned his back to me and, using a key hooked to his belt, unlocked a tall glass case. But before he slid open the door, he looked at me and pointed to a video camera on the ceiling.

He dug into the pockets of his baggy gray slacks and produced a shiny purple cloth, not unlike McPorter's red velvet throw. With surprising dexterity, he laid it on the glass and slid two coins on it.

"Tetradrachms," he said. "Struck in Tyre, somewhere between 125 B.C. and A.D. 70. These are in excellent condition, so I'll do the two of them for three . . . no, twenty-eight."

"Twenty-eight—"

"Hundred."

"Wow."

"All depends on the condition," he added. "Like I said, these are as good as you'll find."

Twenty-eight hundred for two coins, and yet somebody might've been content with $471.

"You want more? No problem. I'll give you thirty, you want."

"Me? I don't want any," I said.

"They're a good investment," Arnold replied as he palmed the coins and ran the purple drape back into his pocket. "They're not making any more of these, you know."

"They used to say that about land." I reached for the coffee.

He put the coins back in the case and redid the lock. "Yeah, I know. But if they put any more land-fill in the Hudson, we'll walk to Jersey."

I knew I was wasting his time, and I didn't have much to offer. I mean, I could've bought Bella a World War I Iron Cross or a Louis XV jeton, but it wasn't going to make the day's rent for him.

Behind me, a handful of milling pedestrians and bargain hunters scanned the stalls of Art Deco jewelry, African sculptures and 15th-century textiles. I noticed that Saleha, the girl with jade eyes, had disappeared.

Arnold ran his yellowing handkerchief over the condensation caused by the coffee cup.

I gave him a business card.

"Send your friend with the Judas coins to me," he said.

"I don't think he's selling."

"No, listen, tell him I got a sliver of the True Cross. Tell him I got Peter's ear. A zucchini looks like Paul VI."

He let out a dry, brittle sound, slapped his thigh. Fred Arnold thought Fred Arnold was a riot.

I was luxuriating in the flowing heat in the back of the taxi when I heard my cell phone buzz.

"That's you," said the cabbie. An aged newspaper photo of Atatürk was clipped to his visor.

"Bella, what's up?" Metallic sunlight sun flooded the avenue.

"Nothing much," she said. "I'm in trouble with Coach Guidry."

"Big trouble?" It was hard to image my daughter in any sort of serious difficulty at school. After more than 10 years in kindergarten, elementary school and now high school, Bella had tallied precisely zero minutes in detention.

"Maybe," Bella said.

"What happened?"

"MSG wants to tape a story on Bolanle, 'cause she's African and six-feet-eight and everything, and Bo doesn't want to do it. So Coach told her that they would do it on me and her, not just her, and that would make it all right. You know, two sophomores. But Bo doesn't want to so I told Coach no and now she thinks that it's my fault that Bolanle doesn't want to."

38

"But didn't Bolanle say she didn't want to in the beginning?"

"Dad, Coach wants to be on TV," she said, cutting to the chase.

"What do you want me to do?"

We were stuck trying to cross traffic pouring into the Queens–Midtown Tunnel. I was close to running late to the courthouse, so I wouldn't be able to get to Whitman until day's end.

"If she calls, be ready," she instructed. "But don't yell at her or threaten her or anything. Just be reasonable."

"What does Daniel say?" I asked. At 15, Daniel Wu was the most judicious person I knew.

I heard her put her hand over the phone. Then Daniel came on.

"Mr. Orr, I suggest you tell her that it is an issue for Mr. Otumu," he said. "This will remove Gabriella from the discussion, and it is likely that Coach Guidry will not pursue the matter with him."

Bo Otumu's father, an influential man in his native city of Lagos, was a cultural attaché at the Nigerian embassy. He had a quiet, studious manner that suggested only issues of gravity could occupy his time.

"I like it, Daniel," I said, as the cabbie lurched between two Fruehauf trucks, dodged a dented Toyota wagon and freed us to move down Second, at least until the next red light. "If she calls, that's what I'll do."

"Yes," he said, "so . . . how are you today?"

I could hear the roar and rattle of young voices, the scuffle of footsteps, the tinny bang of locker doors in Whitman's hallways.

"I'm good, Daniel. You?"

"I'm a little concerned about Dennis," he said, calling Diddio by his first name. "Otherwise, I'm fine, thank you." He hesitated. "May I ask if you've had any progress?"

"With Allie Powell? I spoke to his uncle."

"Really? Already?" he asked with good cheer.

"Yes," I replied, "but no progress."

"Oh?"

"Don't worry, Daniel," I said. "I'm on it."

"Thank you, Mr. Orr."

I'd once told him to call me Terry, but he couldn't bring himself to do it.

The Turk and I passed Kips Bay Plaza, where Julie and I caught a midweek movie when the mood struck and Bella was occupied.

"It's exciting," he said, "in its own way, isn't it?"

"Well, I wouldn't say that, Daniel. But it's marginally better than sitting around doing nothing."

"Yes, but Gabriella said you weren't doing nothing. A book, I thought—"

"Only kidding, Daniel."

"Ah. I should have known that."

I told him good-bye as the taxi approached Stuyvesant Square.

The driver said, "We're still going to the same place?"

"Yes," I told him. "Only faster now, all right?"

The taxi dropped me off at Bayard and I scurried past the old Mulberry Bend to 100 Centre Street. I made it through security and up to the fifth floor just as the midday recess had ended.

Sharon Knight, an executive assistant district attorney, noticed me as I shuffled into the musty courtroom, and she nodded her greeting as she eased through the low, swinging gate and joined her staff member at the dark, unadorned table. She leaned over, whispered in Julie's ear. When Julie failed to react, and intently continued to review the notes she carried in her leather folio, Sharon peered at me through a crack amid the reporters who were chatting behind her, and she shrugged.

No, I thought, the arrival of her boyfriend in court isn't going to throw off Julie Giada. Not today.

Meanwhile, Leslie Richard Perlmutter made his way down the center aisle of the courtroom, leading his lawyers, all three of whom wore suits nearly as refined as their client's, a 62-year-old cardiac surgeon who killed his 11-year-old daughter by flicking a surgical scalpel across her throat, and then waited until her 34-year-old mother returned to her boyfriend's apartment from Parents' Night at her elementary school. According to the blood-spatter

41

evidence, when Anna Perlmutter entered the room, she got the same treatment: scalpel across the throat, a severed carotid artery.

Dr. Perlmutter made sure the last thing she saw was her dead child.

Perlmutter had a semblance of an alibi—he was at a conference in Denver, and his flight landed at La Guardia only 95 minutes before the front end of the estimated time of death for Laura Perlmutter.

Dr. Perlmutter's driver said he took him directly to his home in Sutton Place, and claimed he woke him as they eased in front of his apartment building on Beekman.

The doorman saw the groggy doctor enter his building at 7:42 p.m., a critically important fact to Perlmutter's alibi: At 7:30 p.m., while the doctor napped in the back of his Lexus ES300, Donald Cavanaugh, Anna Perlmutter's boyfriend, received a phone call telling him his mother had suffered a heart attack and had been rushed from her home on East 87th Street to Lenox Hill Hospital. The widower Cavanaugh, a senior vice president at PricewaterhouseCoopers, tried to reach the estranged Mrs. Perlmutter, who was in a conference at her daughter's school, where cell phones were forbidden. Panicked, he left Laura, who insisted she could care for herself, and raced uptown from his apartment near Gramercy Park.

When Cavanaugh arrived at Lenox Hill, he learned that his mother wasn't at the hospital. Nor was she at any hospital in Manhattan. Finally, a call to her home found her in good health, watching TV.

When Cavanaugh returned to his apartment, he discovered the two bodies, and the bloody Bard-Parker scalpel that lay on his living room floor.

While it was physically possible for Perlmutter to travel the mile and a half from Beekman Place to Gramercy Park in the allotted time, no one could recall seeing the portly yet elegant physician leave his building, no one saw him make the trip, and no one saw him enter Cavanaugh's building, where his wife and daughter were staying until their new apartment in Park Slope was painted and its bathrooms redone.

NYPD found the cast-iron gate between Perlmutter's luxury building and its red-brick neighbor unlocked, though the building superintendent insisted he'd re-locked it after he set out the trash bags for early-morning pickup.

The cops had no success flipping the driver, Grigoris Costas, who said Perlmutter often let him take the Lexus back to his home in Astoria, Queens.

The only substantive evidence that linked the wealthy doctor to the murder—not the scalpel, which anyone can buy online or at a medical-supply shop—was the two partial fingerprints, thumb and forefinger, left hand, found on and around the doorbell to the Cavanaugh apartment.

Before his lawyers learned of the latent prints,

Perlmutter claimed he'd never visited the Cavanaugh apartment, insisted he did not know where it was.

NYPD, Sharon and Julie postulated that The Surgeon put on his nitrile gloves after he rang the bell, perhaps while his daughter peered at his face through the peephole.

Perlmutter said he had been asleep in his bed, that his speech and myriad meetings at the conference had worn him down, as had the cross-country flight. Earlier, he had called his daughter's school from Denver International to tell them he wasn't up to attending Parents' Night and had requested a private meeting with the principal for the following Monday.

He lawyered up early, but his defense bordered on passionate. "Of course, I was angry with my wife," he admitted. "Angry, and tremendously, *tremendously* disappointed. But why would I kill my daughter? My Laura. My lovely Laura."

Julie thought the answer might lie in his use of the word "my."

Sharon agreed, saying she thought the aging Perlmutter saw his daughter as chattel, as a polite and proper prize, another real-life indicator of his rise from the middle class to great professional success and the wealth and social standing it delivered.

Anna Chalmers Perlmutter, who started out as the 22-year-old trophy wife, had charged cruel and inhuman treatment, and she had been seeking complete custody, with permission to relocate outside the tristate area.

Perlmutter's associates at New York-Presbyterian described The Surgeon as brilliant, erudite, imperial and cunning. ("Cunning, insofar as it can be a positive attribute," added one.) And as a dedicated physician and loving father who would do anything for his Laura.

One of his colleagues pointed out that he had almost cancelled his appearance at the conference in Denver, for which he received a $20,000 honorarium, to attend the Parents' Night meeting.

Strange, Sharon said, that he hadn't attended last year's parents' meeting, or the one held the year before that.

"Ms. Knight," said one of Perlmutter's lawyers, Alfred Prendergast, "clearly you don't understand what it means to be devoted to a child."

Sharon, who was unmarried and childless, understood the sum of Prendergast's comment.

The highest-ranking African-American in the D.A.'s office and well regarded by local, state and national politicians as well as most media, Sharon had presence as well as stature, and she knew how to use her strengths. Stout, with short-cropped hair and piercing eyes, and tough as blue steel, she wasn't going to let a high-gloss stuffed shirt from a white-shoe law firm get away with a personal affront, especially when rebuking him would help her case.

Sharon drew up and stared at Prendergast and,

as the air grew heavy outside the interrogation room, continued to do nothing but hold him in her glare. Until, Julie said, he started to quiver.

"My apologies," he murmured, failing to meet her eyes.

But Prendergast was an extraordinary defense attorney, Julie conceded. And Perlmutter was wealthy—meaning he had far better resources than the People of the State of New York. Prendergast had his experts, including two psychologists who insisted Perlmutter lacked the disposition for such violence, and, among the character witnesses, a renowned research scientist whose credentials made him seem a modern Pasteur.

"It's stacked against us," Julie said.

But there were those two fingerprints . . .

"Yes, Your Honor," Julie said, as she continued to stand while the rest of us returned to our seats.

"Recall Herbert Küsters," said the doughy court clerk.

Küsters walked to the stand for cross.

She's right, I thought, as I watched him settle in the chair. He is impressive—tall, broad, blond with steady dark eyes. I imagine there were those who'd even find his air of smugness and self-satisfaction appealing.

Küsters, a 38-year-old native of Bamberg, Germany, believed fingerprint analysis wasn't a science but an entirely subjective act reliant on the judgment of fallible law-enforcement officials.

Julie said Prendergast would use Küsters to discredit the reliability of the FBI's analysis of Perlmutter's prints. He'd point out that if the accuracy rate of IAFIS's computers for identifying to whom a fingerprint belonged was 99.98 percent, that meant it made 200 errors per every million scans. Which, he'd claim, could indicate that well over 1,000 adults in Manhattan alone might've left those partials on Cavanaugh's door.

Mathematics, he'd say with haughty certainty, proved it was entirely unreliable as a method for ensuring identity.

And the jury members, who entered the courtroom with the belief that fingerprint analysis was foolproof, would discard the State's best evidence.

Folio in hand, Julie came around the table and moved toward the witness. "Mr. Küsters—"

"It's *Dr.* Küsters," he said, politely but definitively.

Which is exactly what I'd said when Julie addressed me as Mr. Küsters on Sunday night as she grilled me in the living room, pacing in front of the silent TV, Beagle watching her intently.

"I'm sorry, Doctor," Julie said now, as she flipped a page in her notebook.

Küsters nodded. His act of forgiveness, of magnanimity, had caused him to swagger slightly, to puff up even further. Though, I noticed, he did not smile.

"You're a Ph.D., aren't you?" Julie asked, as she continued to search her notes.

"Objection," shouted the lanky woman who sat to Perlmutter's left. "Relevance?"

Julie said, "Your Honor—"

"Overruled," replied Judge Levitch, who'd been on the Criminal Court bench for nearly 30 years. He looked tiredly at Küsters. "Answer."

"Yes," replied Küsters, who then said to Julie, "Yes, Ph.D."

"You testified earlier that your degree was in applied mathematics from MIT. Is that correct, sir?"

"Yes."

"Your Ph.D. is in applied mathematics from MIT?"

"No," Küsters responded. He folded his arms across the breast of his brown tweed jacket. "I have my master's in applied mathematics—"

"And your Ph.D.?"

"From the University of Massachusetts," he said sharply.

"Your discipline?" she asked lightly as she paced toward the jury box.

"Atmospheric sciences."

"'Atmospheric sciences,'" she repeated earnestly. "Is that like meteorology?"

"No, not precisely—"

"You're a weatherman, Dr. Küsters?"

The objection was drowned out by the laughter from the jury box.

But Levitch had heard it, and he said, "Move on, Miss Giada."

"Yes, Your Honor," Julie replied, though not before making eye contact with several jurors.

"Now, Dr. Küsters, you have challenged the FBI's assertion that only Dr. Perlmutter could have left those prints on Mr. Cavanaugh's door. Is that correct?"

"Yes," Küsters replied tersely. His face was red, his jaw clenched.

"You do so on the basis that IAFIS is inherently unreliable on the first pass. Is that correct?"

"Yes."

"What about after the Bureau's trained experts examine the run?"

"I don't understand."

Julie remained by the jury box, so that Küsters had to speak directly to the 12 New Yorkers who sat behind her.

"Do they reduce the margin of error?"

"I don't under—"

"Dr. Küsters," said Judge Levitch, "the question seems obvious."

"May I rephrase, Your Honor?" Julie asked.

"Go ahead," Levitch said with a wave.

At the defense table, Prendergast and his minions sat upright.

"You assert that the IAFIS statistical-probability model is imperfect. Is that correct?"

"Yes."

"But do you question the FBI's ability to analyze fingerprints?"

"No one is perfect," he said tersely.

"Yes," Julie nodded, pausing to permit Küsters's admission to sink in. "But to your knowledge, then, has the FBI ever misidentified a person in court on the basis of latent prints?"

"I don't know," he replied.

"Can you cite an example?"

"No," he conceded, "not at this moment."

"All right, Doctor," she said. "Has it ever been shown that two people share the same fingerprints?"

Küsters edged forward in his seat and made an attempt to hide his contempt for this polite young woman, this pert civil servant in the simple navy-blue suit and white blouse.

"No," he blustered angrily. "But it is my contention that—"

"Thank you, Dr. Küsters."

"You are excused, Doctor," Levitch said wearily.

Küsters hesitated, then burst from the stand. His eyes fixed on the exit, he slammed through the gate and stormed angrily toward the back of the courtroom.

As Julie returned to her seat, across the aisle, Prendergast and the rest of the defense team huddled around The Surgeon. When Prendergast made a motion to recess, Levitch responded with a wry crack about dessert, and granted a 10-minute break.

By the time his gavel hit its mark, Küsters was gone.

Julie turned, found me, and she smiled.

I nodded slowly. You done good, I told her. Real, real good.

I was trying my damnedest to think about Bella and tonight's game, about her arcing lob passes to 6-foot, 8-inch Bolanle Otumu, who had been dubbed by the tabloids the Nigerian Nightmare and, inaccurately, the Ubangi Banger. And Bella's looping jump shot from beyond the three-point line when the frustrated defenders collapsed on skinny Bo.

Bella and her awkward jump shot—left hand over her head, the ball in her right hand above her right shoulder, driving into the air with her sturdy calves, her white socks flopping up and down. My daughter—the only girl on the Whitman team who digs for socks with the elastic all stretched out.

Back in high school, I kept my socks all but starched. Of course, I didn't have a ponytail halfway down my back with a dozen or so tiny ribbons woven into my thick brown braids, as Bella did.

Alicia Guidry called her Rainbow, either after the colorful ribbons or the high arc of her shot.

"Coach," Bella replied, "my name is Gabriella."

Later, Coach Guidry said to me, "She knows who she is, doesn't she?"

I let myself think back to my days at St. Barnabas Prep, when I made second-team all-county as a sophomore. The Barnabas Bees, I was thinking;

how great were those gold uniforms, which were really closer to mustard—

I noticed Sharon beckoning me to the prosecutor's table.

"What's up?" I asked as I came through the swinging gate.

"Hey, Terry," Julie said as the two attorneys stood.

She squeezed my hand.

"Excellent, Jule," I said, as I held on to her.

Despite Julie's expression of affection, I felt out of place in front of the bench in my very casual attire.

"Terry," Sharon said, "go see if Costas is outside."

"Perlmutter's driver?"

She nodded.

"And if he is?"

"Bring him up to seven," she instructed. "It's time to deal."

Julie said, "Terry, we think they'll want to plead this out."

"To what?"

"They'll ask for Man II," Sharon replied.

"And you want Man I," I said.

"And he does the max," she said. "But we need Costas to admit he drove Perlmutter to and from Gramercy Park."

"Will he agree?" I asked. "I mean, to the court he's nothing but a chauffeur now."

Sharon said, "We'll tell him he'll be looking at Murder II when Perlmutter gives him up."

"Terry," Julie said, "you have to—"

She suddenly looked past me toward the back of the courtroom.

Out of the corner of my eye, I saw the court clerk come away from her station by Levitch's chamber door and hustle toward us. She seemed startled.

Sharon peered toward the center aisle. "Now what does he want?" she said softly.

I turned and saw Küsters, the fingerprint guy, storming toward us, a look of raw fury in his eyes.

He reached the rail and, without a word, raised his thick hand and slapped Julie hard across her face.

The crack of the blow echoed in the room.

Küsters stood erect, his shoulders arched in defiance.

Julie recoiled from the jolt and tumbled against the table.

As Sharon darted to her, I reached over the rail, but Küsters, without altering his detached expression, backed away—one step, followed by another.

The clerk grabbed me from behind, and a court officer in uniform, nine-millimeter on his hip, clutched my right arm and pinned it against my ribs. One of the reporters leaped in and, putting her hands on my chest, leaned her full weight against me.

"Terry!" Sharon shouted.

Sputtering in fury, I continued to struggle violently to reach Küsters.

Sharon shouted again. "Not now! Terry, not now!"

She turned to a second court officer. "Rudy, get that bastard. Hold him."

The red-faced cop ran around me to grab Küsters.

"You do *not* embarrass a gentleman like me!" Küsters bellowed. "You common— You do not!"

I looked at Julie. Her cheek was red, inflamed, and her eyes were wide open in shock.

"Terry," Sharon said sharply as the court officer shoved Küsters toward the back of the courtroom, toward the exit.

I continued to struggle with the cop, who now had my left arm behind me.

"Terry, I need you here. Here now. Terry!"

One of Perlmutter's lawyers scrambled into the room as his fingerprint expert was hustled out. He stared at Küsters, then looked at Sharon, who met him with an angry glare.

"Johnny," she said to the cop, who had me in a tight grip. "Johnny, let him go."

The stocky black cop released me, but he kept his hands up, as if ready to jump in again.

"Terry," Julie said, "I'm all right. Really."

The other reporters had moved toward her.

"Terry," she repeated.

I looked at her. "Are you sure, Jule?"

She brought the fingers of her left hand to her stinging cheek. "I'm fine."

Sharon told the cop who had held me to nudge the reporters to their seats.

Then she put her hand on my arm. "Terry," she said, "if you want to help us, you'll find Costas, hip him to what's going down and escort him up to my office."

I was seething, and my hands shook at my sides. "Sure," I said.

"We'll deal with this later."

"Terry, please," Julie added. "We need to get this done."

I took a deep breath. "OK," I said, nodding slowly, as if that would help me regain control. "OK."

"Try Baxter Street," Sharon said, as she gave me a gentle nudge. "Costas's been sitting there all week, letting the engine run. Go."

Grigoris Costas was behind the wheel, enjoying the Lexus's heating system, reading the *News*, blissfully unaware of his impending fate.

In his mid-40s, his hair gone gray, the driver was lean but muscular, and his shoulders pressed against his white, short-sleeved shirt. I made him for about 6 feet, 2 inches, which gave me two inches on him, and I figured I had him beat by at least 25 pounds.

But I didn't care if he was as toned as Schwarzenegger back on steroids. He was coming out of that car and he was going upstairs.

I wanted him to protest. Yeah, I wanted that.

I tapped on the window.

He tried to ignore me.

I punched the glass. It rattled but didn't break. Startled, he rolled down the window.

"Grigoris Costas?"

"What's wrong with you?" he protested, tossing his newspaper aside. "You some kind of maniac?"

"Are you Grigoris Costas?"

"Who are you?" he said.

I stepped back as he pushed open the door, jumped out.

A wave of heat followed him onto Baxter.

"Crazy man," he said, "who are you?"

"Mister," I told him, "if that finger you're pointing touches me, I'm going to snap it off and ram it up your sister's ass."

"My sister's—"

I stepped forward and put my nose an inch or so from his.

"We understand each other?" I asked. My breath, a hot cloud of steam in the January chill, blew into his face.

He calculated quickly, then decided to tone it down.

"Crazy man," he mumbled as he slumped.

"The D.A. wants you," I told him. "Get your coat."

"I don't leave the car here," he said.

"Neither of you will be driving for a while."

"What?"

"It's over," I said, "your little charade."

I reached around him, opened the back door

and grabbed his black topcoat off the leather seat.

He wasn't carrying. No gun, blade or sap. Just the latest-model cell phone, palm-sized, almost as thin as paper.

"Your boss gave you up," I said as I tossed him the coat. I held on to his phone.

"I don't talk to nobody unless Dr. Perlmutter— *What?* What did you—"

"The fingerprint man is an asshole," I told him as he wriggled into his garment.

"No way. He's gold, that guy."

"Well, gold buried your boss."

Costas frowned in confusion. "It's not true."

"And Perlmutter's going to save himself from spending the rest of his life in the can by copping to it," I said. "So it's Murder II for you, chump. You might as well have swung the scalpel yourself."

"I don't know nothing, and I didn't do nothing."

I cut the engine and pocketed the key.

"And drop the off-the-boat routine," I said. "You've got a B.S. in chemical engineering from Hunter."

He looked up at me as we started toward Centre Street. "No. He's going to stand by me. Dr. Perlmutter."

"That kind? You ought to know better."

"I say nothing."

"Well, enjoy your 25 years in Greenhaven."

We walked in silence. At the corner near the concrete park, a hot-dog vendor jumped up and down, jogged in place to stay warm.

Costas let out a low groan. *"Ay hyessou."*

"Sure." I had no idea what he meant.

A moment later, he added, "He threatened me, and my mother."

"That's good." I put my hand on his back and gave him a shove. "Go with it when you talk to the D.A."

When we reached Hogan Place and caught the brunt of a harsh, crosstown wind, I said, "Whatever he paid you, it wasn't enough, you know."

He buried his hands deep in his coat pockets.

"The Surgeon's worth about thirty mil. And the kid was insured for four hundred K."

He turned up his collar and slouched through the shadows on Hogan as we moved toward the D.A.'s office.

After I handed off Costas, I snuck out for the shepherd's pie over at a cafe under the Brooklyn Bridge, where I made some calls, one of which was to an 800 number that sent flowers to Julie's cubicle. And now, three hours after I'd initially arrived at Centre Street, I was sitting in front of Sharon's messy desk. She was sipping a splash of Glenlivet on the rocks, while Julie made do with a celebratory Diet Coke.

"All I'll say is, damn it, Terry, you beat me to it with those flowers."

"I send her some every time she gets smacked in the kisser," I replied.

Julie slid the sweating soda can onto her boss's desk, held her cold fingers against her cheek.

"Hurt?" I asked.

"It's fine. It's fine," she told me, a trace of annoyance, a hint of embarrassment, in her voice. "I wish it would just go away."

"Nothing like getting belted to make you feel self-conscious, huh?"

Amused, Sharon said, "Look at you two. You know, I would've never thought it, but I guess you do make a cute couple."

"Well, we know we can both take a punch."

Sharon put down the plastic cup, using an old memo as a coaster.

She'd played it smart, as usual, letting The Surgeon and Prendergast stew while Costas told his tale. When the driver's lawyer arrived from Queens, Sharon offered Man II, which the two Greeks eagerly accepted. Then she told Prendergast that she had Costas in her pocket, and that Man I, maxed, was the best she could offer. She told him, "I'm willing to let the jury make the call."

The Surgeon accepted the offer, and he was going to have to tell it in open court.

Julie had the task of writing up the plea agreement.

"Terry, take her to Montrachet on Friday night," Sharon said as she hoisted her heavy frame out of her leatherback chair.

"On your tab?"

59

She laughed as she stood. "Better make it Ray's Pizza."

As I started to get out of my chair, Sharon told me to stay seated, and she gestured for Julie to come around the desk, where she gave her a motherly hug, two, three pats on the back.

"Outstanding work today."

"Thanks for the opportunity," Julie replied.

I told her I'd call tonight.

When Julie closed the door behind her, Sharon went to the seat next to me and, standing behind it, put her hands on its curved rail. "Are you going to hurt that girl, Terry?"

She was smiling.

"I don't think so, Counselor."

"She's precious."

I nodded. "So I'm told."

"But you can't go after Küsters," she said. "You know that."

"I do?"

"It comes back here, Terry, if you try to play catch-up."

I kept silent for a moment, then I said, "I hear you."

"I'm thinking you've still got a chip on your shoulder—"

"Because of Weisz?" I said as I shifted in the chair. "No, I'm—"

"On your shoulder," she repeated, "and you're looking for a reason to rumble."

I didn't respond. She hadn't meant Weisz and

we both knew it. It's the other guy, the one Marina was with. Diddio, Luther Addison, Sharon Knight, they all ask; Bella would too, if she knew.

"Terry . . . ?"

"I'm done with ghosts, Sharon. Echoes of the past and all that shit. And I'm not looking to get even."

Now she stayed silent and she bit her bottom lip as she studied me.

"Good," she replied finally, "good. How's Gabriella?"

"Great," I said. "She's got a game today. In about 55 minutes."

She tapped the hardwood rail twice, then returned to her desk. "That's it."

I stood, gathered my coat.

"Terry, don't go after that man," she repeated. "I'll take care of him."

"I understand."

"All right," she said. "Now, go kiss your sweetheart good-bye. And tell Gabriella to score a few baskets for me tonight."

CHAPTER 3

"Oh no," Bella moaned as we left the stinging night air.

"Ghost town. Again," I whispered, coming up behind her. "Damn."

She took off her fedora and let her ponytail tumble out.

Diddio saw her, snapped from his blue funk and broke into a wide, goofy smile. "Gabba Gabba Hey!" he shouted.

The lone customer in the place looked up, then fell back into his book, a Chekhov anthology. Lean, forlorn, with a fuzzy mustache and a hole in the elbow of his thin beige sweater, he looked like he had nowhere else to go.

Gentle techno music with an Asian flavor filled the room.

"What'd you get?" he asked.

"We won," she said, showing D her well-practiced athlete's insouciance.

"Yeah, but what'd *you* get?"

"Three," she said.

"And three assists and four boards," I added, as I slipped out of my leather jacket. She also had two turnovers and three fouls in about six minutes, but she hustled her butt off, up and down the court. And tossed one very nice lob pass to Bo, who caught it in her right hand, spun to her left and dropped a sky hook that would've made Abdul-Jabbar proud.

"Youngest player on the team," D said, explaining the meager output. "You."

Bella frowned. She hated, *hated*, when anyone made an excuse for her unexpected lack of perfection.

Daniel, who helped Diddio in the evenings, came from the back of the bar. He had a damp rag tossed over his shoulder.

"Four rebounds?" he asked. "What happened to Bolanle?"

He and Bella kissed each other on the cheek, Daniel going up on his toes to reach her chilled face.

"The ball kept going long," she shrugged. She yanked an orange scarf from under her cherry-pink parka.

I hung my jacket on the coat tree near the door.

"Hello, Mr. Orr."

"Daniel," I nodded.

He beamed. We were compadres in fighting crime, a regular Batman and Nightwing, Mr. Peabody and Sherman, whatever. What the crime was, however . . .

I'd made two calls over lunch—Silver Haven High and FIT—and Allie Powell was still gone.

Meanwhile, there weren't enough people in here to start an argument.

Diddio's business, formally named the TriBeCa Tea Water Pump but known in the neighborhood as Leo's, was faltering, especially at night. Last year, when our dear friend Leo died and left his tavern, the Tilt-a-Whirl, to Diddio, he decided downtown needed a tea bar. "Think Starbucks, man," he told me, dusted off the liquor bottles, packed them away. "Now forget everything about Starbucks."

D was a rock critic by profession, a pothead by choice, and he had no idea how to run a street-corner lemonade stand, never mind a business that required a monthly intake of $12,200 just to make the bills.

After some ugly wrangling, Leo's sister, who held the mortgage, agreed to float D his seed money. So far, I'd tossed in nearly $30,000 myself. Not that I minded; because of Marina's paintings and my book *Slippery Dick,* Bella and I had no real financial worries. What hadn't gone into my daughter's trust, I put into the house, a few mutual funds, bonds and REITs, and we lived off the skim, with a little mad money tucked away.

But D went nuts, on my watch, I guess, and now the Tea Water Pump was an oasis of fuchsia divans, burnt-orange ottomans, raspberry chester-fields, chocolate méridiennes and one shocking yellow recamier on an oatmeal-tinted floor. Leo's old oak bar was gone—we sold it at a very nice price to a jazz lover who ran a pub in Amsterdam—and replaced by an oatmeal semicircle with a glass front to display the dozens of leaf teas D had shipped in. During the morning hours, when he drew a steady crowd of fresh-faced moms with babies, artists on a break from work, white-collar staffers from Citigroup, and a handful of trendy locals who favored the new until someone declared it passé, Diddio basked in the broad stream of sunlight that filled the room, its rays bouncing off rubber plants and ficus trees, as the chatty customers enjoyed fresh tea and the pumpkin biscotti our housekeeper Mrs. Maoli contributed. The scent of steeping tea, and the occasional whiff of sliced lemon, created a pleasing aroma.

Through lunch and at night, the place was dead, and the colorful furniture, which matched D's unbridled optimism, seemed to mock his dreams.

He handed Daniel a cup of black currant tea for Bella. "Naturally decaffeinated," as he once observed. And he snuck me a glass of club soda from his secret stash.

"How's it going?" I asked, as I perched on one of the cranberry stools that surrounded the off-white, sort-of-beige bar.

"Shit, T, I think I made three dollars since six o'clock," he sighed. "That is, if Daniel over there doesn't ask to get paid."

Daniel told Bella that D needed company when the customers bailed. "He gets a bit depressed, I think," he once observed.

His sister Wendy worked the day shift.

D had cut his long hair, abandoned his collection of ratty black T-shirts, put away the reefer (more or less), upgraded his contact lenses, and told the editors of the media he wrote for that he was moving on, starting a new venture, growing up.

"What are you up to?" he asked.

"I got a case," I said. "Daniel got it for me. A missing boy."

"Oh," he said. "I thought it might have something to do with the guy who whacked Julie today."

"I— You know about that? How?"

"Daniel told me."

"And how—"

"Gabriella, who talked to Julie."

"I am out of the loop."

"Not really, man," he said. "You're like the hub. And I know you, man. You won't let that go, him touching Julie."

Touching her? He tried to knock her face off her head.

I sipped the lukewarm soda.

"Hey, you know who almost came in here today? Harvey Keitel, man."

"Almost?"

D loved celebrities, even though he'd met nearly every rock star and knew few of them were worthy of admiration offstage or outside the recording studio. To walk the streets of TriBeCa, SoHo, the Village, with him was to be compelled to look at every grade-B actor, TV newsreader and marginal pop oddball who walked by.

"Yeah, like, he was walking by, hurrying, and he looked in the window."

"I suppose that qualifies."

"Would've been better he came in."

Yeah, and bought $12,000 worth of tea.

"This kid I'm looking for," I said. "I think he took off with $471 from his uncle's safe."

"That's an odd figure."

I frowned. "Yeah, it is, isn't it?"

"I mean, who puts a dollar bill in a safe?"

Especially when he leaves $2,800 in coins on his chest of drawers.

"I'll let you know," I told him. I pointed toward the door. "Now I've got to go rent a car. Then I've got to see if I remember how to drive."

"I'll drive," he said excitedly.

"No thanks," I said as I went for my coat. He dragged me to see U2 at the Meadowlands in the mid-'90s and, his head full of herb, he drove the rented Impala straight onto the Little Ferry circle.

In back, under the warm glow of D's track lighting, Bella lounged on the recamier—her recamier, she'd said—and was poring over *A History of God* for her World Religions class. Sitting on a stout ottoman at her feet, chubby elbows on chubby knees, Daniel, one of four Taoists in the class, seemed to be quizzing her.

I said, "Tell Bella to be home by 10, OK?" I had to walk Beagle—my daughter's dog was my responsibility. What a surprise. And I needed to get on the Web to learn as much as I could about the Powells of Silver Haven.

"Think happy thoughts," he told me as I went for the door.

Heading for the New Jersey Turnpike, with the morning's pale sun following me and the scent of gas fumes filling the red Ford Focus I'd rented, my head brimmed with ideas, and I realized I wasn't thinking about Marina and her lover, whoever he may have been, her ex-lover, an old boyfriend from her student days in Rhode Island, maybe they had a glass of wine, two, and giddy— Marina struggling in the mire to save Davy— The two of us, young, senselessly in love, Marina unexpectedly pregnant with Bella, as we strode the countryside in Conversano on our way to the Castello Marchione— No, I was thinking about Allie Powell, John McPorter's $471, his two so-called Judas Coins, and Harlan Powell, Allie's father, who, from what I'd learned during two hours in my office last night, was a white-collar, low-life piece of shit if there ever was one.

To my left, proud among the ice floes in the choppy Hudson, was the Statue of Liberty, her back to me, the wan morning light dancing on her copper-green cladding. As I looked at her, a bitter wind ripped through the seams in the little car's body, threatening to toss me onto Jersey City down below.

"Dad, you couldn't get a smaller car?" Bella said, as she heaved her overstuffed backpack into the trunk.

"I don't know," I replied. "Do they make a smaller car?"

When we both got in—me in shirtsleeves, a black pullover sweater-vest and jeans, Bella in a blue knee-length down coat, matching toque and red half-gloves-half-mittens that made her hands look like lobster claws—she said, "You've got to stop living like you're still poor, Dad. Live it up, you know? Gelato, brand names, designer labels, court-side seats . . ."

With as much pep behind us as the little car could muster, we crossed Greenwich, dodging a thin layer of ice at the corner, and went over to Hudson toward Whitman High. "For the record, my dear, we weren't poor, exactly," I said. "I mean, a barber makes a living."

"Yeah, but your dad wasn't a millionaire. Like you," she said, as she jiggled the switches on the inept heater. Muttering, she added, "He finally gets a car and . . ."

I noticed that the Holland Tunnel had already begun to overflow.

"You could've taken the ferry to Hoboken and rented a car there," Bella said, as she surveyed the crawl, pushing the hat off her forehead. "You'll be sitting in traffic for an hour."

"How do you know what's in Hoboken?" I asked.

"Look," she said, ignoring my question, "that's Bolanle's ride."

A black Mercedes limo turned onto Hudson. "Now that's a car," she added wistfully.

I would've taken Davy to the Statue of Liberty. I did all that touristy stuff with Bella—the Empire State Building, the observation deck at the World Trade Center, a tour of Radio City Music Hall, the big whale at the Museum of Natural History, Santa at Macy's, Lord & Taylor's Christmas windows—

Harlan Powell, a native of Freehold, then a ramshackle city in central Jersey, went to Boston College. Married Alexandra Crenshaw, who had gone to Wellesley and came from money. The couple lived briefly in Manhattan—uptown, near Gracie Mansion—as Powell began his career as a stockbroker. He had immediate success, and he and Alex moved to Silver Haven, a wealthy enclave on the northern edge of the Jersey shore. Silver Haven, I knew, was about 10 miles from Freehold. Where personal-income levels were concerned, the distance was measured in light-years.

In Silver Haven, Alex developed into a talented photographer, according to the *Asbury Park Press* archives. And Harlan Powell rode the high-tech wave, making a fortune that exceeded the one Alex had behind her, selling Cisco at $66, Nokia at $45, reaping annual bonuses.

But things got dicey for both of them when the market collapsed and, his lifestyle in jeopardy, Harlan cooked up a classic "pump and dump" scheme, as it's known on the Street. Scouring the new OTC issues, he found a Naperville, Illinois, company called KSFY Inc., an abbreviation for Kids' Safety First—Yellow. The company was raising funds to develop a high-tech, super-safe yet cost-effective school bus with amenities ranging from a seat belt for every rider, padded seat backs and side airbags throughout the vehicle to a state-of-the-art communications system, video monitors, sprinklers, internal gyroscopic devices to prevent rollover. Powell bought 250,000 shares at $1.75 per, which ran up the price to over $4. The gain was noted on MSNBC, and the stock closed at $6.25 the following day. Before the smart guys who wrote the "Heard on the Street" column for *The Wall Street Journal* could weigh in, Powell moved fast and created a consortium of old high-school chums to jump on board. Their buy order of 150,000 shares, which Powell handled, went in at $10.25, and he dumped his holdings, earning a profit of $2,125,000.

Then came the "Heard" column, sparked by a tip that reported KSFY's comptroller as frantic to reach the investor who'd run up the price of the company's shares. The *Journal* was dubious about the long-term prospects of the firm, which had intended to raise seed money by floating its shares and had no real development program for the buses or anything else. By day's end, the stock closed at $0.875 per share.

Powell's friends got hammered, and one or more called the Securities and Exchange Commission. Powell pleaded out, was fined $500,000 and was compelled to surrender his broker's license.

He walked out of the scam with fewer pals. And, if my calculations were correct, more than $1.6 million. Since none of the friends were members of the Silver Haven Country Club—nine of them, according to *Forbes,* still lived in Freehold, and most had drawn their life savings to buy in— Powell went on as he had been, scuffed but not close to shamed. And by then, he was a wheel in town: cocky, attractive, with a substantial bank account behind him; a brush-up with the SEC wasn't about to take him down. He knew that, somewhere along the line, the concept of public censure for crimes involving fiscal gain had vanished.

I'd bet there were people in Silver Haven who admired Powell for getting over on the SEC. They looked at him as a conduit to easy money.

Up ahead on the turnpike, a toll booth, and I had to ease over to the end of a long line, sliding in behind an SUV with eight empty seats.

I lifted my ass off the seat to dig in my pockets for change.

For some people, I thought, money in the pocket is the only value that matters, the only philosophy worth embracing. Loyalty, friendship? With the Harlan Powells of the world? You've got to be kidding.

No wonder the kid boosted McPorter's cash. He takes after his old man.

Sixty-five minutes later, I pulled off the Garden State Parkway and into an Exxon station and body shop on Route 36, undid the shoulder harness and seat belt, and stepped out of the car, and slipped into my leather jacket. I walked over to the attendant, a young man who might've been cutting classes to make a few bucks. He had his hair in a ponytail, something had rotted away a tooth on top, and he wasn't going to come out of the heated office unless the building caught fire. Before I entered his sanctuary, I stomped on the rubber line and made the bell ring. After well over an hour in the little Ford, I needed amusement.

I felt the heat as I opened the door.

"It's self-serve," he said. He was perched on the edge of an old wooden desk, surrounded by bills smeared with greasy fingerprints; maps; a calendar from a national car-parts chain and a vending machine full of cashews, and he was ogling a girlie magazine, the low-rent kind.

"Car ain't worth shit," I said. "But it's good on gas."

73

"Rest room don't work," he added, flipping a page.

"Does anything around here?" I could see the body-shop bay. Save its full array of tools and equipment and an old Econoline van, it was empty.

He lifted a rag from his back pocket and wiped his hands, which were nearly as clean as mine. "What do you want?" he asked tiredly.

"I heard there was an ocean," I said. "Waves, a beach, sand . . ."

The name on his patch was Ezra. Ezra didn't want to chat.

"I'm looking for a kid a little younger than you. Allie Powell. You know him?"

He shook his head and continued to fiddle with the rag, sneak a glance at the magazine.

"I heard his father was a wheel up in Silver Haven."

"Lot of wheels in Silver Haven," he replied casually.

True enough, I thought. Silver Haven had the highest per-capita income of any town in Monmouth County. Median household income was $139,000, which would rival TriBeCa and parts of Westchester and southern Connecticut.

The attendant rubbed the back of his hand against his long thin nose. "Allie Powell and me, we don't run in the same circles."

"I thought you didn't know him."

Flustered, he said, "No, what I mean is, I heard of a kid named Allie Powell."

"He's got a reputation, does he?"

"Allie Powell," Ezra said, "yeah. A reputation."

"For what?"

He stammered, "I said— What I said is I don't know him. I don't know his family. Nothing."

"Almost, Ezra," I told him. "You almost pulled it off."

He stood. The top of his head was below my chin.

"Listen, Mister, I don't appreciate being called a liar, all right?" he said boldly.

I looked at him. "Sit down, son," I said calmly. "I just spent an hour getting pushed all over the Turnpike by trucks and buses, by Jeeps and wagons, and when I passed Newark Airport, I thought a DC-10 was going to land on my roof."

"Yeah? So?"

I nudged him and he stumbled back against the side of the desk, flapping his arms to keep his balance.

"So I could use some exercise," I said, "work off the stress. You get my meaning?"

"I don't know nobody named Allie Powell or his father," he said as he gathered himself. "You know, if you're so fuckin' miserable, you can take your New York ass back home. Nobody asked you here."

I reached for the door. "You ought to work on your customer-service skills," I said, "or they'll never let you run the company."

"Fuck off," he said as I stepped outside.

I noticed, as he had, the New York plates on the little red car.

As I squeezed back in the Ford, slipping into the seatbelt, I saw Ezra, easing back into his seat, pawing the girlie magazine.

He gave me the finger as I drove past his soiled windows.

"Thanks," I smiled.

I drove slowly alongside the craggy retaining wall, and I rolled down the window to take in the briny scent and to see if the ocean mist could reach me over the high rocky divide. Above me, seagulls bobbed and struggled in the blustery winds.

The sun had fallen behind gray clouds, adding to the ghostly ambiance of the gleaming ocean-front lane, serenely quiet in the off-season. For a moment, I felt as if I'd puttered onto an empty Hollywood backlot.

I made a right at Sea Bright, as randmcnally.com told me, and I found Silver Haven, and I moved along, soon passing a stretch of American flags, flapping violently in the wind, on the tapered islands that separated the east- and westbound lanes of the immaculate boulevard. On either side, prominent single-family homes, superbly maintained, tastefully appointed—Victorians, narrow ranches, brick Colonials, bold contemporaries in lavender and rose—all somehow managed to complement one another, creating a neighborly ambiance, one of quiet, restrained affluence. Pure-white snow coated spacious lawns, and a yellow sign at the road's side warned of deer.

It certainly was unlike any Jersey shore town I'd ever visited.

My mother, Regina and I spent two weeks each summer in raucous Seaside Heights, where three fistfights an hour were the norm on the gum-stained boardwalk, as the barkers hustled bleary-eyed vacationers to their gambling wheels, and the aroma of sizzling sausage and peppers overwhelmed the ocean's scent. The chatter of the cigarette-smoking sunbathers concealed the roar of waves breaking against the white sand.

In Silver Haven, the only sound I heard was the putt-putt of my rental car.

At the junior high, where runners in purple hooded sweatshirts and matching sweatpants obediently did laps around a manicured football field, as many as 100 bicycles stood in two long, colorful rows. Not one wore a security chain.

Two municipal workers were taking down a damaged tree limb, and a policewoman waved me around their effort.

I pulled up next to her. "Can you tell me where I can get a bite to eat?" I asked.

"Keep going to the second light, make a left and you'll find a couple of places," she replied. She had soft blue eyes and full lips, and her face was pink from the slapping wind. Her name was Maki, according to the gold bar above her badge, and she wore an 11-round automatic on her belt.

"I appreciate it," I said, and reached to roll up the window. "You wouldn't know how I could find the home of Harlan Powell, would you?"

She tilted her head and rubbed her gloved hands together. "Harlan Powell? No, I don't believe I know anyone named Harlan Powell."

I looked up at her, as she peered over the top of the car as if scanning a horizon.

"He's a player here, isn't he?" I said.

"What's that mean?" she asked. "'A player?'"

I shook my head. "If you haven't heard of him, and the Exxon guy . . . No, I guess not."

I thanked her again, and I drove on, putting her and the workers in the rearview.

He was a big man, broad across the shoulders, thick in the neck and thighs, and his blue topcoat did little to hide his muscularity. As I stepped out of the sandwich shop and into the frigid air, I saw him glaring at me, and then he came off the front of his black Cadillac SUV and walked toward me.

And then, without a word, he punched me in the stomach and I fell hard to the concrete, landing on my knees before tumbling to the side.

The big man put his big shoe against the side of my head and pushed hard enough to let me know how much it would hurt if he went all the way.

"Nobody wants you here," the big man said, his voice surprisingly smooth.

I gasped for air.

"You're going to give back what's ours," he said, "and then you're going back where you came from. You got me?"

I couldn't move, nor could I believe no one was coming to my aid. When I'd walked into the sandwich place, trim White Cedar Street had bustled with shoppers running to the greengrocer's, dry cleaners, cheese store, the ATM at the bank. The big man made them all disappear.

He stepped off my head, reached down and yanked me to my feet.

I still couldn't catch my breath, and I noticed he had brass knuckles across the fingers of his bulky right hand. The metal wouldn't mean much if he went for the midsection again, but it'd crack open my jaw if he snapped a short right at my chin.

"You won't squeeze us," he said, staring hard into my eyes. "We don't pay."

Dizzy from pain, I wasn't strong enough to go back at him. Not yet.

Under close-cropped dirty-blond hair, the big man's wide head seemed more square than oval, and the veins in his broad neck pulsed as he held on to my collar. "Give," he said.

"You—You got the wrong guy," I said, wheezing.

"You want to see Harlan," he said, "you see me."

"Yeah," I replied, "Harlan. Harlan Powell."

"Give," he repeated.

A middle-aged woman, thin, light-blond, in a red parka, cast a quick, stealthy glance at the big man. Head down, she hurried into a vest-pocket appliance store.

"My wallet," I said. Tiny lights danced before my eyes.

He nodded and I dipped awkwardly into my back pocket.

He studied the card I handed him.

Across White Cedar, a young man, prematurely gray, watched from behind the bay window of an insurance office.

"I'm no thief," I said.

"You're saying you didn't break into the car?"

I shook my head. "Car?"

He let go, shoved me.

I regained my footing and I studied him, and I couldn't find a weak spot, at least not one I could work now with my bare hands.

I wiped off the side of my head. Blood trickled from my ear.

He reached into his topcoat and shoved my business card into his shirt pocket.

"What do you want?" he said.

"I'm looking for Allie," I told him.

He looked at me. Then he showed me the butt of the gun in his topcoat pocket.

He snapped his head toward the Darth Vader Caddy.

"Get in," he growled.

He made me put on the seat belt, and then he walked away from the car and he pressed a button on his cell phone. The conversation was brief, and it looked to me like the big thug was taking orders. He nodded a few times, said yes again and again, and then he shut down the little phone and came back to me, though not before shifting his gun to his left side, away from where I could reach it.

The blood from the gash on my ear trickled down my neck.

"Where are we going?" I asked as he turned over the engine.

"Shut up," he explained.

He drove toward Route 36 with the brass knuckles across his fist, and he breathed through his nose as if he was ready to explode in anger at the slightest provocation.

"We going to Powell's?"

Without looking, he threw a right jab in my direction, but I ducked it with little effort, despite the restraining belt and the ache in my gut.

"I told you to shut up," he said.

The big man was slow, and whoever he spoke to on the phone had rattled him. I filed that away, along with the image of him dropping his left when he threw the hard right at me on White Cedar. I knew I'd be seeing him again and only one of us was going to like it.

Ten minutes later, we pulled into the Exxon station I'd visited on my way into town. Parked on the side of the building, near the empty garage bay, was a white four-door Mercedes with gold trim and Jersey plates. Its engine was running, and steam rose from its tailpipe.

"Get out," he said.

I went out into the cold, sneakers on the cracked blacktop, and he came up behind me and nudged me toward the station's door.

In the seat behind the desk where Ezra Exxon had been was a man, about my age, who had to be Harlan Powell. Flabby across the midsection, with a second chin, he looked like the kind of guy who spent most of his day on his ass, and drove the golf cart right up to the clubhouse door. His pricey clothes were immaculate: A thick mustard-yellow sweater covered an ocean-blue silk shirt, and he wore navy-blue wool slacks. Despite the rock salt that had coated the streets since November, his soft black alligator loafers were spotless over sheer socks.

But not even the smell of old gasoline could hide the stench of arrogance that rose from him. Here was a man who'd spent a lot of time being impressed with himself.

"Tell your muscle he had his last free shot," I said, looking into his drowsy blue eyes.

Powell didn't break a smile. I could tell he thought

of himself as a tough guy, despite the paunch, and maybe he'd earned the attitude: He had a deep, crude scar above his left brow, and his wide nose looked like it had been cracked long ago, about the time something cut him near the eye. And though his hands were smooth, he had broad knuckles that suggested he may have had to use his fists before he figured out how to do it with brains.

"Cut your ear, did he?" Powell said, peering at the little wound on the side of my head.

Then he looked over my shoulder at the thug behind me. "Lou," he said, with a snap of his head. "In the back."

The big man went toward the bay without comment or protest. I watched as he squeezed his body through the door frame and edged past the white van.

"You're looking for my son?"

I nodded.

I reached across and grabbed a fat roll of paper towels that sat atop an old, grease-stained phone book.

"And why's that?" Powell said.

"People are worried," I said, as I dabbed the coarse paper against my ear.

"I'm not."

"And there's a problem with some cash. From John McPorter's—"

"He's soft in the head, you know," he said, cutting me off. "Living in that rat hole, praying . . ."

83

"Yeah, but somebody took his $471." A door slammed somewhere deep in the garage bay.

"You notice that the worse it is for some people the more they believe in God?" he mused. "Stupid, right?"

"Maybe that's why they can't wait to get to heaven," I said.

"Heaven? You're kidding, right? Wait, don't tell me you believe in that shit." He looked at the crease in his pants, flicked away a yellow thread. "Here, up there, downstairs—you are what you are, and all you've got coming to you is what you went out and got."

"However you got it . . ."

"Damn right," he said.

An after-the-fact philosophy, spoken by a man trying to justify his misbehavior.

He asked, "And you think Allie took his money?"

"I don't know," I said.

"My son never wanted for a dime in his life," Powell asserted.

"OK, so maybe he can tell me who might've done it."

"Probably some other nut who believes all that bullshit."

I said, "Could be." Another thud from somewhere inside the garage.

"Or maybe there was something else in the safe."

I didn't reply.

"Was there?"

"I don't know," I said. This creep was more

84

concerned about what McPorter had locked away than he was about his own son.

"Who hired you?" he asked.

"Some other nut who believes all that bullshit," I told him.

He laughed as he looked me over. "He can't be paying you much."

I tossed the bloody wad of paper on the dirty floor.

"A guy like you is not going to get too far. Not down here," he said. "Nobody is going to give you the time of day. See, nobody wants you here."

I gathered that he meant Silver Haven, and not a run-down old gas station, and it was clear he considered Silver Haven a special place to be.

For Harlan Powell, it was a long, long way from Freehold.

He pushed himself out of the chair. "I'll tell you what. You keep looking for Allie—"

"So you don't know where he is?"

"What I'm saying is you make sure he doesn't get dragged into this thing, and I'll—"

An echoing crash from inside the bay cut off Powell's pitch. I looked to the open door, and a dented oil barrel wobbled as it rolled across the floor, coming to a halt when it hit the van.

When I turned back to Powell, he had his money clip in his hand, and a spread of $20 bills and a few fifties.

"I'll run a tab," I told him.

"What do you guys get? A hundred a day?"

"Something like that. Maybe more."

He was several inches shorter than I am and I'd bet years of standing behind the brute he called Lou had taken the edge off his game. Not that I could afford to try him now.

He was making things more interesting by the minute, by the sentence.

"You go after top dollar," he added. "It figures. You're all the same."

I figured he meant all humans, not just private detectives. This guy hated everybody but himself.

As he slid his bankroll back into his slacks pocket, he shouted for his goon. Seconds later, Ezra Exxon stumbled into the room, with the big man behind him.

Ezra's nose was bleeding, and his left eye was puffed and purple, and a knot was growing on his left temple, and his little jacket had been tussled and torn.

The big man looked at his sledgehammer right hand, flexed it a couple of times.

Ezra should be grateful Lou hadn't used the brass.

Powell gestured with his head toward the door, and the big man went out to the SUV.

Cold wind swept into the room.

"Clumsy Ezra," Powell muttered. Then he looked at me. "See what happens when you don't cooperate? You find you had some kind of accident. Stumble, fall."

The big man's tires squealed as he ripped from the gas station.

"Ezra," Powell said, "drive Terry Orr back to his Pinto."

Ezra nodded.

Powell went to his white Mercedes.

"Clean up," I said to Ezra. "I'll wait."

I stepped outside, hoping the fresh air would wash away the stench. Not of oil, or industry, but of Powell and his crude play.

CHAPTER 4

On my way back to Route 36, after having been deposited by Ezra on White Cedar Street and driving off in the little red Ford, I saw a police car approaching from the east, and I wasn't surprised when it fell in behind me.

Maki, the cop who sent me to Powell's man on White Cedar. I considered for a moment whether a Ford Focus could outrun a souped-up V-8 Crown Vic with 300 horses, a car that takes off like it wants to trace Glenn's orbit. I laughed aloud, wondering if I could keep ahead of Maki in this thing if she raced after me on foot.

And I laughed even harder 10 minutes later when I caught the drawbridge over the Navesink River, and sat uneasily between two Isuzu trucks.

I looked at the nick on my ear in the rearview. It could take a stitch, maybe two.

"Yeah," I said to the rattling heater, to the bumper of the truck in front of me, the gray water below, "nobody wants me here. They won't let me get out, but nobody wants me here."

★ ★ ★

On the parkway, I grabbed a chicken sandwich at a Burger King, ate it in under two minutes, washed it down with an ice-laden Coke, and used the rest area's men's room to clean up again before I got back into the car.

I intended to go home and work it out on the heavy bag—*pow* Lou, *wham* Küsters, *smack*—and then, and then I'd go back to looking for Allie. But at Newark Airport, I caught a construction slowdown and, as I inched ahead at about six miles an hour, watching four-by-fours, minivans, SUVs and buses zip by on the truck side of the highway, I decided to find out how someone else felt about Powell and maybe see if there was any scuttlebutt on what the big man thought I was trying to sell him. Powell had been ripped off as McPorter had, and his muscle thought I'd come to Silver Haven to sell him back his goods. If Powell thought I had them, he was as lost as McPorter was about his missing cash. Neither of them had an idea about where their stuff had gone.

As I reached Exit 14, I took out my cell and punched in McPorter's number. There was no answer, and no answering machine.

I decided to chance it, and I stayed on the turnpike, passing the Narrow's Gate exit I knew too well, and went up to Route 3 and joined all the other little cars jammed at the mouth of the Lincoln Tunnel. I cursed silently, and not so silently, and 40 minutes later, I came out of the smog under the Hudson. I went north on Tenth Avenue until it became Amsterdam, catching every light and ending up behind a garbage truck and, next, a broken-down school bus just south of John Jay. With the growing shadows stretching over me, I drove over to the 65th Street transverse and rode it across Central Park, passing barren trees and, when I got to the East Side, no more than a few hearty souls and their scrappy dogs, and shuffling doormen outside elegant Fifth Avenue towers. A delivery man on a bicycle, bloated D'Agostino's shopping bag in his basket, went by at breakneck speed.

I puttered over to Madison, saw an open meter on the east side near 63rd, wriggled the red car into the spot, and headed over on foot to 64th, still feeling the effects of the big man's blow to my solar plexus, still amazed at the crassness of Powell's play, the raw display of his coarse code.

Even before I reached the corner, I could hear shouting at the middle of the block and, as I turned east, I saw a crowd forming outside McPorter's apartment building. At the outskirts of the crowd, people were turning away, as if horrified by what they saw. As I started edging cautiously toward the building, my hands buried in the pockets of my leather jacket, a police car came up behind me, and it skidded to a halt near the crowd, blocking the narrow street.

McPorter was impaled on the cast-iron fence outside his building, and his blood dripped onto the cracked concrete, the weeds beneath him. His lifeless eyes reflected the streaks in the late-afternoon sky.

The two young uniformed cops had little trouble fighting their way through the pack—most of the people were eager to go, or at least to turn away. What they'd just witnessed was very likely the worst thing they'd ever seen.

Slick black rods protruded from McPorter's chest and neck, and his arms hung at grotesque angles to the sides.

A man with a small video camera snuck in next to me, and I could see in his viewfinder the red streaks on the rails below McPorter's body and blood drops on the sidewalk.

"Anybody know this man?" one of the cops asked. He was out of breath, more likely from the excitement than from any exertion.

When no one spoke up, I said, "I do. His name is John McPorter." I pointed to the open, third-floor window. "He lived up there."

His sheer curtains flapped in the empty air.

"No way McPorter jumps," I added. "This is homicide."

The cop stared at the open window, turned back to me and went over to his partner, who nodded, then spoke into the microphone at her collar.

"You stick around," the red-faced cop said when he returned.

I nodded. Go. Stay. Sure, why not.

"I need to make a call," I said, as I held up my cell.

The cop agreed.

I turned to the man with the video camera. "How tight can you get to the window?"

He was an odd man, agitated, overly serious, in need of mouthwash and a shave. "I can get right there," he said, nodding rapidly. "Right there."

He probably thought he had the next Zapruder film.

"Any blood on the window guards?" I asked. "The curtains?"

He pointed the camera to the black fence that surrounded the bottom half of McPorter's window.

"I don't see any," he said. "No, I don't see any."

"Let me look," I said.

I didn't see any either.

The poor bastard was alive when he flew out into the wintry air.

The female cop came over with a gray blanket and started to cover McPorter's body, much to the relief of the crowd.

I turned, dialed Luther Addison's number at Midtown North.

I'll be damned. Rather than remove McPorter's body from the rails, they're going to use a buzz saw to cut away the fence and then take the whole thing to the Medical Examiner's.

As the stern mother-and-daughter team that owned the building stood by, glaring in judgment with matching hollow eyes, Addison gestured for me to follow him to his car.

On Madison and all the way back on Fifth, drivers eager to continue across 64th Street slammed their horns, creating a cacophony Addison was able to ignore.

"How can you stand that?" I asked as I slid into his warm vehicle. "You've got the power to fix it."

He adjusted his black tie, which, as always, bore a diamond pattern. "The Queensboro Bridge isn't going anywhere."

I rubbed my hands in the flow of heat from the dash.

"You're saying he didn't jump."

"Suicide is frowned upon by his kind," I replied. "Bad health, bad luck . . . It doesn't matter."

"'His kind' being . . . ?"

"Very devout," I said. "Very religious. Believes in all 10 of them, up and down."

"And how do you know him?"

I went over it: A young family friend gone, more or less at the time the stuff vanished; contents of his safe missing—a few envelopes belonging to his son and petty cash.

"The kid did this?" Addison said. Even though we weren't moving, he had his hands on the wheel.

I told him no. "He's fourteen, and McPorter said he was timid." I pointed up to McPorter's window and its protective gate. "You'd have to be a weightlifter to hoist a guy and throw him over that."

"Maybe the old man snapped."

"And lands on his back? At that angle?"

Addison said, "Don't get ahead of yourself, Terry."

"I'm just saying he didn't kill himself."

"You said bad health—"

"Heart surgery," I replied. "But he seemed pretty robust—"

"Poor health," Addison counted, "suffers a break-in, he's responsible for a young family friend who's missing . . ." He shook his head. "Let's take our time with this one."

I peered out the window. "He wasn't bothering anybody," I said finally.

Sparks flew from the blade of the buzz saw, and the high-pitched grinding sound penetrated the lieutenant's car.

"You've been looking for the kid?"

"Yeah," I said. "In fact, I was down the Jersey shore today, in Silver Haven, where his family lives."

"And?"

"Nobody wants me there."

He frowned.

I told him about the big man, the blow to the stomach, the threat at the Exxon station.

"That explains the ear," he said, pointing. "So you weren't in McPorter's today?"

"Yesterday. Not today."

Under the gray blanket, McPorter's body wobbled and shuddered as the determined city worker continued to drive the saw blades through the rail.

"By the way, somebody ought to call his priest," I said. "And his son, Buddy. Probably John McPorter, Junior."

Addison looked past me toward the curious onlookers who, despite the crosstown winds, remained by McPorter's body, the gobs of blood on the concrete, the hissing sparks of the whirling saw.

He said, "Of course, you have the question of why he'd lock away about five hundred bucks while keeping twenty-eight hundred dollars in old coins lying around . . ."

"I thought of that," I said. "I'm guessing the $471 didn't belong to him."

Or he was soft in the head, like Powell claimed.

Outside, the sparks suddenly stopped. They'd gotten one of the rails free, and now one of the crew held on tight while his partner took the saw to the other side. As the grinding resumed, sparks rushing, vanishing, McPorter's arms, legs jerked and flapped under the sheet. His blood continued to dribble to the ground.

Bella and Daniel jumped from the living room and skittered to the front of the house, their socks gliding across the hardwood, when they heard the dull slap of an open palm on the front door.

I was stirring the minestrone, slowly reheating the sesame *bastone* from Zito's in the oven.

"Great," I said. "A chance to peek at Operation Tip-Top."

"Don't you dare, Dad." She pointed at me, her finger stern.

"Maybe I'd just better get the door," I said. The wooden spoon stood upright in Mrs. Maoli's soup.

With a curt glance, Bella told Daniel to guard their work.

"That Beagle," I added as I wiped my hands on the towel I'd tucked into my sweatpants, "is some watchdog."

"She's great," said Bella, who'd named her Beagle even though she was a basset hound. My daughter had somehow gotten her hands on a red work shirt from the Pep Boys, complete with a patch of Manny, Moe and Jack above the breast. "Don't pick on her."

On WNYC, *Fresh Air* offered a tribute to a trumpeter named Clifford Brown, and lush, romantic jazz floated across the room.

I looked through the peephole and saw Julie out on Harrison. "Christ, I forgot to tell her I changed the code."

I pulled open the front door and let in a cold blast off the Hudson. Julie was down on Harrison Street, a frail, knotty tree at her back. The streetlights on Greenwich spread a lavender glow on the cobblestones, the old snow.

I held out my hand.

She brushed by me, pulling in a rush of frigid air with her.

I turned to her as I shut the door. "You walked? Oh, Jule, don't tell me you walked from Centre Street."

She nodded. Her cheeks were chapped from the wind.

"Are you crying?" I asked.

She looked at her salt-crusted boots, the pale floor tiles.

Bella went quietly to the cabinet, pulled out a soup bowl, took a spoon, fork and knife from the drawer and set a place for Julie.

"Hey, Gabriella."

"Hey, Julie."

"Miss Giada," Daniel began, "let me congrat—"

Bella caught his arm, spun him around and, pulling him past her mother's painting in the alcove, lugged him toward the back of the house, toward notebooks, laptops and hip-hop on TV.

I took Julie's topcoat and slipped it on a hanger behind the laundry-room door.

She blew into her hands and shivered.

"Go by the stove," I said, as I rubbed her upper arms.

She didn't move. "Perlmutter killed himself," she said.

"The Surgeon killed himself?"

She nodded, and I watched as she went into the small bathroom behind her.

I waited a moment, then cut the radio, turned

97

down the steaming soup and poured her a glass of Italian red, a '97 Brindisi Salice Rosso from Puglia that I'd opened to accompany the meal.

When she reappeared, she sat in what had become her seat—to Bella's right, diagonally across from the stove and me. This time, I went to the end of the table so I could be close to her.

"Sorry," she said.

"No need."

We kissed tenderly.

I poured the deep red wine into the stout glass.

"Did you change the code on the lock?" Her round face was still raw from the weather, tears, and yet she managed a warm smile.

The punch code used to be the day and month of my son's birth, followed by my old uniform number. Now I made it the day of Bella's birth and mine, reversed.

In explaining why I altered the code, I told her about my visit to McPorter and how I guessed the combination to his safe.

"Is that what you're working on? The missing boy. Daniel's friend?"

I nodded yes. "It started out as a favor to Daniel, but it's more now. Somebody killed the old man—"

"Oh, no." She brought her fingers to her lips.

"And before that, somebody went after me."

She paused thoughtfully. "And that's how you got that cut on your ear?"

I shrugged. "I'm thinking this John McPorter

was a good man. And somebody has to find this kid."

"And it has to be you?"

I sipped the red. "Better me than his father's goon."

"'His father's—'"

"Later for that," I said. "Tell me what happened with Perlmutter."

At Rikers, she'd met Carolyn Halthauser, a partner at Prendergast's firm, to get The Surgeon's signature on the plea, she said. He skulked into the holding pen wearing bright orange, with his hands cuffed in front of him, the stark overhead lighting shining on his bald head and revealing bags under his eyes and a baleful look of utter resignation.

Julie said he barely acknowledged Halthauser as she began to summarize the document.

He held out his hand and, as Julie watched, the attorney passed the agreement to him. He began to read it deliberately, as if scrutinizing every word.

Finally, he broke the heavy silence. "I am to address the court?"

Julie and Halthauser answered at the same time. "Yes," they said.

Perlmutter bit his bottom lip. "No," he replied softly, defiantly, "I cannot. I will not."

"Mr. Perlmutter," Julie said, "this point is nonnegotiable."

Halthauser added, "Doctor, you have already agreed to this document."

The Surgeon was again silent for a moment, and Julie said she could hear voices in conversation somewhere outside the conference area, and the heat rising in the radiators.

"My humiliation is complete," he said. "My complete and thorough humiliation . . ."

As Halthauser looked at Julie, disgust and embarrassment in her eyes, Perlmutter stiffened, held out his hand and asked for his attorney's pen.

Halthauser reached into her briefcase and passed her client her silver, bullet-shaped Cross Townsend, not before turning it to reveal the ballpoint.

And with unexpected speed and expert precision, Perlmutter jabbed the business end of the pen directly into his jugular vein.

Blood spurted across the table in a stream, hitting Julie on the hand and forearm. Halthauser yelped in shock, horror.

Before either attorney could react, Perlmutter stumbled out of his seat and flung himself against the door. As his blood continued to spurt with each beat of his heart, he pushed his back against the door and, as Halthauser screamed, he slid to the floor, landing in a seated pose.

The first cop who responded couldn't move the rotund Perlmutter to get in the room.

Meanwhile, Perlmutter reached up and raked his blood-soaked throat with the silver pen, ripping open new wounds, shredding the carotid artery.

"Terry, you can't believe how much blood came out of that man," Julie told me.

Halthauser tried to stop the bleeding but couldn't. Julie helped her drag the thrashing Perlmutter from the door.

"When they got the door open, the floor was coated in blood."

The cop at the gate squeezed into the room, and another followed him in, but neither of them could halt the bleeding. On-site emergency personnel didn't reach The Surgeon for almost five minutes.

By the time they got to him, Perlmutter had stopped flailing on the bloody floor and, as they worked on him, he died, as he wanted to.

Julie had gone teary-eyed again, and I said nothing.

"Terry, it was awful," she said. "Blood everywhere—"

She stopped.

Bella and Daniel were in the alcove, staring at Julie, who stood lost in her memory.

"I'm sorry," Bella said. She came over and put her arms around Julie, who for a moment closed her eyes, rested her head on my daughter's chest.

"He tortured himself," Julie said as she looked up, holding on to Bella's hand. "The guilt . . . It must have been unbearable for him."

I left the chair and went to Daniel. "You OK?"

He whispered, "I only heard the last part, beginning with 'all the blood.'"

Though he hung back sheepishly, he seemed intensely curious as he studied Julie, who left the chair to kiss Bella's cheek. My daughter smiled, then gave Julie a tender tap and rub on the arm.

Daniel said, "In World Religions, Mr. Sanchez told us that forgiveness is a principal tenet of Christianity."

"That's right," I told him. "It's the whole thing, really."

"I was going to say that by forgiving that murderer, Miss Giada certainly is living her faith."

"She's very forgiving, Daniel," I told him.

He nodded.

"Dad," Bella said, "I'm going to take Julie upstairs to change."

She gestured with her eyes, and I noticed the right arm of Julie's charcoal-gray suit-jacket was splattered with blood.

"OK, Bella," I said. "I'll get dinner ready."

When we were alone, Daniel said, "I've got some additional information on Allie Powell."

He smiled, and he fussed with the bowls and cutlery. He put my wineglass in front of my seat.

"Well?" I asked as I stirred the thick soup. I had Italian parsley and a mezzaluna on the cutting board, ready to finish the meal.

"He's taking classes in fashion design. He must be gifted, Mr. Orr. Those are college-level courses."

"And he's just a sophomore?"

Daniel frowned. "I'm not quite sure they use those designations at FIT."

"No, I meant at Silver Haven," I said. I should've asked when I had the vice principal on the phone.

"I don't know. Is it important?"

I said no. "What else?"

"He's very fragile, Elixa said. Elfin."

"'Elfin'? Impressive, Daniel. I can see him now."

He smiled with pride as he eased his pudgy frame into his seat, which was to the right of where I sat. Daniel's got a seat, Julie's got a seat, Diddio has a seat. None of us sat where Marina used to.

"You're from New Jersey, aren't you, Mr. Orr?"

"Who told you that?" I asked, as I brought the cast-iron pot to the table, centering it on a man-in-the-moon trivet.

The sound of available food brought Beagle to the kitchen. From under heavy lids, she watched me place a small bowl of red-pepper flakes on the table, next to the Parmigiano Reggiano and the grater. I broke off a chunk of cheese, tossed it to her. When it stopped rolling, she ate it.

"Gabriella. She said you were born in Narrow's Gate, New Jersey," he said. "I've been to the Liberty Science Center. That's near Narrow's Gate, isn't it?"

"Pretty close," I said, as I put on an oven mitt and retrieved the hot loaf of bread. Much closer to the science center than to Silver Haven.

"You never talk about your childhood, Mr. Orr, do you?"

"Daniel, get the extra-virgin olive oil and pour a little into the minestrone," I replied, "about a teaspoon or so, and stir it in. And put a little on the saucers for everybody."

I went off to wash my hands. Upstairs, Bella and Julie were laughing. My daughter had done it again—taken it from worst to best, with a quip, a hug or a smile. What a talent, I thought, knowing how to help others, always trying to make things right.

I had my wineglass, with only a mouthful of the velvety Salice Rosso in its globe, and I was streaming Radio Luxembourg and an old performance of Sibelius's *Humoresques* by Aaron Rosand, and now I was trying to make sense of what I'd learned in the past 24 hours about Allie Powell and his father Harlan, and I was thinking now that $471 had nothing to do with it. The envelopes Buddy McPorter had put in his father's safe: That's it. Worth more than two first-century coins. At least to two people: the guy who took them and the guy who wanted them back.

When I looked up, Julie was in the door frame, and she was about to button her coat.

"Already?"

"Terry, it's 9:30," she replied. "Daniel's gone home and your daughter's gone up to her room. Were you daydreaming again?"

I shook my head. "I'm thinking about something."

"I know," she smiled. "I looked in on you. Twice. But for two hours . . . ?"

"I guess I was concentrating."

She kissed my lips. "I guess you were."

Yeah, I was thinking about what I'd been up to since yesterday morning, thinking about growing up with a scumbag like Harlan Powell for a father, I was thinking about the red mullet Marina and I had near Zagare Bay in Mattinata, sprinkled with thyme; the kisses we shared above the waterfall in the Parc des Buttes Chaumont in Paris; Bella running on the beach at Vouliagmeni—holy shit, me, from Narrow's Gate, in Italy, France, Greece. When I was told, countless times, that I would amount to nothing, wouldn't get off the block. "Smart with the books, but nothing upstairs," my Uncle Eddie said, again and again. Ho-ho! Ha! And yet . . . Incredible. *Me.* And look at Marina, such beauty, pride. Dignity.

The sway of her hips.

The trepidation in Marina's eyes when she told me she was pregnant with Davy.

Nevertheless . . .

Coceau—wrong. Addison, who had faulty information—wrong. Marina was in the arms of another man, yes, but why? Who? An old friend, a former lover, someone to whom she had an obligation.

A fling, and all the while, all the while, she loved me. Because I had become what she needed me to be, and what she needed was what I wanted to be, yearned to be.

Yes.

Yes, but I knew I had lost her. I knew for five

years and I did not let myself remember that I had. Though the signs were there, and I had seen them. Seen them and chosen to ignore them.

I think maybe Leo knew. He had a way of letting his eyes drift when I mentioned her, when Diddio mentioned her.

Was it Leo who first used the word "idealize"?

Loretta knew. "You were meat on the side, Terry," she said.

"Maybe we made the wrong guy," said a cop at Midtown North. What did he mean? I thought he was telling me it wasn't Weisz.

"Terry, I'm saying Weisz is someone we have to talk to," said Luther Addison, several times. A man I trusted. A man I trust.

"Terry, you are corrupting what little we have," Addison, exasperated, told me after he learned I'd spoken to witnesses. "Now they don't know what they saw."

Because they pitied me. Pitiful me.

Why didn't Marina like Diddio? He was always a friend, kind to her, respectful. Loved Bella. Loves her. Loved Davy.

Uncle D.

"T, you go after him . . . I mean, who else is it going to be? You know, like, Deputy Dawg could figure it out . . ."

She told me she didn't like it here, suggested there were opportunities back in Italy. America, she said, was not her home.

Did I drive her away? Did I ever have her?

Did we kiss in the park in Montmartre? Or did I imagine that?

No, we definitely . . . I mean, we definitely went to Paris, met her agent Judy and her local counterpart, the escort, what was her name . . . ? Marina had a show in Montmartre, yes, and I took Bella by funicular to Pigalle. Whoops, that's no place for a kid. What did I expect, they'd be can-canning in the streets? "*Excusez-moi, Monsieur Lautrec, je suppose que vous savez quelque chose . . .* Ah, my French blows. What I'm trying to say, Henri, is that I assume you have a keen eye when it comes to women. The nature of women, to be precise. One woman, frankly . . . Do you think, do you think you could come to a show and observe? Advise, maybe . . ."

Man.

I don't even know what I'm saying. I don't even know if what I think is true. What I say, what I see: Is it real?

Fantasy. Reality. Reinvention lies somewhere in between, sure, but where?

Christ, save me from my own fuckin' observations, my own thoughts.

"Terry?"

"Yeah, Jule," I said as I lifted out of the creaking chair. "I was just thinking about what I was thinking about. You know, maybe there was something I'd missed, something I'd heard that might explain why McPorter went over the window guard and onto his front fence. Grasping at straws, I think it's called."

"You'll get it, Terry. You don't quit."

Who could be more supportive than Julie, huh? She'd put aside Perlmutter's blood-soaked death . . . Christ, it must have shocked her. I mean, she's tough, but . . . She put it aside to hang with Bella, and to see if I'm all right.

"So I asked myself if I could figure out what had been taken from Powell's car," I said.

"Can you?"

"Not really, no. Not yet."

If they were envelopes, I had a pretty good idea where they'd been.

And no idea where they were now.

I'd like to find them just so I could keep them away from Harlan Powell.

I'd like to find them just so I could tell him I had them.

I was certain now that McPorter was thrown out his window, and I knew little Allie Powell couldn't have done it, at least not alone.

"Jule," I said, as I tucked the chair under the desk, "you know what I saw today?"

"Oh, let's see: the Statue of Liberty, two men having an argument while they changed a flat on the Jersey Turnpike, a man's shoe as it stepped on your ear, a gas-station attendant battered from pillar to post, a good man lying on the pickets in his front yard . . . What did I leave out?"

"Not much," I said, as I gestured toward the living room. "You ate three bowls of minestrone. You left that out."

"It was exquisite, and by the way, I can defend my appetite, Mr. Orr, and I weigh what I weighed—"

"Whoa," I said softly. "I've seen you naked, remember? You don't have to tell me you're fine."

She leaned back as if startled. "My goodness, Terry. I think that was a compliment."

"Go."

I followed her as we passed through the living room. Bella's books from her Confronting Evil class—a collection of Locke essays, and John Watson's, a dog-eared paperback of Nietzsche's *Beyond Good and Evil*, Pinker's *The Blank Slate*, Neiman's *Evil in Modern Thought*—were stacked neatly on the coffee table, no doubt for easy access for me, so I wouldn't go into her room to look for them.

"I saw one of those photos of Christ—"

"A *photo* of Christ? That's better than two coins from Judas Iscariot."

"You know what I mean," I said. "One of those paintings. You know, where he's looking up to heaven."

"In the garden at Gethsemane?"

"No, no, he's not crying. You know, Jesus has his head cocked just so, and the light, the way it crosses his face. He's got long, flowing hair, pale blue eyes, a thin nose and a perfect chin with, like, a barely discernible dimple."

"Oh, yes," she said. "The nuns had them in the classrooms when we were kids."

We passed through the brick alcove.

I said, "He's smiling like he's posing for a Hollywood head shot, you know, allowing the spotlight to twinkle in his eyes, to show the glow on his firm cheeks."

"All right, I get it. What's your point?"

"Well, for one, it reduces one of the most influential men in the planet's history to a personality, and a foppish one at that."

"I see . . ."

"I mean, no one really knows what Jesus of Nazareth looked like—"

"But you're going to tell me."

"I'll ignore that," I said. "But it's better than even money that Jesus, an Abrahamic Oriental, had dark hair, dark eyes, and a close-cropped beard he trimmed himself. He was short by today's standards, if Darwin is on target, and looked pretty much like his associates—or the Romans wouldn't have needed Judas to point him—"

"Terry, will you still be talking when I walk outside?"

I looked down at Beagle, made her my audience.

"He was a carpenter by trade, Beagle, a fisherman and someone who traveled without customary comforts, so he was undoubtedly a strong man, and damned capable of taking care of himself among the roughest men."

She reached out and took my hand. "Are you tired?"

"I'm— Why?"

"When you're tired, you think too much," she said. Smiling, she added, "Also, when you're not tired . . ."

I looked at her, the sincerity in her dark eyes, the compassion on her face.

"Go to bed," she instructed. "When you dream, my sweet, try to remember you're at your best when you think with your heart."

I let out a long breath.

"Good night, Terry."

"Hold on," I said, as I opened the laundry-room door, reached behind it to grab my jacket. "I'll give you a ride home."

"Dare I risk it?"

"Be good, and we'll park and make out."

"Mmmm, that might be all right . . . ." She opened the front door.

On the way home, I decided to challenge the FDR and risk a sudden breeze lifting me off the highway and depositing me into the choppy East River. The ride went without incident, and I had just turned onto Houston when I heard my cell phone buzz. With one hand on the steering wheel, one eye on the bumpy, three-lane blacktop, I reached into the backseat, dug through one pocket, then another, and came up with it.

The caller had a 732 area code.

"Is this Terry Orr?"

I said yes, brightly. I was in a good mood. Julie Jewel.

"Fine," said the man at the other end. "Fine."

Alphabet City was crowded, not mid-July crowded, but with enough people to fill more than a few bars and rock clubs.

"This is Sheriff Craw of the Silver Haven Police Department."

"It's a violation of the New York State law to use a hand-held cellular phone while operating a motor vehicle," I replied.

"Then you ought to pull over, Mr. Orr."

"Will do."

I edged the Ford into a bus stop off First. Despite the harsh wind, the tumbling temperature, there was a lengthy queue outside the Landmark Theater across Houston. A shivering man selling hot chestnuts from a battered cart struggled in vain to drum up business.

"OK," I said. "I'm set."

"Mr. Orr, I'd like to ask you to drop into my office tomorrow," he said.

"What for?" It was a 100-mile round trip that felt twice as long, thanks to the stampede on the New Jersey Turnpike. Besides, the car was costing me $78.72 a day, plus tolls. "Does this have anything to do with the murder of John McPorter?"

After a momentary silence, he said, "I'm sorry. The murder of John Porter?"

"*Mc*Porter," I said. "An old friend of your illustrious Harlan Powell."

"I don't know anything about it," he said directly. "I would like to discuss today's unpleasantries with you."

"What an interesting way to put it."

"We can't do this on the phone," Craw said. "If it's not too inconvenient for you, can you drop in at about 10?"

I said no. "Make it noon. This way I don't have to fight rush hour at the Holland Tunnel."

I wanted to hear how the law in Silver Haven handled the attack on a visitor by the strong arm of one of its taxpayers. To see if the old "New Jersey and You" tourism slogan meant anything in Craw's town, in Powell's town.

And I wanted to see the big man, to come up behind him and bring a tire iron across the side of his knee.

"Noon it is, Mr. Orr."

"Maybe I can get an escort," I said, "just to be safe?"

"Noon, Mr. Orr."

I dropped the phone into a cup holder and continued west on Houston.

CHAPTER 5

At 11:48 a.m., I pulled up to Silver Haven's police station, a sort of generic, '70s-style brick-and-mortar job with faux-Doric columns out front, and I parked in a visitor's spot in the rear between two cherry tops—one a monster Chevy Tahoe, the other a standard police-issued Crown Victoria, each with bold purple piping and lettering on white, the same branding color used by the local high school. As I slipped into my leather jacket, I noticed several well-maintained late-model cars parked at an angle to the curb, filling out the small, salt-streaked lot, and I thought, Christ, if you don't have a Beemer down here, a Lexus, a Mercedes, you don't get to play, do you?

The temperature had risen to a whopping 17 degrees by the time I pulled away from the hydrant on Harrison Street, and on the ride down, WNYC said it was going to go up to 30 in Central Park. It was about that now, and water dribbled from the station's gutters across the lot.

I'd lived in and around New York long enough to know that when the temperature staggered above freezing in January, ice daggers would be

114

plummeting five stories off a 19th-century marble warehouse in TriBeCa, 75 stories off a new glass-and-steel building in Midtown, streaking to the ground like falling missiles, making a walk home a treacherous adventure, and killing at least one or two New Yorkers before the March thaw.

That wasn't a problem in a town like Silver Haven, where the tallest point was the flagpole I'd just passed. These people had other problems, though. One of them was Harlan Powell, who let his strongman pummel strangers, grab them off the street, forcing the citizens to scamper and hide behind the shutters, like townsfolk in an old Western.

My sneakers crunched the protective rock salt on the steps and walkway, and then I entered the warm lobby, pausing for a moment at the solemn memorial to an officer killed in the line of duty, and to a pair of residents lost in the World Trade Center attacks. There was no one to greet me at the blond, angular counter, and I followed the purple, rubber-lined carpet to its edge, where a swinging gate stood between the narrow waiting area and an office section that might've been dressed by a buyer at a Scandinavian furniture outlet. Matching the counter, the desks were blond but with rounded corners, and the chairs were purple and sleek, each on five casters. Neither chair was occupied, nor were the two desks, except for framed photos and other personal effects, standard office equipment, and seemingly new computers and top-of-the-line printers.

The purple carpet ran under the gate to a private office. Its glass windows were covered by blinds that had been drawn shut.

I was about to call out, or at least look for a bell to tap, when the blond door to the back office opened, and out walked Harlan Powell.

A tall man in a gray uniform, yellow braiding, black epaulets, followed him, then waited as Powell walked toward me.

Today, he wore a rose V-neck with a white shirt beneath, black slacks and the black loafers he'd had on yesterday.

Unless the big man Lou appeared to carry him to his white Mercedes, Powell was going to soil those soft shoes.

I watched as he came toward me. A heavy gold bracelet hung on his left wrist, and it rattled as he walked.

He brought the thick index finger of his right hand to his lips, and he winked at me. Walking proud, as if untouchable, the cocky Powell pushed back the swinging gate with his knee and kept going toward the exit. Despite his burly form, he seemed to glide along the purple carpet.

"Terry Orr?"

From behind the counter, Sheriff Craw gestured for me to come around and join him. He had a firm handshake and a polite smile. His tight uniform revealed his hard-earned fitness as well

116

as his penchant for sharp lines and crisp creases, and like his deputy Maki, he preferred an Austrian automatic.

"That's Harlan Powell," he said, nodding toward the now empty corridor. "The man you wanted to see."

Craw was six-six, maybe a half-inch taller. He may have played some ball—he had the size and muscle for it—but he walked awkwardly, as if he had either a leg injury or flat feet. But he was proud of his body, and he tried to affect a brawny swagger.

He ran his fingers across the front of his fine, straw-colored hair. "Let's go in my office."

Generic instrumental music, some tone-deaf accountant's idea of muted hip, came from an overhead speaker.

Craw held the door open for me.

He had his desk at an angle so it faced the door. An American flag, with a gold eagle atop the pole, was unfurled behind it.

On the purple leather sofa to my left sat Deputy Maki, in a gray uniform nearly as sharp as her boss's. Her ample breasts strained the blouse, and she knew it. The first cop I ever saw who displayed a manicure, complete with Pepto-Bismol-pink polish, she had her left hand on the handle of her nightstick as it stood at ease against the beige radiator.

The man to her right hung his head, and he didn't look up at me.

117

"Terry Orr," Craw said. "I believe you know Ezra Torkelsen."

His eye was swollen, and a sickly yellow mixed with purple under the egg. The knot on the side of his head hadn't taken on color, but it looked at least as painful as his other wounds.

"You doing any better?" I asked. Yesterday, the kid wouldn't speak to me, or look at me, while he drove me back to White Cedar.

Craw interrupted. "And this is Sergeant Maki."

The blonde nodded at me.

"Sergeant," I said.

Craw told me to sit in the black chair in front of his desk.

"Ezra is considering whether to file a complaint," he said as he went to his seat.

"Good," I told him. "He ought to."

"Is that so?"

His high-back chair let out a wheeze when he sat in it.

"Maybe I should do the same," I added.

Fresh coffee brewed on the credenza behind me, which explained the steam rings on Craw's desk, and the cup, the logo of which told me the Silver Haven football team was called the Zephyrs. Either the sheriff or Maki had served Powell, and at least one of them was going to clean up after him.

"Let's hear your side of it," the sheriff said.

"I came down here to talk to Allie Powell," I replied. "When I got to White Cedar, a cement-headed mug named Lou greeted me. After he got

118

finished smacking me around, he took me to the Exxon station where this kid works. Then this Lou started working him over."

Craw looked past me. "Is that how it was, Ezra?"

"No, sir," the young man said. "That's not it at all."

I turned to him. "When I stopped by your station, there wasn't a mark on your face," I said. "Five minutes with this Lou character, and you look like you went twelve with a cruiserweight."

"You stopped at the Exxon before you went to White Cedar?" Craw asked.

I nodded.

"And you say you went back?"

"Yeah. Not that I wanted to." I looked back at Torkelsen, then at Craw. "What's going on here?"

"Ezra says you beat him after he wouldn't tell you where Harlan Powell lived," Craw replied.

"That's bullshit," I said sharply. "I never touched this kid. Powell's boy Lou did it. And Powell was there."

"And you had a row with Lou Brabender on White Cedar Street shortly after you assaulted Ezra."

I said, "A row, my ass. That guy attacked me. Christ, ask anybody who was out on White Cedar yesterday."

I looked at Maki.

"Did I look like I just came from a fight when I asked you for directions?"

She didn't blink. "I don't know what you're

119

talking about, sir," she said. "I've never seen you before. At least not that I can recall."

"You didn't send me to White Cedar, and you didn't follow me to Route 36, to the drawbridge?"

She turned to the sheriff for counsel.

"Mr. Orr," he said. "I'll ask the questions, if you don't mind."

I stood. "Fuck no," I said angrily. "I won't go for this setup."

Maki dragged her nightstick from the radiator and slid it onto her lap, shifting the butt end to her right hand. Her placid expression didn't change.

I moved back, keeping my eye on the weapon, as I spoke to Craw.

"I came to Silver Haven to find out about Powell's son," I said. "I asked this man for help and he declined. Then your sergeant here sent me to White Cedar, where that Brabender you mentioned attacked me. Then he took me to the gas station where he kicked the shit out of this kid. Anyone who says otherwise is a stone liar."

"Then we have a problem," Craw said.

"Not me," I replied. "I'll talk to everybody in your town until I turn up somebody who can verify what I said. I'll start with the city workers your sergeant was with when I spoke to her."

I looked at Maki. "Instead of threatening me with that donkey dick, why don't you check out Brabender's SUV? Or Torkelsen's van. My prints are all over the dash in both vehicles."

To Craw, I said, "And out of nowhere I'm fighting Brabender, a guy I never saw before. Christ, one of these two tipped him that I was coming. Probably wasn't this guy, though, which is why Brabender pounded him."

"Maura," Craw said calmly, "take Ezra outside."

"The lying fuck," I muttered.

Torkelsen glared at me from under his swollen eyelid.

"Mr. Orr," the sheriff said, "please sit back down."

I waited until Maki took Torkelsen and her nightstick outside, and I held out my hands.

"Do these look like I worked over that kid?" I said. I didn't have a mark on either hand, and none of my knuckles was swollen.

"What do you want to know about the Powell boy?"

"Your Maki . . . She tipped Brabender, didn't she?"

"Mr. Orr," he said, as he leaned forward. "Allie Powell."

I shook my head. "Talk to NYPD Homicide," I said. "Lieutenant Luther Addison. It's out of my hands."

"You believe Allie is involved in the death of John McPorter?"

"I don't know what he knows."

"I've been told it was suicide," Craw said. "I have no reason—"

"Your source is an asshole," I told him. "NYPD

is all over this, and Addison isn't programmed to fail."

"A big-city cop, is he now?" Craw asked sardonically.

"A good man," I replied. "He wouldn't let anybody drop his coffee cup on his desk. Especially a worm like Powell."

Craw glared at me as he calculated his next move.

"You asked me to stop by, Sheriff, and I did," I said. "But I know a setup when I see one. But you won't run it on me. You or Powell."

I saw a blush of red in his cheeks. "You are to stay away from Harlan Powell, Mr. Orr," he said, firmly. "And forget Lou Brabender."

"But I'm not even, Sheriff."

"You're not going to get even. Not in Silver Haven."

"No, not in Silver Haven," I said. "But it's a big world, isn't it? And life's long."

"And you are to stop looking for Allie," Craw added.

"Sheriff, I don't believe your jurisdiction extends to where he is."

He tried to chill me with his dead stare. He was angry, and he fought to keep it in check, but short of caging me, there wasn't much he could do. Not if he thought NYPD might want to know where I was.

"You know, Sheriff, we could've done this on the phone."

He said, "I wanted to do you the courtesy of showing you what you were up against."

I stopped. "So you know it's bullshit. You know I never touched that kid."

He stood. "Have a good day, Mr. Orr."

He waited as I left the chair, opened the door and walked out of his office.

Maki and Torkelsen were gone, but Craw's second day cop was back at his desk, filling out a form that covered the breadth of his flat-screen computer monitor. He looked at me, thought nothing of it, and went back to his two-finger typing, under the sweet gaze of his twin girls, proud of their new purple sweaters in a Sears-style photo near his blotter.

As I came around the counter, I passed the portrait of the policeman who had been killed on the job, and I thought, You must be spinning in your grave knowing these guys are walking your path.

Outside, feathery snowflakes were floating onto the concrete lane, the blacktop, the golden ball on the flagpole.

By the time I reached the red Ford, my hair was coated with downy snow.

I headed for the Garden State Parkway, my wipers pushing away the fat flakes, and I checked in the rearview to see if steam was coming out of my ears. What a dumb bastard you are, I thought, as I got onto Route 36, crossed the drawbridge at Navesink, left 36. Of course, Craw would favor the hometown boy, the local wheel, and Maki wasn't going to go against her boss or the money man. And what did it cost Powell to buy off Ezra Exxon? Maybe only the threat of another beating from Brabender.

"Check out Brabender's SUV. Or Torkelsen's truck. My prints are all over the dash in both vehicles." Christ, what a child.

On either side of the three-lane parkway, thick evergreens and strapping pines caught the drifting flecks before they reached the shadow-coated turf below, and the sky above them seemed to have turned to a muted gray. On the highway, where traffic was midday light, the snow disappeared as soon as it touched the blacktop, but the road was slick, wet. Since I was unfamiliar with the ways of the little Ford on damp road, I clung to the right and center lanes. Keeping it at a steady 60–65 allowed me to think and fume, fume and think.

I'd had it figured by the time I crossed the drawbridge, the icy water below, passing seagulls fluttering at eye level, and I kept going over it on the wide parkway. Craw might've been the badge, but in a town like Silver Haven, people like Powell were the law, and if Powell said I smacked Ezra Exxon, the message he was sending wasn't necessarily about what had happened. The message was about how he wanted it to be, whether or not it played. It was the sheriff's job to make it work.

Craw had known I was in town minutes after I

arrived yesterday afternoon. It was my bad luck to run into Maki, and she directed me straight to Powell's thug. Then she tailed me out of town, making sure I didn't double back on Powell or Brabender.

They'd been waiting for the shakedown, including the cops, and I fit the profile, with my low-budget rental, my sneakers and jeans, the dents in my Buonarroti nose, the way I carried myself: a stranger in town, looking for the victim of the scam.

But what kind of shakedown artist asks a cop for directions to the mark?

In the end, for all their violence and bluster, what they told me was none of them knew where Allie was, nor did they know what had happened to whatever was heisted from Powell's car.

Happens all the time. Guys are so goddamned smart, so goddamned busy looking at the angles, thinking all sorts of shit, they forget what they were supposed to do in the first place.

Powell should've been making sure his kid was OK, and he should've had Brabender working the back alleys, if they had back alleys in Silver Haven, while Craw ran down the break-in of Powell's Mercedes from the straight side.

No, not these guys. Too busy protecting their little thing, these kings of their little world, their Silver Haven.

I don't know what I was thinking when it happened. Maybe I was thinking about the snow, and how it used to pile up to our eyebrows back in Narrow's Gate. Or how I began to blossom as a ballplayer at St. Barnabas in my freshman year, when I shot up seven inches in 11 months.

Or of Marina packing her sketch pad and pastels in her leather satchel and heading off, more often than not leaving Davy with me. "I don't know," she'd reply, perhaps too calmly, her accent surprisingly thick. "I go where I go. I see something, maybe, to paint. It's difficult in New York, so I must look everywhere."

I sent Weisz a copy of Wittgenstein's études for the left hand. Dr. Harteveld said it was OK, that the former prodigy might appreciate a kindness, might understand that I no longer sought to destroy him.

She didn't think, as Lt. Addison implied, that I was cultivating him so he'd one day describe the man Marina was with.

He wrote back a note. His left-handed scrawl was as feckless as a child's.

Mr. Orr:
Thank you for the book.
Thank you for saving me.
Your friend,
Raymond

The letter was mailed from the Rockland Psychiatric Center, upstate in Orangeburg.

On the parkway, a few cars here and there,

motoring placidly, everyone listening to their radio, and I was in the right lane, thick trees and mounds of old snow to my immediate right, and I felt the rush of wind, not from the winter skies, but from a big vehicle, coming out of nowhere, set to pass in the center lane. But the dark vehicle didn't pass. It drew even with me, eased off, then bumped me above the left rear tire. The tap sent me into a whirling 360-degree spin, and then I careened onto the parkway shoulder and off the road.

And the next thing I knew, I was struggling to pull myself out of the Ford, which had flipped and landed on its right side, skidding to a few feet from the dense line of trees, the speckled snow mounds. The air bag had hit me hard, and my face was coated with blood, and I felt a dull pain in my right shoulder, and when I finally managed to get myself out of the car, I stood dazed among the sweet pines, among the brown needles on the pristine snow, the raw bottom of the car right behind me, and then, when I looked down, I noticed that my left index finger had been dislocated.

My eyes watered as I nudged my finger back into its socket.

I decided to move up the incline, wondering if the vehicle that hit me might've stopped, or spun out and smacked the guard rail to its left. Wobbling, I stumbled into the rip and rut the car's tires had made in the cold ground, and I fell. And as I stood again, I realized I wasn't going to make it, that I was about to pass out, and I did, collapsing on the incline, the left side of my bloody face hitting the hard turf.

Moments later, an hour later, a few minutes later, an EMT wagon pulled onto the shoulder, and a young woman, a stocking cap over her blond hair, slid down the incline, her heavyset partner scurrying behind her. They wore matching blue jackets that reflected the sparse light, deflected the falling snow, and rustled as they moved toward me.

"Sir," she said, as she whipped off her dark ski gloves, "can you hear me?"

"The hairline," the heavyset man said as he leaned in, "on the right, up. The gash."

He adjusted his glasses as the young woman tipped open her emergency kit.

"I have a daughter," I told them, with voice wavering. "I need to talk to her—"

"Can you tell me your name, sir?" she said.

"Yes," I replied. "I can."

"Do you know where you are?" She snapped on a pair of latex gloves.

"Yes. But my daughter will worry."

The woman looked at her partner as she tore open a packet and removed a thick piece of gauze. "Is he all right?"

"I don't know," he said. "Looks kind of dazed, doesn't he?"

I turned myself onto my back, rolling on the cold ground, the prickly needles, reviving the pain in my shoulder.

The scent of the earth, and the taste of my own blood.

I squinted to block the rays of silver light that pushed through the trees.

"Do you know what happened to you?" she asked as she pressed the gauze against the top of my forehead.

"Some— Some son of a bitch tried to kill me," I replied weakly.

"You've had an accident," the man began, as his walkie-talkie sparked with static.

"No, not an accident," I told him as I began to fade out.

They brought me to Bayshore Community Hospital, part of a huge, industrial complex in Holmdel, which was about 20 miles from Powell's Silver Haven, and they took 14 stitches in my scalp, and left me with a wide bandage on my forehead and a splint on my finger.

And when the intern who'd worked on me told me the police needed to speak to me, I nodded, asked her to give me a moment to pull myself together, and eased off the gurney, retrieved my shirt, jacket and sneakers from the chair, squeezed between the vents of the thin green curtain and left the emergency room. I dressed quickly in the bathroom, and toweled as much of the blood and mulch from my jacket as I could, and set out for daylight.

At the hospital's main entrance, an old woman with a walker grimaced when she looked up at me as I went for the taxi beyond the driveway.

"Where you going?" the driver asked.

"New York City," I said. I had a bitch of a head-ache, and the brusque intern hadn't done a damned thing about the ache in my shoulder.

"I can't do it," he told me. His face was red, not from the wind, but from some kind of skin condition. Eczema, something.

"Just get me the fuck out of Monmouth County," I said.

Twelve minutes later, I was on a train out of Hazlet, heading north to Penn Station.

I called Bella, got her cell's voice mail. No doubt that's Marcus with her, immortalized on a microchip.

"Hey, dig, it's me," she says, giggling happily, innocently. A boy's voice in the near distance, singing in a goofy falsetto. They're outdoors; a siren in the distance. She turns from the mouth-piece. "Stop it," she demands, but there's no authority in her voice. The boy makes another sound, or maybe just a funny face, and Bella bursts. So does he. "Wait— Stop. Wait for the beep," she manages finally. She turns away again, giggling harder now. "You!"

Beeeeeeep.

I dialed her number again, just to hear her laugh.

CHAPTER 6

I came off the elevator at 100 Center Street confident my swollen nose, scuffed cheek and bloodstained shirt might get the attention of Officer Casey, who insisted always, despite maybe 50 visits in the past five years to Sharon, to Julie, that I present credentials before he'd pick up the phone. But before I could shuffle over to the security desk, I was intercepted by Chad Gayle, another of Sharon's deputies, who was on his way out. Proper, composed, considerate, Gayle looked magnificent in his camel-hair coat, a burgundy and gold scarf.

That man, I thought as I stood in the lobby, is the opposite of me.

A self-deprecating dry wit who loved to tease sweet Julie about her relationship with "an insolent brute of a man," Gayle frowned disapprovingly, took my hand and rested it on his arm. His sleeve felt like a cloud. "If you've come here for sympathy, Terry . . ."

I knew I looked like shit, but I was going to tell Julie what happened. I didn't want her to get blowback from someone in the office who heard the

New Jersey State Police told NYPD they had to talk to me. Then I was going to call Addison, let him know, while it was all fresh in my head. My wobbly, pounding, full-of-fog head.

"Chad," I said, nodding gently.

"Rough night?"

"It's, what, like three-thirty, four o'clock in the afternoon, isn't it?"

"Hey, I don't know what hours you tough guys keep."

I pointed to the bandage on my head with my splinted finger. "Tough guy."

As he lifted his alligator briefcase, he said, "Come on, I'll take you back. I'd say you need to see Julie."

"Maybe I ought to wash up first."

"At least," he said.

A new flock of messengers entered the hall from the elevator behind him, dragging in cold air with them.

Gayle crossed his arms, put his finger on his chin, hmmmed thoughtfully. "I was going to suggest a dash over to Century 21 for a new outfit, but I like that blood on the collar, the mud on your leather coat. Very Steve McQueen."

I sighed in resignation.

"All right then," Gayle said.

"And that's it," I said. "I left the hospital, took a train, decided to get out at Newark, and took the PATH downtown. Here I am."

Gayle gave me a piece of Dentyne, which I used to get the taste of earth out of my mouth while I took off my sweater and shirt and washed off with cold water and paper towels. As I patted myself dry, I noticed my shoulder had begun to go purple, with a nasty yellow soon to follow.

No, I wasn't going to be catching any lob passes from Bella for a while.

"Terry, you could have been killed." She wore a thick, muted-yellow sweater and black slacks, and her crucifix caught the fluorescent lights, glistened.

She let go of my hand.

"Julie, please don't look at me like that," I said. "Like you're going to burst into tears and kick my ass at the same time."

She let out a breath and took a sip from the cold water she'd brought me.

"Yeah, but say something."

She drummed the table, and then said, "What is this all about, Terry? Explain that to me. What are you doing that's worth this?"

On the conference-room wall, the rows of West reporters and other legal books seemed to hover, as if deciding whom to support. I leaned forward, hung my head.

As she dusted pine needles from my hair, she asked, "Is this something to do, Terry, now that Weisz is . . . Your quest for—"

"'Quest.'" I slapped my thigh as I sat back. "Christ."

She stared at me.

"What?" I said finally. "Julie, are you mad at me? That would be incredible, if you were mad at me."

"You could have been killed."

"Julie, I'm here. All right? I'm right here. I got hurt, I came to you . . ."

I thought I saw tears well under her brown eyes. "Terry, every time I think you're moving forward—"

She was interrupted by a single harsh whack on the conference-room door.

Virginia Gonzalez, Sharon's take-charge secretary, pushed her head into the room.

"We're looking for you," she said, pointing at me.

"It's all right, Ginny," Julie replied dryly. "Feel free to come on in."

The black-haired, black-eyed secretary looked hard at her, snorted and turned to me. Considering she was no more than five feet tall in heels and wore braces on her teeth, she looked fairly formidable.

"Ms. Knight wants you now," she said, addressing me.

I stood, gingerly.

"Just give us a minute, Ginny," Julie said. "I'll walk him back."

"I'll wait," she replied, her hand on the knob. "Ms. Knight wants him now."

"I'm coming," I told her. "Thirty seconds, OK?"

She frowned, shook her head and reluctantly closed the door.

"Is it that you don't like her or she doesn't like you?" I asked.

"A lot of both," Julie replied, adding, "I wonder what Sharon wants."

"I guess she's going to tell me again not to beat up anybody," I said as she came toward me.

"Not when she gets a look at you."

"That bad?"

"Worse."

She instructed me to hand over my leather jacket, and she gently brushed the flakes of dried mud from my sweater.

I took her hand, kissed her palm.

"I'm presentable?" I asked.

"I was going to say you look like one of those hard-boiled private investigators—"

"Very Steve McQueen, I'm told."

"—but I don't want to encourage you."

She kissed my bottom lip, and I hugged her tight.

"Such tenderness," I said, "despite this." I stepped back, pointed to my scrapes, swollen nose, the patch on my forehead.

Patting my scored cheek, she said, "We must take the good with the bad."

Sharon was behind her desk, in what seemed to be a casual conversation with a tony, dark-haired woman who sat facing her, her legs crossed in a manner that might define femininity.

"My Lord, Terry—"

The woman turned, and she frowned as if annoyed.

"Terry, this is remarkable," the executive A.D.A. continued. "Even for you."

"Sharon, in my pocket I've got thirty-nine dollars, a train receipt and two Tylenol with codeine I swiped from the hospital," I said as I tried to ignore the disapproving gaze of her guest. "It's all yours if you promise not to lecture me."

She chuckled, shook her head, told me to sit.

I took the chair next to her cluttered table. To my left, afternoon had begun to yield to a winter evening's early descent on Federal Plaza, on lower Broadway. Wan light eased between the slates of the venetian blinds.

"Alex, this is the man I was telling you about."

I turned to my right. Alex wore brown—brown high-heeled boots into which were tucked matching brown ski pants, and a light-coffee cowl-neck sweater, and she held a pair of leather gloves in her tapered hands. The gloves looked as if she'd been wringing them as she spoke. Though hearty, and seemingly resolute, she appeared a bit tired, though her face had a natural freshness that suggested she spent time outdoors.

She had big Jackie O–style sunglasses resting on the top of her head, atop her shining hair which, to avoid concealing her faultless chin, had been brushed back and away from her face, tucked behind her ears. Her gold hoop earrings complemented her wedding band and the big teardrop diamond that sat above it.

"Terry, this is an old college friend of mine. Alexandra Powell."

"Alexandra Powell," I repeated.

I did my best to conceal my surprise.

For a moment, I considered whether I was still lying under the pine trees, still on the gurney at Bayshore Community Hospital, and that I had dreamed of an easy solution to finding 14-year-old Allie Powell.

But I don't imagine I'd come up with one as simple as this.

"Terry, Alex needs your help," Sharon said. "We both need your help."

Powell laid her hand in mine and offered the thinnest smile.

"Her son is missing," Sharon said.

"Alexander," Alex Powell said softly, as she turned away from me. "Allie, we call him."

"'We' being . . ."

She lowered her sunglasses until they were high on her thin nose, and she began to wriggle into her gloves. "His father and I."

John McPorter also called him Allie, I told myself.

"Can you tell me a bit more, please?"

"He hasn't been to school—either school—in days."

At least 14, I thought.

137

"Schools?"

"He's quite gifted, my Allie," Mrs. Powell said. "He attends the Fashion Institute of Technology as well as Silver Haven High School."

"I take it you live in Silver Haven."

Her response was an almost imperceptible nod.

Sharon said, "But he was last seen here, Terry."

"He has some envelopes," Alex added.

If that's so, he also has $471.

"I trust these envelopes aren't empty," I said.

"Hardly."

Sharon said, "Terry—"

"What's in them?"

Mrs. Powell looked at her old college pal.

"And if Allie's been missing for days," I asked, "what's the urgency to find him now?"

"Terry, I can fill you in," Sharon interjected.

"Do we have a photo of your son, Mrs. Powell?"

"I'll get you one, Terry," the executive A.D.A. said.

A photographer ought to be able to provide a photo of her only son.

She stood, and so did Sharon. I stayed in my seat.

"Would you mind . . . ?"

Sharon said, "No, of course not."

I watched as they shook hands. There was little warmth in the gesture.

"I'll have Virginia—"

"No, it's not necessary," she said as she raised her head high. "I'm certain I can find my way."

As Alex Powell went toward the door, Sharon said, "I'll call."

"Please do."

For a moment, it was as if she had pulled the air out of the room, leaving us unable to speak.

Sharon pointed to the door, and I went to draw it shut.

I stood behind the chair Mrs. Powell had occupied. Traces of her perfume: orange, the vaguest trace of ginger, musk.

Sharon sat back as if relieved.

"Why do I get the sense you feel as bad as I look?" I asked. "It's not The Surgeon, is it?"

She shook her head. Then, falling into thought, she went silent, and her eyes began to shift as if she were reading a message written on the air.

"You have something to tell me, Sharon . . . ?"

Still no reply, and I could hear the wheeze of the heat emitted from the vents near the floorboards, the rush of traffic on Broadway.

"I'll go first," I said.

Incredulous, she'd asked, "How in God's name do you know that?"

Then I'd told her about Daniel's request and what I'd learned.

"And you think Alex's husband is somehow responsible for all that?" She pointed to my head, face, splint.

I nodded. "Plus the ass-kicking I got yesterday,

and the scam he tried to run on me this morning with the Exxon kid."

"Then she's got good reason to be concerned," she said as she reached for the telephone, pressed a button.

As I stepped toward the window, looked down at the bare trees in Paine Park, I could hear the buzzer in the outer vestibule.

"Ginny," she said, "see if you can find Luther Addison for me, please."

My tale included John McPorter, his body dangling on the fence, and I told her about his safe, the missing $471.

Addressing me, she said, "I would say this is an incredible coincidence."

"Well, it's at least that," I replied as I turned to face her.

"So now you're working for the mother and the father."

Sharon Knight had a wicked smile.

"I think I'd better find those envelopes."

"You don't think they're with the boy?" she asked as she cast a glance at the silent intercom.

"I'm thinking the mother doesn't come to the D.A. if she thinks her son stole nearly 500 bucks from a family friend," I told her.

"No, she comes if she thinks he's in danger—"

"Or if she wants what's in the envelopes. If it's something else, I'm not seeing it, at least not now."

She hesitated, ran her tongue against the back

of her teeth as her eyes once again went blank. Then she began to twiddle her thumbs.

"I didn't think people actually did that," I said.

"Did what? Oh, this"—she unlocked her fingers as if she'd been caught in sin. "My mother would whack me or my sister with a spatula if she saw one of us—"

The phone interrupted her tale.

"Oh," she said. "Well, leave a message at the precinct. Thanks."

As she returned the handset to the cradle, she looked at me. "Luther's with the Grand Jury."

"This late?"

"Apparently." She abruptly changed her tone, knitting her brow into a tight frown, tapping the flat of her hand in an odd rhythm on her desk. "Listen, Terry, there's an issue here."

"With Addison?"

"No, with Alex Powell," she replied. "With Alex Powell and those envelopes."

I came around, eased into the seat I'd used earlier. "Go on."

As I crossed Greenwich, walking slow, trying to take in the late-evening air to calm my fluttering stomach, I saw the front door of my house open, and our housekeeper Mrs. Maoli come out into the stark evening and she carefully shut the door behind her, squeezing out the glow from our kitchen. The plump Italian, who was somewhere in her mid-60s, carried a small sack of trash, and she was bundled tight against the cold, a black scarf up around her ears, ready for her nightly stroll back to Little Italy. Snow, rain, gale-force winds, the mid-August heat—no cab for her, no. Though she still coddled Bella as if she were her *nonna,* Natalia Maoli could be as tough as weathered leather, and more stubborn than the proverbial mule.

I came up behind her just as she was returning the lid to the garbage can.

She screamed when she turned to me. *"Dio mio!"*

In the dull glimmering of the streetlights, I must have looked monstrous.

"Mr. Orr," she said as she blessed herself, "what did you do to yourself?"

As I started to explain, I heard a voice behind me.

"Well, it was bound to happen," said Bella, coming in from basketball practice, blue toque pulled over her eyebrows.

As she greeted Mrs. Maoli, telling her in Italian not to fret, she went to hand me her backpack and duffel full of gym clothes.

"Can't do it," I told her, pointing at my right shoulder with the splint on my left index finger.

"Come on, then," she said stoically, hoisting the bags. "Let's fix you up."

"Buona notte, signora," I said to our housekeeper as I followed my daughter up the brick steps.

Mrs. Maoli nodded, then, shaking her head, muttered, *"Che ragazzo!"*

As in "What a boy." As opposed to "What a man," and, thus, meaning "What a dope."

Who could argue?

Inside the house, Bella threw her backpack and gym bag on the floor, tossed her coat on the back of her chair and gave Beagle a few crisp taps on her haunch.

I recognized her shirt, an old-school Houston Astros jersey, rainbows around the midsection. It belonged to Daniel; on my daughter, it was too big and too short at the same time. She wore a yellow T-shirt underneath, which matched her socks, a smiley-face earring in her right ear and several rubber bands of various colors on her wrist.

"Feed her and sit," she instructed.

"Me?" I hung my coat on the laundry-room door, not without a grimace as I reached for the hanger.

"Feed her and sit while I warm up my hands," she said.

I went for the sack of dog food at the bottom of the cabinet.

"You look like shit, Dad."

"Eloquent."

Beagle started chomping before I was done filling the dish.

Deep in her authoritative mode, Bella ran hot water on her hands and scrubbed with dish detergent, mimicking a surgeon's zeal.

"I'm sitting now," I told her.

She went to the bathroom, returned with the tin of Band-Aids, a bottle of peroxide, Q-tips and a pair of surgical scissors.

"Do you know where Daniel is?" I asked.

"Home, I guess. Why?"

"I need to—"

"Don't tell me all this is over Elixa. Is it?"

"Not precisely."

"It is," she groaned. She rolled her eyes—and when my daughter rolls her eyes at me, she somehow makes her entire pupils and irises disappear. "You, sir, are gullible."

"Look, I'm trying to help a—"

"Quiet. I'm operating here."

She carefully removed the bandage from the gash in my forehead.

"How many?"

"Fourteen," I said.

"I think they overreacted," she replied. "It's deep, but . . ."

"Yowww!" I heard the peroxide hiss.

She flicked my earlobe with her finger. "Big baby."

Cringing, I waited for her to sting me again, but no.

She blew on the wound.

"How'd it go at practice?" I asked.

"Coach G let me run the first-string offense."

"From the point? Wow."

She was studying the wound. "Yeah, well, Delia had detention, and Becca's knee is sore, so . . .

144

But it was fine, good. I did good." She looked at my hand. "Do you need that splint? I'm guessing no. They put it on so you don't sue their asses. Malpractice."

She tore open a large Band-Aid, carefully placed it on my forehead.

"Perfect," she announced.

I was flexing my hand, splint on the table, when she decided the scrapes on my cheek ought to be left alone.

"Ice for the nose. Ice for the shoulder. You'll live. Disappointed?"

"Don't be so cavalier, Bella," I said as I stood, gathered the splint, the Q-tips, the paper from the back of the Band-Aid.

"Your mission is to give yourself as much pain as possible," she replied. "So today must be a good one in Terry Orrville."

I suppose I should be grateful she's joking about it. For the first year or so after I began trying to work as a P.I., she was furious with me, and embarrassed to the point of shame.

Rightfully so, I've concluded.

How many nights did she stare at her bedroom ceiling while Diddio, Mrs. Maoli or Glo-Bug's mom sat downstairs, biding time, filling in for me while I roamed the streets? Looking for Weisz; no, talking to Marina, listening to Marina.

When I should've been giving Bella what she gave me.

I tossed the trash in the bathroom can, looked

in the mirror. The big Band-Aid she'd stuck up near my hairline made me look like I'd had a minor household accident—a tumble while spackling up near the ceiling or fixing a shelf—rather than a wreck on the highway.

"Thanks, Bella," I said as I returned for the medical gear. "Good job."

She smiled at me, and there was a flicker of tenderness in her eyes.

As I was restocking the medicine cabinet, she said, "By the way, Dad, you should've let Julie stay here last night."

"I don't think so."

"She was miserable."

"No, I think she was all right by the time she settled in."

I pulled the string, cut the bathroom light.

My daughter was drinking cranberry juice out of the bottle.

"I saw her today. She's fine."

Red mustache. "If you're doing it for me, don't," she said. "I like it when she's here. Besides, how is Wednesday different than Friday? I mean, I wake up Saturday morning and she's here."

"Point taken, Bella. And get a glass, for Christ's sake."

"I'm done." She slid the plastic bottle back into the refrigerator, nudging the Tupperware containers filled with the meals Mrs. Maoli made for the week. The freezer was filled too, no doubt. *Nonna* used to cook so many meals because she thought

I'd let us starve. Now she did it to crowd Julie out of the kitchen. The way she looked at the yogurt Julie bought, the sesame flatbread, the corned beef . . .

"But you're still seeing her tonight, right?" she asked as she came around the table.

"Yeah, we're going to the movies. Last night for the new Carl Franklin."

She opened the laundry-room door, tossed the gym bag downstairs.

"Want to join us?"

"Can't," she said, shaking her head. "Busy."

"Ah. You need me gone because people are coming over."

"Dad, stop. Please."

I watched as she began to unload her books. Out came Nietzsche, then *Today's Isms*, followed by her own copy of *Slaughterhouse-Five* and a variety of notebooks, her magic markers. Her journal, chapter 120 or so—one per month since she was five years old.

"Who?"

"If I say Daniel, will you be satisfied?"

"Yes. Of course."

"Or Gloria."

"Sure," I nodded.

"All right then."

"So it's Daniel and Glo-Bug?" I said.

"Dad, don't ask me to lie," she replied. "I'm 15 and I can take care of myself."

I said, "You think so?"

"I know so," she replied as she grabbed her down coat. "And so do you."

She headed toward the stairs up to her bedroom, her coat crammed under her arm. Her mittens and toque still lay on the floor.

"Give me your coat," I said. "I'll hang it up."

"I don't want you to get your blood on it," she replied as she began to disappear.

We left the theater on Second and 32nd to find the wafting snow sticking to the concrete, the blacktop, the parked cars and to my hair.

Julie had a faux-fur thing on her head that was as unfashionable as it was functional and she didn't care. As she took my arm, we both knew her hair would stay dry.

The Franklin noir shoot-'em-up was great—this guy would've been at home among Hollywood directors in the '40s: Curtiz, Dieterle, Wellman—and it took my mind off the things that occupy my mind. And when the film sagged—I suppose there has to be a love story somewhere in the damned picture—I reviewed the conversation I'd had with Sharon, a woman who could be vulnerable and steel-strong at the same time.

"And so what's your issue?" I'd asked her.

Sharon looked at the cuff of her green silk blouse.

"It appears to be a question of what may be in the envelopes," she said.

"Whatever was in Harlan Powell's car," I replied.

"There is an implication," she said slowly, thoughtfully, "that it may be other items as well. Items that were stored at John McPorter's for safe-keeping while Harlan Powell tore his house upside down to find what was taken from him."

"So he thought his wife stole the stuff from his car."

"Or his son."

"Right," I said. "His wife or his son."

"So while he was thinking along those lines," she continued, "Alex said she decided she'd better get some personal items out of the house."

"Such as?"

"Certain photos."

"Of?"

She hesitated. "Of the two of us, among others. Together. Back at Wellesley."

"Oh boy." I sat back.

"You got that right."

Sharon told me she'd met Alexandra Crenshaw at freshman orientation at Wellesley College, where both women were political science majors. That was about all they had in common back then: Sharon was the first in her blue-collar family to attend college, while Alex came from blue-blood lines with 150-year-old roots in Boston's Beacon Hill. But they hit it off, Sharon said, and remained great friends, even after Alex changed her major to Media Studies.

"We were very close," Sharon said. "At times, I felt like she was the only woman on campus who knew where I was coming from, though who knows why."

"So . . . ?"

"Yeah, we were an item for a while. Not long. Alex was experimenting, and it sort of fizzled out."

"All right."

"But not before she took a few photos of us together."

"'Together.' Aha."

"Right," she said, "and she's a packrat, keeps all her negatives. *All* of them."

"Yeah, OK. But who gives a shit? You played around in college. I mean, you've never concealed your sexuality, Sharon. Everyone knows you're gay."

"That's not the issue," she said, edging forward in her seat. She counted on her fingers. "One, to be gay and to pose for explicit photos are two different things. Two, to pose for photos with the wife of a convicted felon is not conducive to maintaining an image as a law-and-order District Attorney."

I waved my hand in the air. "Christ, Sharon, how many years after the fact?"

"Harlan did no jail time. Walked away with his fortune intact. You don't think someone will suggest I might've intervened on his behalf with the SEC? As a favor to my old lover?"

I didn't get it, at least not at first. No one who knew Sharon Knight would suggest malfeasance on her part. The editorial writers at the *Post,* for example, or the drive-time hate-spewers on WABC took their shots, but the people who mattered respected her as hard-nosed, indefatigable, with a record of personal integrity that was beyond reproach.

"Terry, for the past several months," she said, "I've been exploring a new career option, an exciting one. I'm seriously considering running for Congress."

"The eighth district or the fourteenth?" I asked.

"How— You knew?"

"Not really," I told her, "but from the day I met you I knew this thing you occupy now was too small for you. So's the City Council. Congress is about right."

"Well, thank you," she said. "But you see my problem."

I nodded.

"People in the city cut me a lot of slack because I only turn up on their TV when we're putting a murderer away. They don't mind much if I'm gay— or black—when we do that."

"And Alex told you the photos were in the safe?"

"She said she grabbed as many negatives as she could, put them in an envelope and asked her friend Buddy McPorter to stash them away for her. She couldn't say for sure if the shots of the two of us were among them."

The snow tapered off, and soon only a few plump flakes fluttered to the sidewalk from above the streetlamps, above the stalwart trees. The light danced on the fresh coating, and we looked for side streets where no one had trod before us.

Julie was right. It was romantic: For a few moments, we were alone in Manhattan, and high above us, all of it—the gold spire of the New York Life building, the stately clock in the Met Life tower, the Flatiron Building as we exited Madison Square Park onto Fifth, the bold moon hovering above long, wispy clouds—all of it was beautifully romantic.

I told her everything I'd discussed with Sharon, who had insisted I do so, who insisted Julie and I keep no secrets on her behalf.

"Alex Powell sounds like a cold fish," Julie said as we crossed Second.

I couldn't disagree. I thought of her photo of the sun at McPorter's. Despite her apparent mastery of her craft, she succeeded in making the galaxy's source of energy and light look inert, ineffectual.

Or maybe that was her art: turning life into lifeless, the majestic into the indistinct.

"And how did you know about the districts?" she asked. "I thought it had to be the eighth."

"If she declares her residency as her condo on West End and 87th, it'll be the eighth," I said. "You ever hear her talk about her sister Joan?"

She nodded.

"Sharon owns the apartment on Roosevelt Island where Joan lives, and that's the fourteenth."

"I didn't know that. About Roosevelt Island," Julie said. She was walking on my left, away from my bum shoulder, and holding on tight, as if she might slip in the snow.

"I think I went over the edge a little there when I first met her," I said. "I ran a dossier on her. Addison too. I didn't think I could trust them."

"And? You trust them now?"

"Yeah," I said. "Yeah, I do."

"And what about me?" she asked, looking up.

"You have to ask if I trust—"

"No, no, what I meant is, did you run a dossier on me?"

I laughed. "I didn't know you then," I said. "You were just the very pretty woman in Sharon's office. Pretty and focused, and compassionate. Or so I was told."

"So you asked about me?" she said. "Admit you did."

The brisk night air felt refreshing on my face, and I ran a bare hand across a car roof as we continued east, leaving four long marks in the snow.

We walked in silence until we reached Julie's block.

"You coming up?" she said when we stopped in front of her brownstone.

"I don't think so," I told her as she went up the first step, brushing aside the virgin dusting. "I've got aches and I've got pains. Headache . . ."

"Are you sure? Look at you: snow in your hair,

your denim jacket all crumpled. The bottoms of your jeans are wet. Your feet must be freezing in those sneakers. Your hands. You need to get out of the cold."

"Give me a rain check, huh? A snow check."

"Of course."

"Besides, maybe if I rush home, I'll get to meet Marcus. The mystery man."

She began to remove her gloves. "He's a nice boy," she said casually.

"So we're told."

She reached into her pocketbook, dug for her keys. "No, he's fine. I met him."

"You met him?"

"Sure. A few weeks ago."

"Where was I?"

"At Leo's," she said, "pulling linoleum, chasing out the rats, selling the bar to the Dutch, whatever. Being busy, daydreaming. Being you."

"She introduces you to him, but not me? Unbelievable."

She found her keys, closed her bag. "He's afraid of you."

"Oh. Great."

"No, he's a big kid. Strong. They look good together. They fit. But he's afraid of you. He's seen you in the neighborhood."

I craned my neck, stared at the starless sky.

"You don't realize it—or maybe you do—but whatever is going on in that head of yours doesn't have much to do with what the world sees. You may be thinking, 'Oh poor me, I'm so . . .' you know, but the rest of us see a big, angry man. A man who looks like he could snap off your head."

"I'm going home," I said, pointing south, gesturing.

"Especially with that nose tonight, and those scrapes."

"Were that it was Halloween, huh?" I said. "My sack would be full of Snickers and pennies and apples. Chunkys."

She reached for me, and I backed away, only an inch or so, but away from her outstretched hand.

"Oh, I hurt your feelings? I'm sorry."

"Don't tease the dead man."

"Come here, cutie," she said. "If I can't, who can?"

We were eye-to-eye. I stepped up, reluctantly, put my hands around her waist.

"You want to see hurt feelings?"

"Not really—"

"Watch." She put her lips to my right ear. "I love you," she whispered.

She kissed my cold cheek.

A moment later, she cut the quiet.

"See? That's hurt feelings. On a night like this, and my lover stays silent."

She flipped the keys in her hand, turned and went up the stairs, kicking aside new snow.

I walked past my house, to West Street, to the river, and waiting for two *Daily News* trucks to rumble by, came back, and passed my house again. My shoulder hurt like hell, I had an awful headache, but I knew where I was. Not lost, but pacing. Lost. Juggling, living now: the boy Allie, the mother Alexandra. Well, we knew who was wearing the pants in the family when he came along, don't we? "I'm naming him after my favorite person in the whole world—me!" she said, without irony. No, what she probably said was, "You shall give him your family name, and I shall give him the name my family bestowed upon me." No, not that either. Probably somewhere in between. And Harlan? Harlan didn't give a shit. "*You* wanted him. *You* change his fuckin' diaper." Yeah, I can hear him now. No wonder the kid skipped. It wasn't $471. It was Dad, and icy Mom. The poor boy. Fourteen, and now out there; where?

Yeah, deep in the *now,* back to the river, crossing Greenwich toward where Leo's restaurant used to be. Where Marina and I took baby Bella.

Damn it.

Julie, whose lover stayed silent. Bella, whose boyfriend— Well, that's enough right there: Bella's boyfriend.

Davy, he's vivid tonight.

Wide smile. Round head. Bright eyes. He recognized me when I entered the room. Bella once told me he'd get all excited, giggle gleefully, start kicking his legs inside his Knicks pjs the moment I announced I was home—"I'm *ho-ome,*" I'd sort of sing, let the door slam behind me, drop the backpack filled with notes I'd taken at the library, a couple of books from the Strand, maybe Coliseum, including at least one for Bella.

"Dad, we're up here," my daughter shouted. "In my room."

"Bella, stai calma! Sto lavorando, eh? Dio!" Marina, from her studio down the hall, shouting.

"Sorry, Mama."

I shuddered, remembering what it was like to be excited as a child, and then told to be quiet, told that something more important than a child's happiness was going on nearby.

Suddenly, Davy started to wail.

I looked up and saw, on the west side of Greenwich, near my steps, a familiar face. Lee Rauch, who lived around the corner, first-floor apartment, rubber plants in the window, black *pow-mia* sticker. Another nightcrawler, 50ish, pug of a man, felt-green U.S. flag on his forearm, served in Nam, worked at a Crazy Eddie's warehouse in Long Island until a forklift rolled on him. Hooked up with a lawyer who had an 800 number, an ad on late-night TV. Lee's a millionaire now. His daughter Celia is over in Iraq; regular Army, like her dad. I remember when Celia was Bella's age.

Nighttime, he told me, was the worst. If Celia was going to get it, he knew it'd be at night. Night here, night there. Somewhere, it's night.

He said it like it was a done deal.

"Hey, Orr," he said when I joined him under

the violet light at the corner of Greenwich and Harrison.

If Beagle showed any kind of initiative, she'd be barking now.

"Been out long, Lee?"

He smiled, grabbed at his collar to cover his thick neck, the top of his pajamas. "You passed me twice, Orr."

"I did? Sorry."

"Cold as a tit." He feigned a shudder.

"Isn't it though?"

I thought we'd exhausted subjects for conversation.

"Listen, Lee, I've got to get in."

He nodded, dug into his jacket for his pack of Marlboros, smacked the pack against an open palm. "I'll say hi to the wife for you."

Behind him, a big black barge headed north, crunching ice.

"You pray for my Celia, huh?"

I told him I would.

"That is, if you start praying again, Orr."

Taxis rushed south. Limos. A woman in flats, nice overcoat, jogged no faster than she walked, but I could tell it made her feel like she was getting somewhere, making progress.

CHAPTER 7

I slept in, made short work of a call from a clerk at Avis, then went back to sleep. When I finally got out of bed, it was past 11 o'clock, and I returned a second call from the rental-car company. The conversation, which had grown as contentious as it was tedious, ended with me saying something like, "I guess I was lucky I took the extra insurance, wasn't I?" Her response, which clearly wasn't in the company playbook, was "You'll never rent another car in this town again, fucker." I went off to the shower, emerging 20 minutes later, pink as Sergeant Maki's nails had been, and I shaved, and I felt close to all right. Achy, swollen, still sleepy, out of sorts but close enough to all right.

In fact, with the exception of a dull headache and a little lightheadedness, I felt better than I had any right to expect. Apparently, I'd done a decent job of popping my index finger back into the socket, so I didn't need to replace the splint. The ice pack on the nose and left cheek while I watched Cassavetes' *Killing of a Chinese Bookie* had done its job. I couldn't do much with my shoulder, though maybe the scent-free Ben-Gay

159

I slathered on might eventually make it work as it should.

I came downstairs, in black jeans, a blue Oxford and a navy six-button sweater-vest Julie got me for Christmas, and I threw back my vitamins, washing them down with cold bottled water. I did the same with a pair of 500-milligram acetaminophen.

A plate of pumpkin biscotti, earmarked for the Tea Water Pump, no doubt, sat in the center of the kitchen table. I thought, "*Perfetto,* Mrs. Maoli," as I entertained thoughts of a quick cookie brunch.

As if on cue, she arrived, passing through the brick alcove, lemon wax and chamois mitt in hand.

"And how do you feel today, Mr. Orr?" she said, her accent typically thick, yet pleasant, mellifluous. As she stepped into the kitchen, her green clogs clattered on the pale linoleum. Beagle padded in behind her, and the droopy-eyed dog didn't look at me.

"*Molto meglio,* Mrs. Maoli," I replied. "*Grazie.*"

An old gray sweater covered the top of her apron and dress, and her bulbous nose was red, as if she had been dabbing at it with a handkerchief.

"I didn't wish to disturb you."

"No, no," I said. "You didn't."

"I didn't put on the washing machine," she told me. "The vacuum."

"Well, I'm going out, Mrs. Maoli. So you're on your own."

She frowned, stiffened. "Out? With your head?"

160

Conversation could be awkward with her, and not merely because of her limited English and my fumbling Italian. It was Marina who brought Mrs. Maoli to us, and her loyalty had been to her and her babies. Bella she loved, always. Me she tolerated. I suspected she had a good thing going with Beagle, who sat at her feet while she crafted our dinners, feasting on scraps of marinated pork, flank steak, homemade pasta.

Further, she had a way of pronouncing judgment with a word, a raised eyebrow, a downward glance, a sudden frown, though, if quizzed, she would insist she kept her thoughts to herself. Her judgment this time? This chucklehead doesn't know when he's beaten. Terry Orr: punching bag.

I wonder how you say that in Italian.

"So I'm . . . I'm going uptown," I said, as I edged toward the laundry-room door, pointing with my thumb.

"Mr. Orr, Gabriella says you cannot wear the leather jacket," she informed me.

"No, I guess not."

"I bring to the cleaners."

I grabbed the denim carpenter's coat off the back of the door and carefully eased into it, trying in vain not to jar my shoulder.

"Mr. Orr, you will be cold," she said.

"It's lined," I told her, as I reached for a cookie.

"But you don't have gloves."

To my surprise, there was a black leather glove in each pocket.

When I produced them, pumpkin cookie in mouth, she said, "Ah, Gabriella. She's the smart one."

I put the gloves back in the pockets and told Mrs. Maoli I'd see her tonight.

"Be careful," she advised. "You know . . ." She pointed to her head, then mine.

As I turned up the denim collar, I told her I would be.

A rocky ride on the 1-and-9 subway line brought me to 27th, and I stationed myself on the east side of Seventh Avenue, in front of a sandwich shop called Manhattan Heroes. Stifling a yawn, I put the sole of my sneaker against a brick wall, leaned back and faced the broad beige buildings of the Fashion Institute of Technology, where Allie Powell was a part-time student.

Addison had been here already, no doubt, or had sent one of his charges, and now Allie was deeper in hiding than he'd been before—not only far away from his parents but the cops too, driven off by John McPorter's murder, the theft of $471 and his mother's negatives from the dead man's safe, and maybe what had been taken from his father's car.

Maybe that's why he'd decided to spend his weekends at McPorter's: He was tired of his old man accusing him of swiping something from his car.

Or maybe he knew who did it, and that's why he had to run.

I looked up at the distant sun beyond the pale sky. What little heat it provided was an illusion, a harbinger not of warmer days, but a suggestion that winter would last until mid-April. Probably cold as Kirovsk along the water in Silver Haven this morning, thought not as cold as it would be for a young, frightened boy on the run.

Across the street, FIT students emerged on a cigarette break, to head for the subway.

I had asked Daniel to contact Elixa, see if she'd meet me.

She would, he told me, and added that maybe I'd better not tell Bella any more about this.

"She's mad at both of us," he said, as I took his call last night in the lobby of the Loews Kips Bay. "Disappointed, I'd say. Which is worse, wouldn't you agree?"

About 15 minutes into the watch, I noticed a young girl, younger than most of the students, who'd come out, looked north, south, looked at the sun. Hooded sweatshirt under her peacoat, its hood up over her head.

With my hands still deep in my pockets, I skated across Seventh as a fleet of yellow cabs rushed by.

She had on old blue jeans and thick black boots, and there was a silver ring through her left nostril, and dark green, tusk-like tattoos came from

163

somewhere on her shoulders to the sides of her neck. She had nibbled her fingernails almost to the quick, and the index and middle finger of her right hand, which extended from her fingerless gloves, were stained with nicotine.

In the window of the school's museum behind her was a tall, thin swan of a mannequin in a long, sequined dress that clung close to its body. The mannequin had its arm extended just so, and the cigarette at the end of its holder seemed to be waiting for Gatsby to appear with a gold-plated lighter.

"Fuck off, perv," the girl said.

"'Perv'?"

"Yeah. I saw you checking me out," she said, and she spit on the sidewalk.

"I'm Terry Orr. We're meeting, remember?"

"Yeah, yeah." She looked away, focusing on some object in the distance, way uptown. "Of course, I remember." Under her breath, she added, "I'm not the one who's got the dent in his head."

"I need more on Allie Powell," I said.

"I thought you were going to find him."

"Well, it's gotten a bit complicated. I mean, with what happened to his uncle."

She looked at me, squinting, shielding her eyes from the deceptive sun. "It's not his—What do you mean 'what happened to his uncle'? What? What happened?"

"He's dead," I said, "and somebody killed him."

She flicked the cigarette butt into the street. "No shit."

"None," I said, and I told her what I'd seen on 64th Street—the blood, the body on the rails, the sickened onlookers.

"That made their day, I'll bet," she said. A tough cookie, this one.

A UPS truck pulled to the west side of the street, and the driver hopped out and scurried to the rear, where the packages were stacked. No brown shorts, brown knee socks, for him today: a parka worthy of Amundsen at the South Pole.

"And still no word from Allie?" I asked.

"Nobody's seen Allie."

She walked into the shade, and I called to her. When she didn't turn, I followed, and we were under the building's overhang, and I was adjusting my eyes to the shadows.

"Look, man, I don't know where he is," she said. "I tried to find him, I couldn't. Now you're supposed to find him."

"I need something to go on," I told her, adding that I'd been to Silver Haven, met his mother and father. I didn't mention the square-headed thug Brabender or the crooked cops. "Only take you a few minutes."

She thought about it, moving her jaw as if she were grinding her teeth as she looked uptown.

Finally, she said, "I haven't had lunch yet."

I pointed to the other side of Seventh. "Pizza?"

She said, "Let's do it."

★ ★ ★

165

Allie was a troubled boy, and Silver Haven a war zone. Not necessarily the entire town, Elixa told me, but the high school and the Powell home. Harlan Powell had a favorite nickname for his 14-year-old boy: faggot.

I asked her if Allie was gay.

"He doesn't know," she said, as she nibbled on the crust before moving on to a second piece, which until moments ago had been mine. "He doesn't know who he is, what he is. He's just a kid, man."

I could've made better pizza by pouring ketchup on cardboard, but Elixa seemed content. She went at the second slice as she had the first, picking at the bubbles in the dough.

At least I was enjoying the Pepsi I'd ordered. The caffeine, I figured, would keep me alert and help speed the painkiller through my bloodstream. At least I hoped so: My headache was coming back, and I feared it was intent on revenging its banishment.

"So what gives his father the idea his son's gay?" I asked.

"You know how many of us have to put up with that shit?" she replied, pointing over my shoulder at the school. "Like you've got to be weird or something to like design." She shook her head. "Assholes."

The older students in the back of the pizza parlor looked happy enough to me. Maybe it was because they shared the same dreams, or simply had made it through high school.

"What about his mom?"

"She's an artist," Elixa said, "a photographer. So she's cool, I guess. I don't know." She dashed garlic powder on the bland crust. "She hates her husband. I know that."

"Really?"

"People need love, man."

I took a sip of the cold cola, let a piece of ice slide into my mouth. So far, Elixa hadn't given me anything I didn't know or couldn't have guessed.

"Tell me about his work," I said, as I rubbed my temples.

"He's good. Real good. His age and already he's got a vision."

She said it like she was 20 years older than her classmate.

"He loves traditional Asian apparel. Updates it. And it works, man. None of this looks-like-a-kimono shit neither. Great sketches—the best in the class. Stitches like a tailor. Knows cloth, color. Man, he's great. No bullshit."

She wiped her mouth on the sleeve of her sweatshirt, looked at her watch—a small face surrounded by a wide, tattered leather band.

"I need a smoke," she said as she dug into her coat pocket. "Let's take it outside."

Just in time, I thought. In here, the rank odor of tar and nicotine blended into the scent of bad pizza, lackluster tomato sauce, the clang of aluminum trays, and the static-laced blare of Mega

97.9. I couldn't take it, the smell, taste, the sound, not with my stomach empty and my head starting to pound. I reached behind me, grabbed my jacket with my left hand.

"Hurt yourself?"

I nodded. "Not too bad," I said.

I started toward the exit to Seventh, as she ducked under her hood and wriggled into her coat.

"Wait," she said, "I want to ask you something."

She skidded after me and joined me outside the pizza joint. I stood with my back to the restaurant. An Econoline van with Jersey plates that stood at the curb.

Elixa put her hand over her eyes to dull the sun, looked at the van.

"Gabriella Orr. She's your daughter, right?"

Had to be a rhetorical question. "Yep."

"She doesn't look like you."

Wasn't the first time I'd heard that.

"Man, she's, like, the best student at Whitman, plays on the basketball team and shit. Everybody thinks she's great."

I shoved my hands deep in my jeans pockets. "Thanks."

"I heard you were a writer," she said, "and your wife is, like, some super-fantastic painter."

"True." As in "was true," not "is true."

"Gabriella, she wrote some kind of book too, didn't she?"

I said she did.

"Shit, man, you must be proud."

I nodded, but said nothing. I was uncomfortable talking about Bella while I was working, as if refusing to acknowledge her would somehow shield her from what I heard and saw.

Behind me, somewhere near the General Post Office, a car horn let loose a piercing wail that careened off brick façades. When it faded, I could hear the rear doors of the Econoline van creak open.

"She doesn't like me, your daughter," Elixa said. "Not that I give a shit, but she doesn't. Being popular and shit? Fuck that." She blew a stream of cigarette smoke toward the cold sky. "I don't need that shit."

"Who told you she doesn't like you?" I said. "I don't think that's true."

She eyed me suspiciously. "It's true."

Everything this kid said and did told me she wanted acceptance, didn't think she'd get it so she decided to strike at the world before it went after her.

I believe Bella would forgive me a white lie.

"I'm not sure you're right, Elixa. Bella was there when Daniel was telling me good things about you, and she told me that you had a good heart. And she thought we ought to help you find your friend, so—"

Suddenly, I was slammed from the rear and I felt a man's forearm lock tight across my throat. Before I could react, I felt myself being wrestled away from the girl.

"Go," the man shouted. "Goddamn it, go."

I couldn't wriggle free of the man's rigid grip. Though I struggled, he was strong enough to lift me off the ground as he dragged me backward, and I couldn't catch my breath.

Elixa seemed to disappear.

Just as I lifted my arm to ram an elbow into his gut, we fell, landing in the van's cargo bay.

The man got his leg around my hip.

He shouted something I couldn't hear, and then the van ripped from the curb. The rear doors swung wildly as we tore south, made a squealing turn onto 25th Street.

The sharp curve sent us both rattling hard against an inside wall, allowing me to wriggle free of his grip, and scraping my sneakers on the floor, I scrambled backward toward the front of the vehicle.

Though he was on his knees, the man gathered himself to bolt across at me.

I didn't recognize him, but I saw, below his short-cropped hair and fierce scowl, the fury in his eyes and the veins pulsing in his thick neck: a stranger, wired, determined to take me down.

I put my left hand up on the passenger's seat for leverage. But I had no chance with this bull of a man, not with my injured shoulder and pounding head. The plunge into the van, and the tumble across the cold floor, had left me dizzy and disoriented.

I looked to my right. Ezra Exxon was the driver.

I had no choice. Though we were speeding, I

reached up awkwardly and grabbed Ezra by the ponytail. As he screamed, I brought my left hand around and snatched at his face, catching his nose, his eyes.

The other man leaped on my back just as the van plowed into a car parked on the north side of 25th.

The airbag exploded and slammed into Ezra Torkelsen's face, chest. White powder flew into the back of the vehicle. Outside, a car alarm screamed.

I bounded off the seats and skidded toward my rival.

I kicked at him as he tried to square himself, driving my heel against his jaw. When he fell back, I sprang toward him and threw a looping left to the side of his head. It didn't do much.

I decided to roll out through the open door, to chance it on the street. As he grabbed at me, I heard the wail of a police siren, drawing closer.

He threw a wild right at my head, but by then I had dropped out of the van and landed hard on the cold blacktop.

As I hustled to my feet, ready to take the brunt of his furious charge, the blue-and-white came up behind us, and the tough guy stopped. He bent at the waist to catch his breath, clutching at his jeans.

The cops' arrival made him think the fight had ended. But it hadn't, and I kicked him hard, ramming my heel into the top of his head. He stumbled back, struggling to stay on his feet.

I squared up for his reply, the flashing red and

white lights sweeping over me. When one of the uniforms grabbed me by the crook of the elbow, I let out a breath, opened my fists and followed him meekly to the south side of the street, avoiding the gaze of the gathering crowd.

"What the hell is going on here?" Claire was the lanky cop's name, according to the gold bar on his coat.

"The guy jumped me," I said, trying to steady myself. "Pulled me into the van."

"You know this guy?"

My opponent had been nudged toward the patrol car by Claire's partner, who looked about as tough as the guy who'd been beating on me. I would've liked to hear what they were saying.

"No," I replied, "but I know the driver. Kid works in an Exxon station in South Jersey. Torkelsen."

I felt lightheaded, and I knew my face was bright crimson. I couldn't seem to get my bearings.

Before the cop could get out his next question, I said, "Call Lieutenant Addison at Midtown North. He'll vouch—"

At that moment, I felt a sharp, stinging pain in my temple, and I felt terribly nauseous. When I doubled over, neither the excruciating stabbing in my head nor the squeamish feeling in my stomach disappeared. Yellow lights danced before my eyes.

And everything seemed to melt.

★ ★ ★

I woke up in the emergency room at St. Vincent's Hospital, on a gurney in between two rows of way stations hidden by thin floral curtains. Bright fluorescent lights stared dead into my eyes, and I could swear I smelled rubbing alcohol and roses. The nurses' rubber soles squeaked and squealed as they hustled by.

Someone had opened my sweater-vest and shirt, and hadn't rebuttoned either of them. My sneakers were gone. But not the sharp stabbing in my skull.

At least it was warm in here.

"Edward Orr?" said a young man in a pale-green uniform. He had a stethoscope around his neck, and he absently clicked the top of his plastic pen.

"Yes," I replied, trying to rise.

He quickly jabbed out an open palm. "No, no," he said. "Don't get up."

"What happened?"

He was pale and tired, and his dirty-brown hair looked like it had been cut in the dark. But he had a nice smile, and the stubble on his chin and cheeks made him look like an adult. "Well, that's what we're going to find out."

A piercing scream—high-pitched; a woman's voice—came from a distant corner of the emergency room. The young man didn't react.

"No, I mean, how did I get here?"

"You collapsed, Mr. Orr. On the street," he said, looking up and down the sheets on the metallic clipboard that had been hooked to the gurney. "I'm Dr. Thaddeus, incidentally."

We shook hands.

"I'd say by that wound on your head and the swelling on your face that you suffered a blow in the past day or two. Am I correct?"

"Somebody tried to kill me," I replied.

He gave me a few patronizing taps on the chest. "Yes, that's right," he cooed before returning to his clipboard.

"No, I'm serious," I said. I tried to lean up on my elbows, but the jiggling sent a new shock wave through my aching melon. I groaned and said, "Pushed my car off the highway. And then some guy just grabbed me on Seventh Avenue . . ."

He wasn't listening.

After a silent moment or two, he looked at me. "Hurt?"

"Like hell."

"And now?"

"Worse."

"Are you a gambling man, Mr. Orr?" young Dr. Thaddeus asked.

"No," I told him. Not since Starks threw up that airball in Game Six of the '94 NBA Finals.

"I'll bet you that you've got yourself a slight concussion," he said, scribbling on the paper.

Again, a scream. And behind one of the curtains to my left, a discussion in Spanish was building to an argument.

"I'm not going to get better here," I said, as he continued to write. "Give me something to kill the pain and I'll rest up at home."

He looked at me and smiled. "No, I think we'll run some tests, a CAT scan, just make sure there's no bleeding up there, no intracranial pressure."

"Maybe I didn't eat enough," I offered.

"We'll have somebody come over to get your insurance information and check you in," Dr. Thaddeus said. "Relax, Mr. Orr, you're going to be with us for a while."

I heard a string of profanity from the Hispanic couple. Any minute now, blows and blood. Thaddeus could stitch them up between rounds.

"Don't I get one phone call?"

He laughed. "You don't need your lawyer, Mr. Orr."

Oh, yes I do.

Three hours later, and they were all pissed at me, especially Julie, who couldn't believe I'd left the lab and had taken an elevator back up to the room they'd given me. In the bed closest to the door, my roomie, who earlier had introduced himself as "Tim Pfeiffer. Gallstones," was trying to sell his boat to somebody who'd responded to an ad he'd placed in *Newsday*.

"I'm sure someone would've come for you," Julie said testily, as the disapproving nurse walked out.

"I was tired of staring at the ceiling." I kept seeing Brabender and his brass knuckles, Maki and her slack, passive expression, Powell and the waves of arrogance that rose from his corpulent body. The black tank that pushed me off the parkway, and the bull-like thug who wrestled me into the van on Seventh.

Marina, whispering softly, her head on the bare chest of her other man.

"When are you going to understand there may be someone who knows more than you do, Terry?"

"Sssh," I hissed. "You don't want Gallstones to know we're fighting."

The CAT scan was a breeze. I fell asleep in the plastic tube, though my nose nearly touched the inside of its curved hood. Something they'd given me had made me dopey and drowsy. This, I thought, is how Diddio feels all the time, or used to feel in his marijuana glory days—slightly tipsy, unable to focus, inappropriately giddy.

Gallstones wasn't going to take $4,200, and now he was trying to explain what the expression "best offer" meant.

"They forgot about me," I told her, and only the drugs kept me from blowing up over it.

"Terry, must you always be so vituperous?" Julie said, shouting in whispers. "You probably have a concussion. At least a concussion."

I waited until she stopped shaking her head.

"What did Bella say?" I asked her. "Is she all right?"

"She's down the hall," she told me, "in the lounge."

I swung my legs around and started to leave the bed.

"Terry, no."

At that moment, from behind the thin green curtain appeared a young man in an elegant black topcoat and mustard paisley-patterned silk scarf, an ensemble far too stylish for a cop on duty. His blue necktie was done up in a double Windsor and, as he slowly removed his black calfskin gloves, I caught a trace of his woodsy cologne.

"Orr," he said.

"Julie, this is Rey Twist."

She seemed to swoon when he shook her hand.

I wasn't sure if Twist still hated me. Whatever happy dust the nurses had sprinkled on me made it OK for me to ask.

"Lieutenant Addison sent me," he replied coolly.

Julie's wide eyes told me the question might've been out of line.

She didn't know that about four months ago Twist and I had had three run-ins, one of which found him cuffing and running me to Midtown North. Sergeant Twist, it turned out, had been working on my wife and son's case, and he knew Raymond Montgomery Weisz hadn't hurt them. He thought I was harassing Weisz, a hapless psychotic, by trying to track him down.

I hadn't seen him since I pulled Weisz away from the roaring subway train that took the troubled man's right arm and most of his right leg.

"Mind telling me what happened today?" he asked.

177

He had unbuttoned his coat to reveal a crisp navy-blue suit and lightly starched pale-blue shirt.

"Are you sure this one's for Homicide?" I asked. "I'm not dead."

"Yet," he said as he withdrew a notepad from an inside pocket.

I inched back into the bed. "How much did Luther tell you?"

"You think the jumper on East 64th was pushed."

I nodded.

"And now you say you got pulled off the street by . . ." He flipped to another page in his book. "By Ezra Torkelsen and Erik Torkelsen."

"They're brothers?"

Twist ignored the question. "They say you assaulted Ezra Torkelsen and they came up to get even."

"Well, that's not right."

"Meaning?"

"You've grown awfully taciturn, haven't you?" I said.

Julie interrupted. "Terry . . ."

With my head full of clouds, I didn't know how I felt about Reynaldo Twist. Addison approved, which ought to mean a lot, and Twist had been right about Weisz—I had harassed an innocent man.

Twist also knew Marina had been cheating on me. Maybe that's what irked me most.

Maybe I should ask him if she was just closing an old account, if it was love or lust.

I said, "A guy named Lou Brabender smacked

the kid around. At the Exxon station outside Silver Haven."

Twist scanned his notes. "Brabender. And this is the man you told Lieutenant Addison might be involved in John McPorter's death."

I nodded. "Powell, Brabender. The same thing."

"So then why are these Torkelsens after you?"

I didn't know and I told him so. Lying on the gurney outside the lab, waiting to be retrieved, I'd thought Powell might've sent them to rough me up or, worse, to finish what Brabender tried to do on the parkway.

"And they waited until you were on Seventh Avenue to grab you."

"Or they might have been looking for the kid—"

"Allie Powell."

"—to snatch him back to Silver Haven," I said. "Then they saw me."

"Unless they followed you from TriBeCa."

"I guess. Maybe." Craw could've given out my address, or Maki.

"Tells me you ought to stay home," he said, still staring at his notes. "Keep an eye on your property."

"You forget," I told him. "I've got a watchdog."

He shook his head. "No, I didn't forget."

Twist was there when I first met Beagle, last year on Riverside Drive. The dog had been on the other end of a leash in the hand of Jean-Pierre Coceau, a man who took a bullet in the chest, a bullet meant for me.

"I think you tried that before, Twist. Telling me to stay home."

He looked at Julie, then he turned to me. "Sounds like good advice if you want to keep your head in one piece."

Meanwhile, on the other side of the curtain, Gallstones wasn't going to take a dime less than $3,900. Or $3,800.

Twist closed his notepad and squirreled it in his pocket. "I'll be in touch," he said.

"Thanks for stopping by," I told him.

He said good-bye to Julie and left.

"What was that all about?" she asked when the green curtain came to rest.

The floor was cold against my bare feet.

"Remind me to tell you," I replied.

"He's—"

"I know," I said as I stood. "Denzel handsome. Billy Dee."

"Young Marvin Gaye."

Maybe. "Did you get me the information on Buddy McPorter?"

I'd asked her to find out where McPorter lived, and for whatever else she could find out about the man who put the photos and other items in his father's safe. Maybe he was the kind of man who'd take them out, stealing $471 from his own father.

"I'll give it to you," she said, "when you're up to it."

I started toward the door, ready to pass the

negotiating Gallstones. "Is my ass hanging out?"

She looked at the back of my flimsy gown, and she nodded.

"Good," I told her. "I'm walking the halls, ass out, protesting my shabby treatment."

I stuck my head into the lounge, and Bella, reacting as if I'd opened one of her private journals, scrambled to gather the papers she and Daniel had spread across the table.

"What's that?" I asked. "Tip-Top?"

"None of your business," my daughter replied.

"Hey," I said. "A little courtesy. I'm a sick man."

"You have a concussion," she replied, as she crammed a calculator into her pocket. "And you have high blood pressure."

"High blood pressure? No, that's impossible," I said. "I work out, I eat right . . ."

As she nodded in judgment, Bella's blue toque flapped and wobbled on her head. "Argue with your doctor," she said, "not me."

Daniel took the papers, and he shuffled them until they fit back into the folder.

"At least you got color in your cheeks," she added, pointing at me. "That's a good sign."

"Could be the wind."

"Mr. Orr, can I ask how you feel?" Daniel said, hesitantly. His red down jacket was on the scuffed floor, leaning against a vending machine as if waiting to catch a landslide of mixed nuts, mini nacho chips and Wint-O-Green LifeSavers.

"Good," I said. "Better."

"But not best."

"No, not yet," I said. "I'm a little disoriented, you know?"

He ran his hand through his soft mop of black hair. "Dennis says hello," he added. "He wanted me to bring tea to you, but we weren't sure if it was appropriate."

Bella took the folder from her friend and shoved it into her backpack. "I'm missing practice," she told me.

"Will Coach Guidry be pissed?" I asked.

She shrugged as she removed her tie-dyed cell phone from her backpack, jiggled it in front of me. "Since you're not dying—*again*—we'll hook up with our friends."

Daniel and I watched as she went toward the elevator bank.

"She was concerned, in her own way."

I sat, bare ass on plastic.

As he turned to face me, he said, "Mr. Orr, I can't help but think this is my fault."

"Absolutely not, Daniel. No."

"But I was the one who—"

"Daniel, did you throw me into a van, try to beat the daylights out of me?"

"No, I did not." His face still bore its solemn expression. "But I introduced you to Elixa Oostenbrugge. I've been thinking that Gabriella might be right about her. She's been suspended a number of times. Fighting, absenteeism and such. Pot, I think."

"Yeah, but, Daniel, we're helping her friend. A boy in trouble. The rest of it, I mean, what does it matter?"

"But you are in the hospital," he said, "and you have stitches and your finger . . ."

I reached over, cupped his chubby face.

"You did a good thing, Daniel," I said. "That boy needs help."

I thought I saw his eyes well with tears.

"We're going to make sure he's fine. You got it? Me and you."

I looked up to see Bella, and she gave me a harsh frown. "What's this?"

"We were talking," I said, responding to her accusation.

"Are you trying to get him to tell you about Tip-Top?"

"Yeah, that's it," I said. "I'm shaking him down so he tells me all about it."

Daniel stood, went to collect his coat.

"We were talking about Elixa," he said as he took a handkerchief from his pocket, dabbed his eye.

"She witnessed what happened today," I told her. "Be prepared for her side of the story to get back to you."

"Elixa," she said disapprovingly. "I told you, Dad. She's more sinner than saint."

She waited for Daniel to wriggle into his globular coat.

I asked, "And you'll be home at what time?"

"Julie said midnight."

"Oh. Julie said."

"Dad, it's Friday, and Julie will wait up."

"Don't make me leave my deathbed to find you," I added.

"Yeah. OK, Dad," she said matter-of-factly.

Daniel's sleeves covered his plump hands.

CHAPTER 8

After midnight, strange surroundings, strange scents, no books, and I was thinking, I was thinking, I was thinking, I was thinking, I was thinking, I was thinking. I was thinking.

And I started to boil.

And I told myself, I said to myself, "Look at you. You're a victim, again, and you make yourself the victim." Up on my elbows, I said, "You're a victim because you refuse to seize control."

I used that exact phrase: Seize control.

But I can control nothing in my head. Nothing.

I need a plan, that's what I need. A plan.

Make a plan. Seize something. What you ought to do, you ought—

Marina's sister Rafaela arranged a rental for us. Did it by phone, though the agency was maybe 800 meters from her flower shop. An old Fiat, *buona fortuna*, with a map of the countryside of Foggia, suitable for a stranger. And when I got behind the wheel, my knees almost touched my chin.

Red-haired Rafaela, freckle-speckled Rafaela, hands on hips under the golden sun, unflappable

185

Rafaela said calmly, "Maybe he has to drive from the back seat."

I wonder if Rafaela knew—

Damn.

As if I was going to devise some sort of plan with Diddio's brain in my head.

Hungry, I decided to whip up a frittata with leftover fried artichoke hearts and some grated Parmigiano Reggiano, maybe a fresh plum tomato on the side, sprinkled with a little salt.

Beagle heard the refrigerator door open, and Julie padded down the stairs right behind her.

"I don't believe this," she said as she leaned her hip against the banister.

"Nice jammies."

Scotch plaids, tops and bottoms, and they looked like they'd been ironed. Must be for Bella. She usually wore an old T-shirt or tattered henley, nothing more, when we went to bed.

"What did you do?" she asked as she came off the last step.

"I left," I said. "I took my stuff out of the closet and I left. I had it. Enough."

"At 4:30 in the morning?"

I looked at the clock in the face of the stove. "Actually, I left at 3:30," I said. "I walked home."

"You walked? You walked and it's 10 degrees out?"

"I had to get the hospital smell out of my nose," I said. "Once I got going, I was fine." Which wasn't true—I froze as I came south along Seventh, through Sheridan Square and crossing over to Hudson at Houston, waiting for cars zipping into the Holland Tunnel to Jersey, passing the blue-and-whites outside the First Precinct house over on Ericsson. But I needed to do it, despite the remnants of the headache, the last of the light-headedness from the drugs: I'd realized, as I talked at myself, stared at the TV hanging from the ceiling, listened to the silence outside my door, watched and listened as my mind wandered, that I'd had enough, simple as that, nothing more, and I got out of the push-button bed.

I'd had it with The Surgeon who killed his daughter, his wife; with a fingerprint expert who slapped an earnest A.D.A.; with Lou Brabender, dropping me on the street; Harlan Powell, a slug in cashmere; Craw and Maki, mocking the good cops, the ones who bled; the Torkelsen brothers, if Hollywood wants to remake *Deliverance* . . . Had it with Alexandra Powell, her nose in the air; with Buddy McPorter, and I hadn't even met that son of a bitch yet. Had it with Elixa even, looking at her watch; she was looking for the van, wasn't she? She walked me into it, didn't she?

Yeah, I'd had it with everybody.

Almost everybody.

Had it with lying in hospital corridors, waiting

to be retrieved, and pissy little rental cars, settling for what's left in the garage.

Most of all, I'd had it with me.

If I didn't walk out, they were going to have to pull me off the ceiling.

Or a ledge.

"Did you tell anybody?" She had her arms folded beneath her breasts.

"Gallstones was sleeping," I said, as I cracked two eggs into a coffee cup. "He snores." Pillow over his mouth, 45 seconds, a minute. He struggles, then bye-bye.

"Did you get your blood-pressure medicine?"

No, but I grabbed a fistful of Tylenol with codeine.

The frying pan was hot enough for the drizzle of olive oil.

"Hey, Jule. You want in?"

She sighed. "Terry, if you're all right, I'm going back to bed."

I thought I heard a rustling in the living room, and I went to the alcove. In his black sweater and a pair of my gym shorts, Daniel was rousing himself from sleep, slowly untangling himself from the comforter he wore.

"What's—"

"He's protecting us," Julie whispered. "He's such a gentleman."

Half awake, he sat on the sofa and rubbed his nose with the back of his wrist.

"Daniel," I said, "frittatas. You in?"

He mumbled, murmured yes.

I tossed the artichoke hearts into the microwave to take off the chill, edging by Beagle, who was waiting for the kind of treat Mrs. Maoli offered.

"The info on McPorter?"

"Yes, Terry," Julie replied. "I put it in your office."

I came up with two more eggs and the cheese.

"You need sleep," she told me as she went toward the stairs.

I looked down. "You might as well go with her, Beagle," I said. "There's nothing for you here."

"Terry . . ."

"I'll be up," I said, as I cracked one egg, then the other. "Keep it warm for me."

She stepped aside to let Beagle lumber by, and then followed the dog upstairs.

More asleep than awake, Daniel Wu wobbled in on round feet. "What's a frittata?" he asked as he scratched his weary head.

"You are about to find out, son."

I pointed toward a chair.

By the time I had the eggs in the pan, cheese sprinkled just so, and was ready to drop in the breaded artichoke hearts, Daniel had fallen back to sleep, his head on his arms on the table.

I felt Julie's kiss on my forehead, heard Julie tiptoeing to avoid waking me, heard her whisper a good-bye to Bella, and then she headed back uptown to ready for a Saturday brunch with a visiting friend from her Rosemont College days.

As soon as the front door shut, I was up, and I showered, feeling if not fully invigorated, at least energized.

I had a choice, I had a plan, I could turn this thing around, maybe the whole thing, and all I needed to do, one step at a time, was choose between heading straight to where Julie told me Buddy McPorter lived, or following a hunch to find Allie. As I eased carefully into a gray T-shirt and pullover sweater, ouch, over jeans, hair still wet, new Band-Aid on my melon, I decided to look for the boy. More than two weeks on his own: He needed rescuing. He needed a frittata, at least.

I noticed that Julie had kept the note I'd left for her on the mirror, and that made me feel good too.

I took two high-test Tylenol, just in case, and a vitamin, and I washed them down with a Fig Newton.

Christ, I wonder what Mrs. Maoli thought of Julie's Fig Newtons . . .

There were three cabs over by Bazzini's, three drivers chatting over coffee in cardboard cups.

Let's see who among them has the will to succeed.

I decided to start at 70th Street and Park, and I entered the modern, pink-granite Asia Society building promptly at 11 a.m., when its doors opened. I quickly checked in at the red reception desk, paid the admission, grabbed a brochure and, taking off my denim coat, set out.

Unless Allie spent the night squirreled away from the maintenance and security staffs, I knew that I wasn't going to find him here, not yet. So I went up the vertebrae-like stairwell to glance into the galleries, and ducked around *shoji* screens, and past tree lilacs and zelkovas that prospered under a glass ceiling, my sneakers squeaking on the hardwood floors as I moved past ceramics, bronzes, paintings bursting with reds and vibrant earth tones. Near the elevators, I found an authoritative-looking security guard, a stout black woman in uniform complete with a snap-on bow tie, who told me she hadn't seen, or heard anything about, a boy returning to the gallery time and again, sketch pad and crayons in hand, hanging around until he had to be chased away. Telling her about his interest in Asian fashion did nothing to jog her memory.

"Do you have a photo?" she asked.

I silently cursed Alex for failing to provide one, and myself for neglecting to search the Web for one.

"He's small for his age," I said. "Elfin."

"'Elfin'?"

No luck in the kitchen either, as the help busily prepared for several midday luncheons, including one to celebrate the opening of an exhibition on 16th-century Persia. The space overflowed with the scents of saffron, leeks, grilled lamb, lime powder. Clanging pots echoed against stainless steel.

No one had noticed a boy who looked in need of a free meal.

I gave my card to the guard, two men in the kitchen, the reception staff, and I headed out, crossing over to Fifth, where I jogged, dodging doormen with dogs, kids with skateboards, a female street-hockey team and jiggling, half-frozen hotdog vendors until I reached 82nd Street and the Metropolitan Museum of Art.

Twenty-one degrees and the vast front steps were crowded with tourists. At least they had the sun on their faces.

A bus passed, then another, blue fumes, and I crossed Fifth and bounced up the stairs, passing under flapping banners of a reproduction of a Delacroix, a red-pine bust from St. Petersburg, armor. As I entered the vestibule and saw it was already shoulder-to-shoulder crowded—a queue at the security checkpoint, another at the coatroom; and it had already been open for two hours—I abandoned my plan to search methodically for Allie, and I went instead to the Costume Institute's library. Though it was closed, and available weekdays only with an appointment, I found an administrator, a young woman with a jutting jaw and a small vinyl briefcase with a laptop, part of its black cable peeking between the zipper's teeth. She listened carefully, only looked up at the bandage on my forehead eight or 10 times, then told me she hadn't registered any appointments for an Allie Powell in the past two or three weeks. I gave her the whole spiel, nod, nod, nod and she took my card, not before advising me to call the textile center when it opened on Tuesday, visit the Institute's gallery on the ground floor where there was an "exquisite example of *shibori*," and the Asian Art galleries on the second floor, where she'd seen "a great many students with sketch pads, some of them quite young."

I thanked her and set out for Asian Art. The Costume Institute's space was too tight on a busy Saturday for Allie to work.

As were the Asian galleries, I discovered. They were packed to the point where visitors were up on their toes, craning necks, or bending below elbows and shoulder bags, and I was surrounded by the low buzz of conversation, the rattle of shopping bags. Despite a torso of a Bodhisattva draped in flowing garb and a gold-embroidered Koh robe, there were no FIT students at work that I could see. In fact, no one was sketching in the busy galleries.

Undeterred, I went to the security office, prepared to tell the tale, to leave cards.

I was moving now.

Getting my ass kicked a few times: inspiring, motivating.

Moving keeps the head clear, gives you no time to think about anything but now.

★ ★ ★

I got out of the cab at 23rd and Seventh, looking over my shoulder to make sure another set of Torkelsens wasn't on my tail, not that I thought they'd tail me from a museum, not unless I visited the Museum of Douchebags. But they might've been staking out Buddy McPorter's block, looking for him as I was, though not with the same intent.

If they'd made bail, that is.

Arriving at a little before 1 p.m., I went to Buddy McPorter's place between Seventh and Eighth, next to an old YMCA and across from the Chelsea Hotel.

The apartment building, which I'd put somewhere between homey and seedy, had in its lobby a list of names next to buzzers, and I stood on the faded terrazzo tiles and started to search for McPorter's name, running my finger down the list. A young blonde, two pillowcases swollen with dirty laundry in her rolling basket, looked at me with sympathy.

"Too many," she said with a kind smile.

She hadn't put on makeup to rush to the nearest laundromat, and I could see she had pristine skin that was dotted with freckles here and there, and they somehow matched her pale brown eyes. She wore a beige trench coat over a camel-colored, terry sweatsuit, which might've been the last thing in her casual closet, and new running shoes.

"Thomas Hardy," I replied, as I took off my gloves.

She looked for Hardy on the list of names.

"No, *Jude the Obscure.*"

I could tell she regretted stopping to help.

"Sorry," I shrugged. "An affectation, I guess."

She started to tug her basket toward the flat, silver light on 23rd.

I said, "I'm looking for Buddy McPorter." I pointed to the list of names.

She stopped. "Oh, he's not home," she said, deftly pushing her long hair up and away from her face. "He's at a funeral."

"His father's?"

She nodded, and I explained to her how I'd been working with the elder McPorter to recover goods stolen from his safe. My business card seemed to convince her that I might be telling her the truth.

"I'd like to talk to him," I added.

"Well, I know he's working later today," she said.

"On the day of his father's funeral?"

"He's always working," she said, "one job or the other, health club or juice bar. Has to, I guess."

She told me to visit Chelsea Fitness on Sixth.

"Ask for Val," she said. "He usually knows his schedule. You can tell him you spoke to me."

She introduced herself as Christine. She had a nice smile, and she thanked me when I carried her basket onto the cold sidewalk.

After the brisk walk past several florists', specialty shops and coffee bars populated almost exclusively by gay men, past the PATH station and the trains to Jersey, moving under white cast-iron canopies and alongside terra-cotta Roman columns that shone despite the muted light, I arrived at the club. Steady work had kept the headache at bay. I felt fine. Maybe not fine enough to go zipping up a StairMaster or make like I was skiing the Dolomites, but better than I could've expected. The only remnants of my accident were the tenderness around the wound on my forehead and the stiffness in my right shoulder, both of which were now mere distractions.

Christine said McPorter was always working. "Has to," she said.

John McPorter, Jr., aka Buddy, who had gone to Freehold High School.

Along with a bunch of other guys who made up the consortium that got scammed in Powell's pump-and-dump.

Buddy had lost his life savings.

But he wasn't one of the guys who complained to the SEC.

Julie had put a Post-It note on the top of the report she'd created for me.

Way to go, Julie. When she digs, she digs until there's no more hole.

BEST I COULD DO, it read.

I stuck it on the bathroom mirror with another one underneath it.

"You're the best I'll ever do too," I replied.

Fuck it, right?

Chelsea Fitness was on the second floor of the

old B. Altman's Dry Goods Store, between 18th and 19th streets, and its high-tech treadmills, stationary bicycles and other machines were occupied by men fit enough to model swimwear. Behind the counter, a man in a red tank top expected me to present a membership card.

"Is Buddy in?"

The man, blond with dark streaks so obvious they could've only been intentional, looked over a schedule in a plastic sheath. "No, not today," he said, with a polite shrug.

"Val?"

"Upstairs," he told me, pointing at the ceiling.

I thanked him and went past a mirrored room filled with twenty-somethings who were shadow-boxing with serious intent, accompanied by pounding, pulsing music and the exhortations of an instructor who wore a microphone headset and danced like a spry welterweight.

Wavy techno dance music engulfed the weight room beyond the short flight of red, rubber-coated stairs. As I entered, I heard the clank of metal on metal, smelled the plastic mats, forced heat, sweat. By the door, a 30ish woman with close-cropped red hair and a tight electric-blue workout suit was doing curls with a 15-pound dumbbell, and as she stared at herself in the ceiling-to-floor mirror, she let out a curt grunt with each snap. To the rear, beyond the racks of free weights of all sizes, a man with broad shoulders under a black T-shirt sat on a big orange ball and struggled to balance himself

197

as he tossed a smaller plastic ball around his back. The exercise looked like murder on the calves, thighs and lower back, and he was going at it with caution and grave intensity.

I passed a beefy man doing squats with about 320 on the bar, and headed to the only instructor at work in the room.

Val was spotting a lanky black man as he bench-pressed a modest amount, 180 pounds if I was reading the weights right. His client had a dancer's body, lean, sinewy, and the guy was going for definition rather than bulk.

In other words, he didn't want to look like Val Politano, who, under his yellow sleeveless work-out shirt that he'd knotted just below his sternum, had the most impressive pecs I'd ever seen—broad, flat, smooth as stone. His brawny arms were as carved marble, muscles against muscles, veins pressing against his bronzed skin, and the bulk on his thighs threatened to burst the black bicycle shorts he wore. If there was an extra ounce of flesh on that six-pack abdomen, I didn't see it.

He looked like he could've tossed the 180 pounds over his slicked-back hair, his long ponytail, with a pair of index fingers.

The weights wouldn't have had far to travel. Politano was about a foot shorter than I am, which made him about five-four, five-five.

I took off my gloves, left the coat on. I sat on a bench by the racks of free weights, and, as various men who'd strolled in to refine their already fit bodies looked me over with suspicion, curiosity, a discreet display of available sexuality, I made it clear I was waiting for Politano.

He walked over when his work with the black dancer was done. At least, I assumed they were done—the man slapped Politano on the shoulder before he grabbed his towel and peeled away, bouncing on his lean legs.

"Christine sent me," I said as I stood.

He wiped his face, his broad Roman nose, with a hand towel, and he looked up at me.

"I just can't take on another client," he said, lisping slightly.

He was eager to move on.

"I wanted to ask you about Buddy McPorter."

"Sorry," he replied. "I can't help you."

He started to walk toward the stairs, passing a machine that sold vitamin-enhanced water, annoyed that I followed him. For a moment, it seemed, he'd forgotten that the room was lined with mirrors, that I could see his face, his expression.

"I need to talk to him," I said to Politano's thick neck. "About his father."

"No, you don't."

"Look, I'm just trying to—"

He spun around and pressed close to me, as if to threaten me. "Leave Buddy alone. All of you."

I held up my hands and showed him my empty palms. "I'm not looking for trouble here," I said.

"Trouble is what you'll get," he replied sharply. "More than you can handle."

"Listen, you fuckin' monkey," I said, staring down at him, "put me in the mood and I'll kick your puckered ass up and down Sixth Avenue, you hear me?"

He glared hard at me, and he was calculating.

Meanwhile, I knew it was one good shove and he'd bounce me down a long flight of stairs.

"Save the rough stuff for the dancers," I told him.

He looked past me, as if he wanted to be sure no one had heard what I'd said.

"I went to talk to Buddy's father—"

"Somebody killed Buddy's father," he said.

"Yeah, I know," I told him. "I found the body."

He stepped to his right, put his hand on the newel post.

The towel was in his left hand.

I eased back. Politano's bulky arms would be a handicap in a street fight. I could get off three, four jabs before he reached me, break his nose.

"I've been looking for Allie. I need Buddy's help."

"Who sent you?" he asked.

"If you're asking me if Allie's father sent me, it's no."

"Alex, then," he said.

"Maybe. And I know the D.A."

That seemed to calm him. He looked up at me, slapped the towel across his brawny shoulder. "Well, Buddy's not here," he said finally, as he inched away. "I don't know where he's gone."

"Sure you do," I said. "He's at his father's funeral."

"All right—"

"I only want to talk to the guy, OK?"

I dug into my wallet and gave him a card.

I said, "He can call me. I don't give a shit. I'm just trying to turn up Allie."

Politano looked at the card, looked at me. "If I see him, I'll tell him."

I followed him down the stairs toward the main floor, toward the big window onto Sixth.

"Who else has been around to see him?" I asked.

When we reached the landing, he said, "Nobody's been here."

"What about Buddy's apartment? Anybody come to see him there?"

He started to reply, but he held his tongue.

"You'd better talk to him," he said finally.

He walked away, went behind the desk, tossed my card in a drawer near the register.

By the time I stepped into the dull sun, shoppers scurrying around me, I had it in my mind that if I was going to see Buddy McPorter, I couldn't press him, and I couldn't let Politano be the messenger.

If he was going to help me find Allie, he'd have to believe I didn't care what was in the safe—$471 and whatever else could fit in a couple of manila envelopes: 28 more 2,000-year-old silver tetradrachms, a cache of stolen rubies, St. Cuthbert's knucklebone, a few bags of Mexican black tar, photos that could damage Sharon's reputation, whatever had been stashed in Powell's trunk.

If he thought I was after him for clearing it out, or if Politano told him I'd been aggressive, he'd hide and I'd have lost what could be a valuable source.

On the other hand, John McPorter had made it sound like Buddy was the only other person who knew the combination to the safe. He'd have to know that someone would think he'd done the job.

I wondered if Addison had talked to him yet.

Should've asked Twist.

Should've asked Twist instead of mouthing off.

If I called Addison to ask him if he'd met with Buddy, he'd tell me to go home, rest my head, walk the dog.

I wondered if Sharon had told Addison about the photos, about Wellesley.

I had to find Buddy, get him to tell me where he thought Allie might be hiding. Since he knew young Powell from the womb, according to his old man, he might have an idea.

I bounced from juice bar to juice bar in Chelsea, all 26 of them, looking for Buddy, fresh from a funeral. They blurred together now in my mind, all the colorful syrups, stacks of bananas, baskets of mangos, whirring blenders, magic powders, frothy drinks in plastic cups, big straws, the *ch-ching* of cash registers, customers smiling as they took their change, sipped their drinks. The pretty boys behind the counters, each and all tanned, miraculously, despite the sub-freezing weather.

And then I saw him, coming out of a juice bar I'd visited two hours earlier when I'd begun circling the neighborhood, torn page of the Manhattan phone book in my hand. He looked as he did in the photo in his father's living room—strong, well-proportioned, though concern now crossed his face.

Buddy McPorter was leaving the Chelsea Market on the northwest corner of 15th, several manila envelopes under his arm, walking purposefully, hurriedly, toward a silver BMW with Jersey plates, and he hopped in on the passenger's side.

Alex Powell was behind the wheel, Jackie O sunglasses covering her eyes.

Before I could hustle across Ninth, before the traffic rushing south had to hold up for a red light, the BMW pulled away from the curb, slipping around a delivery van lettered with Korean characters. It sped away, and I imagined it zipping uptown toward, among other things, the entrance to the Lincoln Tunnel to New Jersey.

I went into the market. The manager at Victory Juice told me McPorter had stopped by to pick up his check and a few effects he'd stored in her office safe. Envelopes, yes. No, she hadn't felt obligated to tell me he worked there the first time I'd come in. Yes, she'd told him I'd been looking for him. No, she didn't know what was in the envelopes. No, he hadn't said where he was going. No, she didn't know if he was coming back today. No, she'd never seen him in a suit before. And I ought to buy something if I was going to ask so many questions.

Only if I could use the men's room, I told her. Her Merry Berry Passion Punch, $3.49 for a small plastic cup's worth, was the third fruit drink I'd had in the past 90 minutes.

The cabbie picked me up on Ninth outside the Old Homestead Steak House, and it was time for the obligatory phone call to authority, the one where I'd get told to back off, cool down, wise up, move on.

But this time, it wouldn't be Luther Addison at the lecture, wagging his fingers.

"I went looking for Buddy," I told Sharon, "and I found him. With Alex, wrapped in black fur, big Jackie O sunglasses."

"And?"

"And they had several envelopes. They could've had negatives in them, or photos. I couldn't tell."

"Alex," she muttered.

"One was kind of stout, like it had a book in it, maybe. Or a three-ring binder."

The old cabbie wore a stocking cap with the Rangers logo above his ear, and he must've thought he was paid by the hour. He kept us at a steady 12 miles per on the West Side Highway heading south. Bicyclists, bundled up like Kalaallits, blew by us.

"So much for keeping us informed," I said.

"Any word on Allie?"

"None. You?"

She said no.

I told her I'd checked two museums, a health club, too many juice bars.

"Terry, you're not thinking he's fallen in with some men in Chelsea?"

"Sharon, I wish I knew. Besides, just because a kid likes design, it doesn't mean he's gay."

"Thank you for raising my consciousness, Terry."

The Clarkson turnoff was next, after the Washington Market, maybe three blocks away. I was hoping we'd get there before the river thawed.

"I've got a couple more places to look for him."

"All right," she said. "It sounds to me like you're getting somewhere. You keep pushing. Stay on it."

Hadn't heard that one before.

CHAPTER 9

I entered the gym beneath the visitors' basket and found Whitman up by 17 with less than four minutes to go in the first half. Perhaps 75 people sat on the bleachers to my right, across from the scorer's table and the two benches, the bellowing, clapping coaches who prowled the sideline, both in gray skirts. As I walked behind the baseline, with action called to a halt at the other end by an official's whistle, I thought, Not a bad crowd for a non-conference game, and I thought, Doesn't Julie look awfully nice for a frigid Saturday afternoon?

"How are we doing?" I said as I reached her. She'd saved a seat for me, halfway up toward the cinderblock back wall.

Daniel replied. "Becca's been hot, so Gabriella's only been in for two minutes or so."

"And?"

He stared at the action. "She has two points, both from the free-throw line, and two assists, both to Bolanle. And a steal. Kind of a steal. She kicked it, so . . ." He looked at me. "We're just glad Coach Guidry her put in. Because Becca was very hot."

Julie nodded.

I looked to the far end of the court, where we had worked out earlier in the week. The girl from Mother Cabrini covering Bo Otumu was about nine inches shorter than the Nigerian Nightmare. Bella took the inbound pass from Vlada Sanchez, dribbled twice, three times to her left and lobbed it in to Bo, who had crossed over to the post.

The pass flew behind her, high but well over Bo's head and to her left, and it went out of bounds.

The tranquil expression on Bo's face never changed.

As Cabrini's cheerleaders stomped and hooted, my daughter wiped her forehead, then her lips, with a green wristband and backpedaled to play defense. She looked at me out of the corner of her eye. When I shook my fist to encourage her, she grimaced, looked away.

Daniel and Julie spoke in unison. "No sympathy," they said.

"She told us," Julie added, as she peered at the Band-Aid on my forehead.

Daniel excused himself and, black sweats bagging around his ankles, carefully made his way down the bleachers.

I removed my coat, straining to avoid jostling my sore shoulder. "How was brunch, Jule?"

"Fine. Nice," she replied, keeping her eye on the action, clapping her hands with polite enthusiasm. "We went to Café des Artistes."

The Whitman zone defense was moving nicely,

following the flow of the ball, the girls on their toes, hands high.

"Wow."

Cabrini did the only thing they could: Their guard penetrated until she reached Bo, then kicked it back out. But Gillian Gunn, a lanky Whitman senior, was waiting and she jumped out, stole the ball and held it, butt out, elbows high, until the defense collapsed. Then she tossed it to Bella, who led the offense down the court.

"She treat?" I said, as Bella dribbled across the half-court line. Guidry called out a play.

"Yes, *he* did," she replied.

Bella stopped at the top of the key, looked left, held up the dribble and slapped the ball. Gunn came around a Bo pick and Bella snapped the pass, maybe a bit too hard. But Gunn caught it chest-high and drained the jumper for two more points.

Down below, the college scouts scribbled in their notebooks.

Bella, with the wristband: this time, forehead, lips, chin.

Wipes per assist? I could never figure her tics, her tells.

I said, "I thought you said your friend went to Rosemont." Rosemont, outside Philadelphia, was a Catholic college for women.

Coach Guidry, who had an admirable killer instinct, had put on a full-court press, and one of Cabrini's stout little guards was having trouble inbounding the ball. Frustrated, she called a time-out.

"I said I *knew* him from Rosemont," she replied.

"The 'knew' part I got." My eyes traveled from the huddle by the Whitman bench to Julie and her burgundy turtleneck, rosy cheeks. "By the way, you look great."

"Thanks," she said demurely.

"Was it a date?"

The teams huddled and the Whitman cheerleaders, a rag-tag bunch, took over center court.

She turned to me. "I don't know. Are we seeing other people?"

"I guess you are," I said. "I don't."

"I don't believe we've ever talked about it, Terry. Terry?"

Under the visitor's basket stood Elixa, the girl I'd met yesterday outside FIT. From beneath her dark hood, her thumbs sticking out of holes in her sleeves, she scanned the crowd and when she saw me, she nodded discreetly, turned and walked out.

Struggling to get back into my denim coat, I followed her out of the building and caught her on the corner of Clarkson and Varick, where traffic was jammed tight back a half-mile from Canal and the mouth of the Holland Tunnel.

We were surrounded by the scent of mesquite from the stovepipe above Brothers BBQ, by gray afternoon shadows.

"I fucked up, man," she said as she turned toward me. "I've got to get it out of my head."

Her nose was running.

"You ran me into it, didn't you?" I said.

She stepped back, looked up at me, glaring angrily, incredulously. "Fuck no," she spit. "Those guys, those two guys? They were after *me*."

I pulled back, and I could feel a look of skepticism cross my face.

"You don't believe me?"

"Elixa—"

"What? They came to FIT to find you? That's weak, man."

"The guy with the ponytail and I had a run-in a day or so before, Elixa. Down in Silver Haven."

"And the other guy was at the school, like, every day for a week," she said. "He was asking about Allie and some asshole pointed to me. He threatened me."

"When?" I asked.

"Last Thursday," she replied. Agitated, she shuffled in place, scratched her neck near her dark-green spikes.

"What did he say?"

"He said if I don't tell him where Allie is, he was going to fuck me up. That's what he said. All right? Shit."

The traffic on Varick lurched ahead for several feet, then resumed its hesitant crawl.

"So you talked to Daniel," I said.

"I believed him, that guy. You saw him," she said.

"He'd do it. I knew he would, and he came back, didn't he? Wasn't for you being there and they would've took *me* in that van."

She wiped her nose on the sleeve of her jacket.

"You find Allie and they stop looking at me," she said. "Find him, man."

I stared at the traffic, at the soiled snow near the hydrant, and I said, "You still have no idea where he could be?"

"I don't even know him. Not really. He's just a kid in my class. We talked a few times. We didn't hang, man. I like his work. It's original."

Asian-influenced, yes. I had two more places to go, and I'd intended to visit them tomorrow after I spoke to Buddy.

But I realized that I had to go now. If a shrewd city kid like Elixa was frightened, little Allie must be terrified.

She said, "What's going on? I mean, do you even know?"

I looked down at her. Though her street uniform, her untied work boots and the menacing tattoos tried to say otherwise, the soft, red cheeks of her freckled face told me she was still a girl, fragile in her own way despite her brand of smarts, and in jeopardy because of the risk she'd taken.

"Somebody stole some things from Allie's uncle's apartment," I told her. "Somebody in Silver Haven thinks he's got them. He doesn't."

"You should tell them," she said urgently.

Not until I figure why Alex came to Sharon, her

college friend. "I think it's better if I find Allie."

"No," she said. "Tell them. Get those guys off my ass. And yours."

I reached, dropped my hand on her shoulder, gave it a gentle squeeze. "Go home to your family, Elixa," I told her. "Get something to eat, stay warm, sleep in. Blow off FIT until you hear from Daniel." I pointed west toward Whitman. "If you want, I'll talk to Security."

They had some brutes at Whitman. They'd love to take on the Torkelsens.

"Stay home for how long? These guys don't quit."

"For one, Elixa, they may still be in jail. And two, I know who's got the stuff from Mr. McPorter's safe."

"That's not his uncle—"

"Yeah, I know, Elixa."

A sudden gust of wind whipped from the west, and she turned her back, stood next to me.

"This thing is about at its end," I told her. "NYPD is looking into who killed Mr. McPorter, and the District Attorney's office is paying attention."

"That didn't do too much good when—" She stopped herself, shrugged, jammed her hands into her coat pockets.

"If you want, I'll call your father," I said. "Explain how you tried to help."

"I live with my mom," she told me, looking east at a scraggy crowd outside the check-cashing dump. "And half the time, she's nowhere."

"I—"

"But I can crash at my stepbrother's over in Alphabet City. I do it all the time."

The thought seemed to relieve her, at least for the moment.

"Call me if you need anything," I said. "Call me if your brother's not around."

We stood in silence as a metallic-beige Suburban eased into the intersection, blocking traffic from proceeding over toward Bleecker Street. Horns blasted, but the mid-30ish, turtleneck-wearing couple in the Suburban stiffened, ignored the cacophony and refused to back up.

"How much does this suck?"

"Big much," I replied.

She turned to me. "You want to do something for me?" she asked.

I nodded.

"Tell Gabriella I helped you," she said. "Tell her I'm not a dweeb."

"I told you: She doesn't think you're a dweeb. I heard you've got real talent. You'll be a big, famous designer someday."

"She said that?"

I reached, turned up the collar of her peacoat. "Go home."

Suddenly, she frowned.

"Naw, she didn't say that. Daniel, maybe."

"Look, Elixa. You don't have to care what other—"

"Hey, fuck it. Right?" She shrugged and, stepping

over a pile of black snow, she scurried across Varick, snaking her way through angular shadows and manhole steam, between cars, delivery vans, around a FedEx truck.

Halftime was almost at its end, and the gaggle that had been smoking near the rec-center entrance started to file back inside. The players were running layup drills, the Cabrini girls were glancing warily at Bo, Bella was fixing her socks. I ducked my head into the gym, caught Daniel's eye, called him to me with a discreet gesture.

"Yes?"

"I've got to run, Daniel," I said. "Do me a favor and tell Julie I'll see her at home."

High up the stands, Julie was talking to a woman about her age who was struggling to keep her wriggling two-year-old on her lap. Delia Gardner's mother, and she had two more besides the baby and Whitman's starting two-guard.

"Your home or her home?"

"Harrison."

He nodded. "Might I ask . . . ?"

"Yes, but I've got nothing to tell you."

"I saw you leave with Elixa," he said.

I put my hand on his shoulder. "I'm afraid Bella was right about her, Daniel."

He sank as if dejected.

"But you were right too," I said quickly. "Allie is in trouble. Like I told you, you did good."

He looked up.

"Smile," I said.

He did.

I told him I'd probably see him tonight.

It wasn't until I was halfway to Chinatown that I remembered that Bella's Saturday night was for her Marcus, and I wouldn't see Daniel Wu at least until Sunday.

I figured I'd find him at the Tibet House, over on 15th Street, quite near Union Square Park. For some reason, Tibet was hot with teens. They thought the Dalai Lama was a teddy bear, an outsider kept from his rightful place, and sanctified; a model then, the physical representation of their idealized selves as righteous outcasts. The Tibet House Web site had told me they had a display on Buddhist art by Siddhimuni Shakya, whose paintings contained images of deities in colorful garb, and an exhibition of photos of Tibetan monastic life, men in swaddling clothes. Plenty of inspiration there for a young designer, and maybe a place to hide from his father, Brabender and the Torkelsens. A sanctuary of sorts.

But instead, with a sort of hasty imprudence that suggested I was merely getting it out of the way, I went to the Museum of the Chinese in the Americas, over on Mulberry near Columbus Park, which sat roughly where the old Five Points' infamous Mulberry Bend did, the site of the seminal crime in Bella's book and Scorsese's *Gangs of New York*. Now, in the shadows of the Criminal Court Building, it was a blacktop ball field: softball in spring and summer, soccer and basketball all year round. And it boasted the cleanest public restrooms in the city.

As I reached Mulberry, surrounded by bold Chinese characters on handmade signs, vegetable stands with bok choy, and bean sprouts in water, old cars parked fender-to-fender, a teeming crowd of tottering elders with craggy faces nearly hidden behind upturned collars and snug hats, I had a premonition: He's going to be here.

No, not a premonition. A conclusion. The museum was as nondescript as any I'd ever seen. It was in an old public school building, P.S. 23, which had been constructed when the second wave of Italians arrived in the 1890s, and it was surrounded by scaffolding that all but hid the battered structure. Only a red banner, covered now in shadows, announced its presence.

I'd bet not even the art-minded Alexandra Powell knew it existed.

I entered the old building, went up the steel steps of the square stairwell to the second floor, and I walked on creaking planks past brick walls painted white, gated windows, dusty rubber plants.

At the end of the corridor, beyond the home of the HT Dance Company, was a sign for the museum and its current offering on the history of Cantonese opera in New York.

Plenty of colorful costumes in Cantonese opera.

There was no one at the cash register, which stood on a platform by the entrance.

The inventory of the gift shop fit on a lone table.

I put three singles on the sign-in book and went inside.

And there, on the floor beyond the wall that held a diorama of old paper lion heads and antique laundry irons, sat a young boy in black cords, sketch pad in his lap, drawing with pastels and pencils, looking up at bright robes bearing dragon faces with emerald eyes, peacock wings, gold egrets, tiny circular mirrors. Looking up at magentas, oranges, stunning yellows and reds.

He was the only person in the museum.

"Allie."

He kept working, drawing, erasing with his little finger, shaping, looking up, looking at his pad, drawing.

"Allie."

He jumped, turned to me, and a look of terror formed on his suddenly ashen face.

"Allie, my name is Terry Orr," I said, as I held up my hands. "I'm here to help you."

He started to backpedal while he remained seated, and his pad slipped from his lap, scattering his rainbow of pastels.

"Allie, no. Listen, your mother asked me to find you," I said quickly. "She's friends with a friend of mine in the District Attorney's office. I'm not going to hurt you."

He didn't believe me, and he was edging toward a glass case in the corner that held programs from various operas, photos in black-and-white.

His pink Polo dress shirt wore a rainbow of smudges on the pocket, collar, sleeves.

"They're friends from Wellesley, Allie."

Didn't mean much to him, and he kept going until he was up against the case.

"I know about John McPorter, and I know about the safe," I said, as I inched toward him, avoiding his pastels. "And I know you're scared, Allie, and I would be too."

I reached out my left hand.

"Come on," I said. "Let's go talk."

He had begun to tremble.

"Maybe get something to eat," I added. "You look like you could use a meal."

"Don't—" His voice caught in his dry throat. "Don't make me go home."

"I'm not going to make you do anything, Allie."

He stared at me. He seemed to be trying to look behind my eyes.

He reached, gave me his hand.

It was covered in oranges, stunning yellows. Reds. Magenta.

After slipping into his preppy L. L. Bean kind of coat, he'd stuck his pad and pastels under his arm, and we walked east on Bayard, passing an old cobbler under rusted steps and a woman selling jade trinkets from a folding table. On Mott, we went south past a stand that sold dried mushrooms, and the Transfiguration Church—another landmark in Bella's book—and into Wo Hop, a restaurant Diddio had introduced me to in the St. John's days, a favorite at 3 a.m. among glassy-eyed New York twenty-somethings. I knew the layout of the room, and I asked the man at the cash register to take us to the back, away from the red booths, to a table near the kitchen. He did, placing us across from a man who was shucking peas and dreaming of someplace he yearned to revisit. Someplace where he didn't have to shuck peas.

Or a woman he'd lost. A child, a son.

I gestured for Allie to take the seat in the corner, where the walls met, and he sat between two tinfoil pictures, birds in flight, faded red on faded gold.

I looked at him, as he nested his supplies on an empty chair. He was small, and he had big dark eyes that sank at the outer corners. And he was soft and no match for whatever he feared he'd have to face back in Silver Haven.

A bored young man, black slacks, white shirt, black vest, brought us a pot of tea, two cups and saucers, and fried noodles.

"Go ahead," I said as I pushed a menu toward him. "By the way, if you're feeling uncomfortable, those stairs over there lead down to the bathrooms. They've got sort of an annex downstairs, another restaurant that the natives prefer. You can go down there and escape, if you want."

He nodded as he took a noodle, ate it hungrily and, as I stood, noticed that I'd grimaced as I removed my denim jacket.

"Yeah," I said, as I hung the jacket on the back of the chair, "I met Lou Brabender."

He took another crispy noodle, stopped just before jabbing it into his mouth.

"We'll order first," I said, as I sat, picked up the menu, called over the waiter.

Across the room, two guys, burly old friends, second- or third-generation Italians, whined about their bosses. "Me and him, we're always banging fuckin' heads, this guy," said the mutt on the left, the one with the mustache, the guy who was slipping Jack Daniel's into his Diet Coke. The other guy nodded.

I eavesdropped while we waited for the food, while Allie snacked, drank violet-scented tea. (D, name that brand.) Five minutes, and the other guy, chomp-chomp, said nothing while mustache prattled on. "I told this son of a bitch . . ." "And this prick, he says to me, he says . . ." "I mean, who do I got to blow to get out of this fuckin' job?" "I says to him, 'Do I look like some kind of *arruso* to you?'"

The other guy: He's either family or deaf.

"What's going on?" I asked, when the egg rolls arrived.

I pushed the plate to his side of the table.

"I don't want to go home," he said, as he cut into one of the fried rolls.

"Is that why you've been hiding?" I asked. "Are you afraid of being sent home?"

He nodded.

"What's at home, Allie, that makes you afraid?"

"My Dad. And Lou. Lou Brabender."

I nodded.

"I don't have it," he said, with a tired voice. "I don't have what they're looking for."

"Did you open the safe?"

"No," he said, "I didn't. I didn't know the combination."

"It was pretty easy to guess," I said.

"Why would I want to guess? I didn't want what was in there."

The waiter brought the hot mustard and sweet-and-sour sauce, a Coke for Allie, left the water pitcher for me, two glasses with shards of ice. I took a taste of the mustard, cleared my sinuses. They ought to serve it to everyone who gets his bell rung.

"Did you know what Mr. McPorter had in the safe, Allie?"

He hesitated and then he nodded. "Yes. I did, yes. Sort of."

"What?"

"Money," he explained. "And the stuff Buddy put in there."

"Which was . . . ?"

"Envelopes," he said. "I didn't know what was in them."

I rubbed my forehead below the wound, the Band-Aid. "What about the money?"

"I don't know," he said.

"If you were going to take off, the money would've come in handy."

"I wasn't going to take off," he said. "I liked staying with Mac. I liked it. I liked living here. I wanted to move here, go to high school here and everything. Get into Whitman."

"So why'd you run away?"

"Because I thought my dad was going to come after me."

"Because . . . ?"

He hesitated. "Because he wanted what was in the safe."

"I don't understand."

"I told him that Buddy put new stuff in it. The safe."

I leaned in, sliding my elbows, forearms on the table, waited until he finished chewing. "Why did you do that?"

He shook his head. "I don't know. He was asking. He asked me if I saw Buddy, if my Mom came by ever, and I just told him."

"When was this, Allie?"

He looked at the ceiling as he tried to recall. "I can't remember," he said.

"Maybe if—"

"Wait," he said suddenly. "It was a Wednesday. I had first-period Bio."

The stuff went missing two days later. It took two days for a warning to get to Buddy, word that he ought to move whatever he had stashed inside.

"So your father was interested in what was in the safe?"

He nodded.

"Didn't you tell him you didn't know what was in there?"

"Yes, but he didn't . . . He never believes me and then he gets furious."

"You were afraid."

He said, "I *am* afraid. Of him, and Lou. They're crazy to find what was stolen from my dad's car."

"And they think it wound up in Mr. McPorter's safe?"

"I guess. I don't know. Maybe."

"Do you think they believe Buddy ripped off your father?"

"I don't know," he replied. "But how could he? Buddy works all the time, and he never goes down there. He doesn't even have a car."

We sat in silence as the waiter returned with the beef chow mein, the roast duck lo mein, a plate of steamed dumplings; young Allie had ordered enough starch to fuel him to run a marathon. I'd ordered asparagus in garlic sauce for myself, and I figured we'd share the brown rice.

"What are we going to do with you, Allie?"

He had started to fill his plate, but he stopped and looked at me.

Allie didn't know what was next, and in his eyes, I could see he had learned the world was a vast, forbidding place.

"Who can you trust?" I asked.

"Nobody."

He couldn't go to Buddy and he didn't want to return to Silver Haven.

"Any of the teachers at FIT?"

He said no. "I'm too new."

"I can't put you up, Allie. A lot of people know I'm looking for you."

"Don't tell the police," he said. "They'll make me go home. They will."

"You're right," I said. "They will."

"Then I'll be killed. Like Mac."

"Allie . . . 'killed'?"

"No, really," he said. He dropped his fork, slouched in the seat. "Really."

"Your father is going to kill you?"

"He said he would. He said, 'I gave you life and I can take it away.' Lots of times."

I could imagine an asshole like Powell saying something like that. But saying it didn't mean he meant it literally.

"Or Lou. He's crazy. Violent crazy."

No shit, and he's got trainees.

"And all this because they think you have what was in the safe."

He nodded.

Or, I thought, if you don't have it, you know what it is.

"And you're sure there's no way you can come clean with your father? Just tell him what you told me?"

"He won't believe me."

The kid was probably right. Once an arrogant, money-and-status-driven bastard like Powell got something in his head, it would take more than a blood bond to dislodge it.

If I was Allie's age, and his size, I'd stay the fuck out of Silver Haven too. "And your mother?"

"I can't find her. I tried."

"You left messages."

He sipped his Coke. "I can't. He'd get them, even on her cell. He'd figure a way. He probably has Lou following her."

I put a spoonful of brown rice on my plate.

"She wants you back, Allie," I said.

He shook his head. "My mom knows I'm better off far, far from home."

"Allie, play me straight, OK? Did you take Mr. McPorter's money?"

"No, I swear."

"You don't have to," I told him. "I believe you."

"No," he said, "I can prove it."

He reached into his coat pocket, came up with a handful of crumpled singles and receipts, passed them to me.

A dime fell between his fingers, rattled on the table.

ATM receipts. Forty bucks here, twenty bucks there. From machines in different parts of town.

"Smart," I said. One receipt was from a machine at New York University, another from a bodega on the Lower East Side.

The last one said the transaction wasn't permitted.

"He knows," Allie said. "My father knows I need money."

"He cut you off."

He nodded.

"And you've got, what? Three dollars and ten cents."

He didn't reply.

He kept eating and eating, and in between he told me that he spent the first weekend across the river at an AmeriSuites near the Meadowlands, running a tab on an AmEx debit card his mother got him for emergencies. And he wasn't thinking about going home because he was living a young teen's dream, and he had his sketches taped on the walls, and clippings from *Women's Wear Daily*, swatches on the floor, as if he was in his own little apartment, and he almost forgot about his bullying father and Brabender and the risk he faced. On Monday, he took a bus into town so he could attend his late-afternoon class, and he called McPorter, who told him his safe had been emptied. Frightened, thinking Brabender had cleaned out McPorter, he went back to Secaucus, gathered his stuff, got himself as much cash as he could at an ATM in the Port Authority, and he hid, illogically, at FIT until Security caught him during his second night in an upstairs student lounge. He bought himself a bed at a youth hostel on Amsterdam, and he found himself imagining he saw Brabender in the crowd at the Manhattan Mall on 33rd, at the Museum of Arts & Design on 53rd, at the Tibet House (I knew it). The streets weren't his way, so, defeated, he decided he'd return to McPorter's and ask him to call his mom, who might be able to find a place to hide him from his father's wrath as well as Brabender's rage.

And when he turned the corner of Park and 64th, he saw a gathering crowd outside of McPorter's place and, as he drew closer, he saw the body on the black spikes of the fence outside the house.

He admitted he'd lied to the old man. "I told him I'd stay with friends."

As McPorter said to me.

The waiter hovered, looked at how much Allie had consumed and, when he returned to his pea-shucking partner, let loose a string of Mandarin that had both men laughing aloud.

"We've got to hide you, Allie, until we clear this up."

He looked at me, waiting for a solution to his dilemma.

I had to stash him somewhere, and it had to be with someone who could deal with any heat that came his way, someone sturdy who wouldn't sell me out, who could handle a sensitive kid.

"Go clean up," I said, as I gestured to the bathroom downstairs. "I've got to make a call."

CHAPTER 10

It was a small apartment, a two-bedroom, not far from the Metro North station on 125th, and I could hear the rattle of an express train, see its lights, as he took me outside, asking his wife, daughter and inquisitive toddler to wait in the kitchen. We left Allie on the sofa, and he put his hands between his knees and stared at the blank screen of the TV.

Now we were out in the cold, on the balcony that overlooked a meticulous courtyard. The city had put up these apartments, and the tenants made it special, one of a number of bright spots in lower Harlem.

Pale-yellow rays of a lamplight shone on his shaved head, and steam rose from his mouth, his wide nostrils.

"What's it about?" asked Mabry Reynolds.

"I've got to stash the kid."

"And you're bringing him to me?"

He was incredulous, and I didn't blame him. I'd met Reynolds at the Zora Neale Hurston Elementary School almost four years before, and we nearly came to blows: A security guard who took his job seriously, he tried to prevent me from leaving the school after I'd been insulted by a vice principal who accused me of racism. We smoothed it out, and Reynolds went on to help me solve my first big case.

I persuaded Luther Addison to chaperone him through the process of getting accepted into the Police Academy. But Reynolds, who aced the exam, had an arrhythmia and couldn't pass the physical, though he looked leaner, hardier than at least half the cops I saw on the street. He went back to the Hurston School, and I met up with him last year when the principal asked me to help collect from a deadbeat dad or two on Wall Street.

Mabry Reynolds was a solid man, good to his word: someone who understood the world exists for more than the take-all-you-can philosophy that these days gripped so many people, rich and poor, regardless of race or religion. It didn't surprise me that he lived in the new Maple Plaza complex. It took good people like him to create beauty and order amid so much neglect, amid the presumption of failure.

"Let me explain," I said.

"Yeah," he replied. "You'd better."

I told him what I knew, and I didn't leave out the part about my dustup with Brabender, and the follow-up with Powell, Craw and Maki.

"Addison is working the old man's death," I added. "So he's looking for whatever else was in the safe from that angle. But the kid is right. The cops will send him home and his father will bust his balls until he breaks."

"The mother—"

"Can't make her," I said. "Allie thinks she'll help, but I'm not sure. I mean, if it was your boy, what would your wife be doing?"

His expression told me she'd be turning the world inside out to find him, instead of gathering envelopes from an old friend after a funeral mass. She'd bang down doors at One Police Plaza until a citywide search was underway, instead of merely coercing an old college roommate in the D.A.'s office to bring in one private investigator.

I said, "The $471 can't mean anything to Powell, so whatever's missing has as much to do with his reputation as it does with anybody else's."

"What's that mean? 'Anybody else's.'"

I couldn't tell him about Sharon and her ambitions.

"Someone broke into Powell's car and stole something," I told him. "I'm thinking maybe it ended up with Buddy and he tried to bury in it his father's safe."

"Unless this Buddy broke into the car . . ."

"Could be," I said, shrugging, shaking my head, nudging the dull ache above my eye. "He was one of the guys Powell played in the pump-and-dump, so he's got a solid gripe."

He gestured for me to go on, and he shoved his hands into the pockets of his jeans. I couldn't imagine that thin, black-fleece pullover he was wearing was doing him much good against the early evening's cold, the wind off the Harlem River.

I said, "Or maybe it was somebody who knew exactly what Powell had back there."

"Whatever it was, they think it's worth enough that somebody would try to sell it back to them."

"Somebody who'd go down to Silver Haven from New York City to do it," I said. "Which tells me Powell thinks the stuff could've ended up here."

He hesitated, and then he said, "Let me go talk to Millie."

I nodded. While I waited, I watched the sparks tumble down from the elevated tracks as another train rumbled by, and I saw planes easing down on their path to La Guardia, and for a moment I forgot I was standing on a balcony in Harlem, trying to hide a teenager both Luther Addison and Sharon Knight wanted to see, and I had asked a strong black man to do it, to try to help me get over on his own kind.

I was willing to bet that, for Mabry Reynolds, the expression "his own kind" meant more than race. That being a parent, and protecting a kid, meant more than anything else.

It'd better, or he was calling Addison right now, and I'd be standing here when the sirens

231

cried out and the red lights whirled and I found the lieutenant or Rey Twist chewing on my ass while little Allie got dragged back to Silver Haven.

Reynolds shut the door and stepped into the cold.

"Fine," he said. "But Millie says he's coming to church with us tomorrow."

I thanked him. "Run a tab, OK?"

"He don't look like he eats much."

I laughed. "You'd be surprised."

"When it's going to end?" he asked.

"Somebody's got to force it."

He looked at me. "You."

I shrugged. "Why not?"

"Because you owe somebody a beating."

"Maybe so," I told him. I shifted from side to side, trying in vain to build up body heat. "On the other hand, there's that kid in there, and an old man who didn't deserve to die. And down in Silver Haven, there's a guy who knows how to make an ass out of what's right."

He nodded.

"Listen, Mabry, I got to ask you for one more favor," I said. "If I'm out of line, you tell me, and we'll let it blow."

He bit the inside of his lip as he stared at me, but he didn't change his expression, didn't take his eyes off mine.

"I need to carry," I said, "and I'm empty."

"I can't let you have the Beretta," he said. "It's registered to the school."

"Do you know where I can pick up something?"

He snapped back. "Now?"

"Yeah. Now."

He studied me, trying to figure how much he ought to let me know. Since I'd trusted him, I was hoping it would come back in kind.

"You licensed to carry?"

"Hell," I said, "I'm barely licensed to drive." I pointed to the Band-Aid on my head, the scrapes on my cheeks.

"I was wondering about that . . ."

I turned when I heard another train rattle by, and down below the tracks I saw two young men strolling south, walking briskly, confidently. Dressed in their Saturday-night finery, they were getting an early jump on a long night of good times.

What I wouldn't give to have that guy's ankle-length fur coat and his matching hat, both of which seemed to shimmer in the starlight.

"Can you fix me up?" I asked.

"I've got to make some calls," he said.

"You think—"

"Yeah."

I told him where he could find me later this evening.

"It won't be me," he said. "I've got company."

Reynolds already had my cell number, so I knew I'd hear from him, one way or another.

I thanked him again, and Millie, shook his hand and asked him to tell Allie I'd be in touch.

"Watch your back, Terry," he said as he went for his front door.

I arrived home after six to find the house empty save for Beagle, who lifted her head from the arm of the sofa, looked at me with her droopy eyes and went back to sleep.

Julie had left a note on the table. I read it as I blew into my hands, as I went for two more acetaminophen.

> *Terry:*
> *At the Water Pump—giving Dennis at least one customer.*
> *Gabriella is off to the movies in Battery Park City. Home at midnight. (She scored 6 pts. Daniel was very proud.)*
> *Hurry.*
> *Julie*
>
> *P.S. I walked Beagle. Poor dog is lonesome.*

How can you tell if a basset hound is lonesome? Thing looks miserable always.

A mistake to stay in an empty house, even to soothe my shoulder under a hot shower, change a bandage, check to see if Addison called, or Sharon. Sit in my office for five minutes, stare at the monitor, listen to the heat drift through the vents, the traffic on Greenwich.

Maybe she was kissing him good-bye.

From the fuchsia divan they shared, Julie and Diddio turned toward the door as I entered, their eyes filled with hope, expectation. They were the only two people in the place, and he sank when they saw it was me, and she drew herself up, a sympathetic expression crossing her face.

I hung my coat on the tree in the corner and walked past the oatmeal bar to join them. A solo cello, playing something austere, floated softly above the empty furniture, languid plants.

My sneakers squeaked on the buffed floor.

I put my arm around D and hugged him. His head leaned against my hip.

"T, does this blow or what?"

"Blow it does," I said, as he leaned back and looked up at me.

The scent of dried leaves, of citrus fruit, of cleanliness, surrounded us.

"It was such a good idea, man," he moaned.

"It still is," I told him. "Don't get down, D. This is a good thing."

"Good and empty," he muttered.

He wore a black denim shirt, black jeans, and he looked like he could just cry.

"Hello, Miss Giada," I said.

"Mr. Orr."

D stood. "Let me get you something, T. Something special, man."

A water sounded right, but I knew he wanted to display his skill, to show me he'd done all he could to make the place a success.

Allie had drunk two pots of tea at Wo Hop. He was wired by the time we got to Reynolds's. Wired, yet he fell asleep in the cab.

"Dealer's choice," I said as Diddio scuffled across the room, dodging one of the burnt-orange sofas.

"You got it," he said brightly.

I sat where D had been, and looked at Julie, who, as always, was fresh-faced, smart, though at the moment, she seemed subdued, almost sad.

Who wouldn't be? We were watching a friend's dream die.

"Thanks for taking care of Bella, Jule."

"Not much to do there."

My hands were too cold to touch hers.

"Marcus pick her up?"

"Right on time," she replied. "He was beaming with pride. Apparently he scored 15 baskets this afternoon."

"He's on the Whitman boys' team?"

"He's quite a player. Even Daniel says so," she said. "And what about you? Did everything work out with that girl? Elixa, is it?"

"I've got the boy," I said, and I told her about Mabry Reynolds.

"I don't think I know him," she said, as she reached for her cup of tea. A blend of chamomile, lemongrass and orange flower, if memory serves.

"A good man," I said. "You'd like him."

I heard the door open, turned and saw two women enter. They shivered as they shook off the cold, removed their gloves, undid their scarves and, as they wriggled out of their heavy coats, scanned for good seats.

Behind the bar, D tried to conceal his glee.

The women, working-mom types who'd managed to escape for a few hours, chose a raspberry chesterfield, and they nodded at us as they passed to look over the menu. Wendy Wu's whimsical turquoise penmanship on a Plexiglas board made teas with vague names like Golden Mystic and April Dew sound appealing.

Their arrival gave us an opening to leave.

"Hungry?" I asked.

"I haven't eaten since brunch," she replied, nodding, smiling.

"Oh, that's right. Your date."

I stood and extended my hand. She took it and lifted off the divan.

"Let me tell D we'll be back," I said.

Twenty-five minutes later, we were sitting in Ivy's Bistro, a couple of blocks from my house on Greenwich; a table in the corner, sharing a bowl of mussels in a garlic wine sauce. She ordered a glass of Pinot Grigio. I thought that I ought to stick to sparkling water, in case Reynolds's man showed up.

The light from the table candle flickered unevenly.

"Powell thinks his son knows what was in the safe," she recounted. "And you believe John McPorter was killed for the same reason. Because he knew."

"Or because Powell thought he knew where Allie was. Or maybe he just wanted to frighten Allie into coming home."

"And you have to find what was in the safe to protect the boy."

"Not 'find,' not as in it's missing or lost. It's with Buddy and Alexandra. They've got it. It's Buddy that I've got to find."

"What's Sharon think about this?"

"She wants what was in the safe too," I said.

"She's encouraging you?"

"As remarkable as that may seem, yes." I put down the slice of *bastone* that I had been about to dip into the broth. "I'm doing good here, Jule. I can feel it."

"I suppose . . ."

I leaned forward, elbows on the table. "Bella's gotten to you, hasn't she?" I asked lightly. "She sent you out tonight to tell me to give it up, to write again. Is that it?"

"Exactly."

"I knew it. I—"

"Of course, it's not it. Boy, you sure can be dense when you want to be."

238

She took a long sip of her white wine.

"So that's why you've started dating," I said. "Because I'm dense."

"Are you serious? Do you really think I'm seeing someone else?"

I didn't see it as her style. "No—"

"Oh, Ron is as gay as they come. But I can talk to him. I can tell him what's on my mind and he listens. And," she added, "no one is trying to kill him."

"Point taken," I said quickly. "Sorry."

"But let's put the issue on the table. Is it going to be just you and me?"

She was looking me square in the eye, just as she had when she was preparing to cross-examine Küsters.

"Terry?"

"Wait," I said. "The defense may object."

She smiled. "I'm pinning you down." She rapped the table with an index finger. "Right here, right now. In Ivy's."

"OK." I reached over the candle, brushed her cheek. "I'll put it like this: I'm with you. It's great. I'm not looking around. I'm . . . What else? What else do you want me to say?"

She glared at me.

"Come on, Jule. Don't ask me to say something that isn't within me."

"So you don't feel the same way I do?"

"I didn't say that. I'm saying . . . What I'm saying is I can't say it. I'm not in the right place to—"

"Oh, that is such bullshit, Terry. You've been telling me that you've got some sort of emotional disability since we met and it's simply not true."

"Julie—"

"I mean, I don't know exactly what goes on inside that head of yours but I've got a pretty good idea—"

"Julie." I pointed toward the waitresses' station. The two women in white shirts, cute black bowties, were staring at us, awaiting the next volley.

We sat for a moment bounded by the convivial sounds of the diners around us, and laughter at the bar and the light jazz from hidden speakers.

"OK, Jule," I said, "let's nail it down."

"I think the moment has passed, Terry."

"No, I'm up for it."

She hesitated, and then she said, "Go on."

"All right. As I see it, you want me to be different," I said calmly, evenly. "For whatever reason, that's what you want. And I told you, and I told you as clearly and honestly as I could, that I am what I am."

"Yes, but you can be so much more."

"And maybe that's the guy you love, Jule. The guy you think I can be."

"Well," she said, "at least you acknowledge that I love you."

"Of course I do," I said.

"Yes, but do you love me?"

"Julie . . ."

"Do you know that you have *never* said it? Not

240

once." She leaned closer to me, to the flickering candle, and she whispered, "Not even while we were making love."

I watched as she sat back again, lifting her napkin, folding it, returning it to her lap.

"Well, shouldn't that tell you something? You're, like, my favorite person in the world and I can't express myself to you."

She blinked, shook her head. "What did you say? I'm your favorite person in the world?"

"Well, certainly in the Adult, Female category," I said.

We both laughed.

"And does that make you think of the future?" she asked after she took a mussel with her fork, savored it, washed it away with the white.

"The future? Julie, have you noticed that I'm having a little trouble with the present?"

"I—"

My cell phone buzzed, and I held up my index finger.

"Terry," Reynolds said, "where are you, man?"

"I don't—"

"He's at your house."

"Who?"

I signaled to the waitresses for the check. Their evening's entertainment was over.

"Pulpo. With the thing you wanted."

I reached for my wallet, my AmEx card.

"What's it going to set me back?"

"Four bills," he told me.

I said, "Tell him to go north on Green—"

"Terry, get home, man. Now."

I had to go to an ATM for the cash.

Julie looked at me with concern.

"OK," I told Reynolds. "Tell him five minutes."

"Is everything OK?" she asked when I put the phone away.

"I've got to see this guy," I told her.

"Is it about the boy? Then go."

She handed me my AmEx card, reached for her handbag, her wallet.

"Meet me at D's?"

"I'll wait," she said, "but only for three or four hours."

Pulpo wore a black ski mask, but, perhaps to indicate we were co-conspirators in crime, kept it rolled on top of his head as he looked me in the eye, showing his impatience. A light-skinned Latino, with pockmarks and carbuncles on his face, he sat on a scooter, the kind they drive in Rome to duck and dodge traffic. His long legs let him balance the bike on the slick cobblestone.

"I'm waiting, *pavo.*"

I handed him five $20 bills. He had six fingers on each hand; hence his inaccurate nickname, which means "octopus" in Spanish.

"What the fuck is this?"

"The bag," I said. "Open it."

He sneered defiantly at me, and then he swung the battered leather backpack from his shoulder to his lap, and he let me look inside.

Five more twenties went his way.

"Unwrap it."

He reached in and undid the red bandanna. I saw the outline of an automatic.

"Where's the clip?"

"It's juiced, *pavo*."

I said, "Pass it over."

"You take it."

I lifted the Smith & Wesson. The nine-millimeter had eight rounds in the clip and one in the breech. I shoved it into my coat pocket.

He said, "*Todo está bien chévere, pavo.*"

"You call me turkey again, Pulpo, and you'll need another fuckin' dentist," I said as I pushed the remaining $200 at him.

He opened the front of his black vinyl jacket and flashed me his piece, a .357 Magnum. It looked like a silver cannon under his arm.

"Draw," he said, and he showed me his gold tooth.

Then he kicked over the little engine and went off toward the river.

CHAPTER 11

I used to lock the guns I'd borrowed or stolen in the cabinet in my office. But it nagged at me that Bella might find one—she of the boundless curiosity, for whom a lock would create an irresistable challenge—so I took to hiding them where she'd never look. Now, as before, I went downstairs to the musty space off the laundry room and opened a box that held about 20 unopened copies of my Connolly bio. Surrounded by the smell of paper, of cedar and cloying detergent, I shoved the gun in among the pristine books. For good measure, I put the box under other boxes, the ones that held my notebooks, photocopies and research papers, the stuff I'd buried when I knew I'd never write again. When I pulled the string dangling from the bare bulb above me, the room and the stairway went black.

Beagle greeted me again as I entered the kitchen. As I started to go for her red leash to take her out before I caught up with Julie, my cell phone buzzed and I snapped it off my belt. Reynolds, no doubt, checking to see if the deal was done.

He was the kind of man who'd follow up.

As I brought the phone to my ear, I heard loud, bass-heavy music and the clatter of voices trying to talk above the din.

Bella? Not in a bar, not for a few years yet. Unless Marcus can pass for 21, 22 years old . . .

"Hello."

"Is this Terry Orr?" a woman bellowed.

"Who's this?"

"Terry Orr?" Christ, that was some god-awful music.

"Yeah. Terry Orr."

"It's Saleha," she shouted. "Remember me?"

"Sure," I said. "The Art and Antique Center." The girl from Afghanistan. Green, almond-shaped eyes. Full, inviting lips. Killer figure.

"Come out," she said. "Come out and I wait for you."

The coin dealer, Fred Arnold, must've given her my card.

"It's Saturday night," she added, fighting off the booming drums. "It's time to dance."

She sounded drunk. Enthusiastically drunk.

"Saleha," I said. "I can't get away."

"Make an excuse," she said. "Come on. We all take a risk, everybody."

"No can do," I told her.

"You're missing something."

Apparently so.

★ ★ ★

245

"Where's Julie?" Bella asked.

I was sitting at the table, sipping the last of the Brindisi red, listening to *Evening Music* on WNYC—a mixed bag: Scodanibbio in the hands of the Arditti String Quartet and a sampling of Lester Bowie's *Brass Fantasy*—and reading *Evil in Modern Thought*.

"TV, upstairs," I said, as I put a Post-It note in between the book's pages. "And shut the door." The bitter wind snapped at my bare legs below old gym shorts, my feet.

She took off her toque. Her pigtails flopped onto the back of her bright-blue down jacket. "What did you do?"

"I didn't do anything," I said. "She's watching *I Love Lucy*."

"And you hate *I Love Lucy*. The only woman, man or child who—"

"How was the movie?"

"Great. Scary. Boo!"

She dropped her coat on her chair.

"And how is Marcus?"

She stopped, pulled up. Went to tug a rubber band, but there were none on her wrists.

"He's fine," she said hesitantly, cautiously.

"You should have asked him in."

"It's late," she said finally. "I'm tired."

"I like to meet your friends. Shake their hands."

She headed toward the refrigerator, thought better of it and went toward the stairs.

"I heard he got 30 today."

She didn't know what to say. Really. Bella Orr did not know what to say.

"I heard you two look good together."

She turned to see if I was teasing her. When she saw I wasn't, she said, "How do you know this stuff?"

"I'm a private investigator, remember?"

"Oh, yeah," she said, recovering. "That lump on your head, the shoulder thingy . . ."

She headed upstairs, and a moment later, I heard her and Julie chatting, laughing at old TV, agreeing to search for a movie to watch when *Lucy* ended.

"Dad!" Bella shouted. "Make popcorn!"

I finally joined Julie in bed, and I stared at the ceiling as she purred contentedly next to me, and I chased away the past by trying to feel what Allie felt as he bunked with strangers, terrified of his father, dubious about his mother's will. And for a moment I was terrified too—back in Narrow's Gate, alone, threatened, desperate for affection, to be understood, to be forgiven. Terrified of my irrational mother, dubious about my father's will.

I sat up, lay back down and watched the headlights sweep across the ceiling.

I slept for a while, fitfully, tossing, cursing the pillow, the tangled sheets.

In the darkness, I looked at Julie, listened. Maybe I could hold her, I thought, but then something told me that Allie had no one to hold, no one to hold him in return.

I was getting closer, I knew, and the boy was safe. But it wouldn't mean shit to a tree if I didn't come up with the envelopes, hand them to Sharon.

So . . .

I threw on the jeans I'd worn all day, a fresh gray T-shirt and black V-neck sweater, running shoes, went down and quietly dug out the gun, wriggled into my denim coat and stepped onto the deserted streets, accompanied by the wind whipping off the Hudson.

Not yet dawn, no, and I could hear the slap and groan of the river as I started north along Greenwich, looking in vain for an empty taxi, and I stepped carefully over the patches of ice that had settled against the curb. Above me, there was nothing but darkness behind windows in the lofts, old brick buildings, behind the honeycomb shades, and I counted not a single car crossing from west to east. An empty New York street, with only splashes of pale purple reflected on the gray cobblestone, thick clouds of steam billowing from the manholes, the white light of the Empire State Building a beacon in the distance.

Julie and I were walking in midtown, over by the Algonquin, and we caught a glimpse of Grand Central. The sunlight, as thick as honey, cast shadows that seemed to hide between the columns, beneath the cornice.

That was a good day, easy, sweet; last August, but

mild, a bit of a breeze as we headed toward the Park, holding hands. Julie could be so damn endearing without trying, and she knew what was right and what wasn't, and she believed life was full of little joys, little surprises that made it worthwhile, and that a family was a good thing, loving and true.

By the time I reached Canal, the tips of my numb ears no doubt a bright red, I'd started thinking I'd have to head to Chinatown to find a cab, and then I saw a yellow Crown Vic ease to a stop on Spring. The cabbie got out, stretched his arms over his head as if he wanted to touch Jupiter, his ample stomach showing as his shirt and sweater jumped out of his pants, and then he did a few old-fashioned toe-touches. As I approached, he grabbed his head and twisted it hard until his neck cracked.

"That looks like it hurts," I said.

"Nah. I'm as fit as a fuckin' fiddle," he replied.

Squat, bloated, he looked like he ate bacon at every meal, but I went along with it.

He twisted his head to the other side, and the sickening crack echoed off the dormant buildings.

"I'm going uptown," I said.

"Good for you," he replied. Then he let loose a phlegmy laugh, slapped my arm and gestured for me to get in.

I stepped into the arc of sallow light in front of the Chelsea Hotel and, tucking my change into my jeans, walked across the four lanes and yellow lines of 23rd, as desolate now as TriBeCa's Greenwich Street had been, its storefronts gated, weatherworn cars cold against the curbs on either side. As I stepped over a stretch of black ice near a hydrant, I saw a bread-delivery truck, racing south on Seventh, land with a thud as it hit a bump in the intersection, leaving sparks in its wake. I looked farther east, all the way to the other side of town, and saw no sign of sunrise. My watch made it 4:20 a.m.

I rang Buddy McPorter's bell, rang it again, and I didn't get an answer. I thought about pressing Politano's buzzer, but I figured if the weightlifter hadn't helped me in the afternoon he wasn't going to do it 90 minutes before sunup. And I couldn't bother Christine, the young woman who'd let me in when I last visited. I didn't know her last name, and four of the 28 tenants had the letter C as their first initial.

I noticed that the oily glass door that separated the vestibule from the old building's shadowy lobby had a spring lock, and when I nudged the black bar that ran across its center, the door fell back as easily as if someone had pulled it for me. When I looked at the latch, I saw that it had been pried open—silver scratches on the triangular bolt, and a subtle dent in the lip of the strike. Kneeling on the cold, salt-and-mud-streaked terrazzo tiles, I took off my glove and ran my finger on the lip and studied the scratches on the bolt. No signs of caked grime—the break-in had happened recently. Had to be: There were still enough junkies and thieves circling West 23rd that the tenants wouldn't let management get away with a broken lock for long.

I entered the building, and I was greeted by the scent of dust, of arid heat. To my left, a small, wizened man who might've been in his 70s slept upright on the lobby's well-worn sofa, snoring gently, arms folded across the front of his tattered cloth coat. I stopped to look at him, and then saw myself in the round, gilded mirror above his head. I saw my disheveled hair, the beige bandage on my forehead, the determination in my eyes along with a vague trace of fear, and I saw that I could not convince myself that the busted lock was a coincidence and that I would find Buddy McPorter tucked safely in his bed. Slipping off my other glove, I withdrew the Smith & Wesson from my pocket, and it was cold in my bare hand. Feeling the heft of it, I watched myself and I remembered there was a round in the breech, and I was surprised to see that my expression did not change.

I left the sleeping man and, ignoring the elevator, took the stairs up to the third floor; McPorter had apartment 3C, one of six on the level. Dull bulbs provided a dim light in the stairwell and yet, when I reached the landing, the red EXIT sign at the end of the long, narrow corridor seemed unusually bright in the gray surroundings.

McPorter's door was open, and his living room

had been ransacked: His green futon was overturned and his shag rug had been flipped and tossed aside; two dozen or so books had been pulled from their shelves and now lay scattered on the floor. I shifted the gun to my left hand, went over to the corner, lifted a plastic lamp off the floor and snapped its switch. Despite the broken base, it worked and raw light spread about the area.

Drops of blood led from a wide pool in the center of the room to the door, the threshold.

I tugged the cheap lamp as far as the cord would allow.

I had walked on the blood stains, smearing them, grinding them into the hardwood.

I put down the lamp, hustled to the bedroom, the tiny kitchen. No sign of McPorter, and both rooms had been tossed as badly as had the living room. The one telephone in the apartment, in the bedroom, had been yanked from the wall, and the cord was gone.

Back in the living room, I opened McPorter's front door, held it back with the edge of the coffee table and put the lamp on its side. A wash of light spread across the floor and out into the hallway.

The blood drops ran to the stairs heading up.

Politano lived in Apartment 4G.

His door was closed but unlocked, and I opened it slowly, carefully, with my left hand and forearm, my body away from the ray of light that swept into the murky hallway. And when I heard a low moan, I turned, gun in hand, and swung to face the apartment, the living room.

Politano was on the floor of the disheveled room, his hands tied behind his back with his phone cord. As I straddled him, I saw blood dribbling from his mouth, and an egg-sized lump above his eye that was spreading to his temple. It had come from a blow that was meant to put him down forever.

I bent down and whispered, "Is he still here?"

He couldn't focus his eyes, couldn't speak.

I looked around Politano's apartment: stereo on the inverted rug and pad, the sofas overturned, cushions thrown aside, and books and CDs scattered everywhere. Politano's ficus tree had been ripped from its pot, flung across the room, where it had landed on a red-and-blue crocheted throw.

And no Buddy.

Politano moaned, but he couldn't form words.

I left him, went to the bedroom, snapped on the overhead light, and saw more chaos. Politano's bed had been thrown aside, the mattress flat against the wall to my left. Dresser drawers had been emptied, his clothes scattered on the floor. The phone had been ripped from the wall and his cell phone was smashed to pieces. Several trophies, testimony to his weightlifting skills, lay amid the ruins.

I stepped back, took a deep breath and edged

toward the kitchen. It was empty, and it too had been taken apart. And, as it was in McPorter's place, the window to the fire escape was locked from the inside.

The man had walked down the stairs. With McPorter, a gun jabbed into his back, exiting onto 23rd Street by the front door.

Politano's bathroom was empty. In the sink, the contents of the medicine cabinet.

I returned to the bedroom and I heard breathing.

Stepping around the fallen chiffonier, I raised the gun and went to the closet.

The breathing, in short, staccato bursts, was coming from behind its vents.

I snapped open the door, pointed my gun.

Clothes were in a pile on the floor. A single hanger swayed on the dented bar.

And on the shelf above me, crumpled into a ball, was Christine, the young woman who'd held open the front door for me some 20 hours ago.

She wore only a thin, sleeveless undershirt, and she shivered frantically. Sometime during the ordeal, she had wet herself, and her urine soaked the shelf, and had dripped onto the mound of clothes below her.

Her face was a ghostly white.

"Christine," I said as I reached up. "Christine, give me your hand."

She looked nowhere and she continued to shiver and quake.

"Come on, Christine," I said, cajoling her. "Let me help you."

She moved her head slightly and studied me with raw, vacant eyes.

Finally, she reached out her hand, unfolded herself from the small space and fell onto me.

I held her in my arms, carried her past the chiffonier.

Her lower back was clammy and cold, and when I put her down she struggled to stay upright.

I led her by the elbow to the bathroom and I waited.

She staggered out of the room, still naked below the undershirt.

I edged her to the wall next to the open door, lifted a towel from the floor and handed it to her. She looked at it, and then she wrapped it around her waist.

"Do you remember me?" I said.

She stared at me, but did not reply.

"I was looking for Buddy," I said, nodding hopefully. "This morning? I was looking for Buddy? I made the crack about Thomas Hardy?"

The towel fell from her waist. She collapsed.

I knew I had to call the police, and I had to do it soon. I'd untied Politano, but I couldn't do a damned thing with his jaw, and the grotesque lump on his head was filling with blood. Christine was sitting on a chair in the kitchen, but she was

255

pale and she trembled so hard she seemed to clatter.

She didn't give me much, but what I got was useful. Christine had been in a deep sleep in the weightlifter's bed, but she woke up when she heard the racket in Politano's living room. By then, Buddy, his torn T-shirt, was covered in blood, and Politano had confronted the intruder. She heard a bitter conversation.

"He wanted . . . He wanted Buddy's things," she said. "Buddy's stuff."

"What stuff?" I asked, though I believed I already knew the answer.

She shook her head. "I don't know."

"Christine . . . ?"

She frowned. "The stuff that was in his father's safe."

"He said that? The guy who beat Buddy said that?"

She nodded.

"And did he get them?"

"Buddy told—" Her dry throat caught as she tried to explain. "Buddy told us he returned it all to Alexandra. All of it, everything."

Returned, not gave. "When?"

"He told us . . . He said this afternoon. Today."

I went to the sink, drew a glass of water.

She sipped slowly. Her hand trembled.

I took the glass. She looked at me, shuddered, and vomited. Bile mixed with the water she'd taken.

She lifted the towel, wiped her mouth, chin. "Where's my—Where's my Val?" she asked. "Did he take him too? The guy . . ."

I pulled my cell, punched in 911.

I told the operator what I'd found, and I gave her my name.

When she told me to hold the line, I told her I couldn't, and put the cell away.

"Christine." I knelt down so our eyes were parallel. "Did you see him?"

When she hung her head, I reached and lifted it by the chin.

I said, "Did you?"

She sobbed. "No. I was— I was in the closet. I didn't want to die."

I touched the side of her face.

"I didn't see him," she repeated. "But I didn't want to die."

"That's right," I said softly. "Nobody wants to die."

She cried, "Oh, poor Buddy . . . I want— Can I still help him?"

I stood. "Wait for the EMT guys," I said. "Make sure Val is all right."

"Are you— You're leaving?"

I nodded. "I don't want to get hung up with the cops."

I felt her eyes on my back as I returned to the living room.

Politano was leaning against an overturned sofa, staring at the raw marks on his skinned wrists.

Blood continued to trickle down the sides of his chin.

"Brabender?"

He closed his eyes, shrugged, shook his head, shrugged.

"Did Buddy call him by name? Was it Lou? Did he say Lou?"

Politano nodded.

Had to be. Either him or Erik Torkelsen.

"What's in the envelopes? What's Alexandra got?"

He coughed, and a spray of blood issued from his damaged mouth.

"The stuff from Powell's trunk?"

Again, he nodded, slowly, painfully.

"Anything else?"

He held up two fingers.

"I don't understand."

He grimaced as he raised his index finger toward his eye, and he flexed it repeatedly. As if he were snapping photos.

"Is Buddy going to give her up?"

I looked over my shoulder. Down the hall, the elevator rattled as it climbed.

When I returned to Politano, he was shaking his head. Wiping blood from his chin and shaking his head.

"He's not going to give her up?" I asked, as I edged toward the door. "Even to save his life? Why not?"

Politano took his hand from his chin, tapped his

chest with his bloody fingers, tapped it several times above the heart.

I was on the stairs, heading down, when a thin man in his mid-50s came out onto the third-floor landing. He wore a tattered bathrobe, pajamas and scuffed leather slippers.

"What's going on?"

"You're too late," I said.

"I didn't hear anything," he said defiantly, crossing his arms in front of him.

I looked at him with all the disgust I could muster.

"What?" he said. "I'm supposed to be a hero? Not me."

"No," I replied, "not you."

I kept going, heading down to the lobby, to frigid 23rd Street.

CHAPTER 12

I ran over to Sixth Avenue to the PATH station, paced the empty platform and caught a westbound train, and I arrived in Hoboken and emerged into the murky morning light a few minutes short of 5:45. Up the block, a middle-aged man in a heavy coat, stocking cap, earmuffs and worker's gloves was using a box cutter to tear the twine around bundles of fat Sunday newspapers, and stacking them on a wooden plank held up by two plastic milk crates.

The two other guys who had been on the train with me, and the uniformed nurse, whose black, fur-lined boots clashed with her cap and stockings but matched her overcoat, went north to walk along the other side of the Hudson. I went to the man at the newsstand.

"I hear there's a rental-car place around here," I said.

He looked up at me and held up a callused finger. Then he walked to his stand, passing a pyramid of candies and gum, and threw a switch. A spotlight hit me, the cracked sidewalk, ribbons of ice, slush at the curb where the buses pulled in.

"You know Observer Highway?"

I did. It was how we used to get to Hoboken from Narrow's Gate.

An old Italian, he was lean enough to be skinny, and he was freezing his bony ass.

"Go five blocks."

"Will it be open now?" I said.

"Oh no. Not now."

I gave him two bucks and took a pack of Clorets.

I was outside the Thrifty place, stomping my feet to stay warm. They had cars, but no one to offer one to me. Bella was right, though: The signs told me I'd save about $20 a day versus Manhattan prices. A lot more if I didn't leave the car in a ditch off the Garden State Parkway.

"Sharon Knight," she said, trying hard to conceal that she'd been asleep.

"It's Terry." The cell phone scraped against my frozen ear, the scab on its tip.

"What's wrong?"

She was alert enough to understand I hadn't called to chat.

"Somebody took Buddy McPorter," I told her. "Lou Brabender."

Empty trucks sat idle at the rusted bays of the old terminal across the old four-lane road. To my left, Manhattan's downtown skyline hovered over the river.

"When?"

"This morning," I said. "And he beat the daylights out of McPorter's friend. Gave him a broken jaw. At least a broken jaw."

"Where is he?"

"The friend? Probably in Saint Vincent's," I said. "As for Buddy . . ."

"And where are you?"

"I'm on my way to Silver Haven and, Sharon, I've got Allie."

"You do? How is he?

"He's all right. Frightened. Rightfully so, I'd say, given what happened to Buddy."

"Where is he?"

"He's safe—"

"Terry, where is he?"

"Look, Sharon, he's afraid that he'll be turned over to the police. Let me see what I can find out down in Silver Haven before we have to think about doing that. All right?"

"Have you called Luther?"

"I'm calling you, right?"

A young Hispanic woman, bundled in a long down coat, came toward me. She had a ring of keys in her hand, and her eyes were on the Thrifty front door.

"Terry, he's not with Julie, is he?"

"No. Nor is he with me," I said.

"But you're sure he's safe?"

"Well, he's not going to be safe until you've got everything, Sharon. From John McPorter's and from Powell's car. Everything Buddy stashed away."

The lights went on inside the car-rental office, and the young woman pulled up the blinds. I heard the rattle out on the empty street.

"Sharon, do you have any news on the Torkelsens?" I asked. "Did Luther see them? Have they been released?"

I wanted to know what I'd be walking into.

"The Torkelsens? I don't know, but I'll find out."

The woman threw back the gates to the small parking lot, then disappeared.

"Terry, be careful. Terry. Please."

"I will," I told her.

"Terry, don't put yourself at risk. You've got the boy. That's good enough. The other stuff isn't worth—"

"I've got to go, Sharon," I said.

In a crisp pale-blue uniform, the young woman opened the front door, smiled warmly and waved me inside.

I told Sharon I'd call her later. I turned off my cell phone, and I thanked the pretty woman for holding the door open for me. For a fleeting moment, her peachy perfume reminded me of summer.

The turnpike was Sunday-morning empty, and as the sky turned slowly to a pallid blue, I drove the midsized Buick past the Statue of Liberty, the eroding church steeples of Narrow's Gate. Over by the ports of Elizabeth, ocean-bound container units were held high by impossibly agile straddle carriers.

The V-8 handled well, I thought, though it was tested only once—near Newark Airport, when a jackass alone in a Tahoe cut across three lanes to make the exit. The power brakes worked fine. As Irma had said they would. Baby-doll Irma, who could not take her eyes off the Band-Aid on my forehead, the tiny nicks on my cheeks and ear.

I paid the toll and eased onto the Garden State Parkway and, as I approached a rest area and service station on the left, I decided to make a pit stop. I followed the scent of cinnamon and frying oil, and found a parking spot close to a brick way-station, where seagulls milled and flittered near a Dumpster, pecking at scraps.

I left the car, took out my cell. It was too early to call, I knew. But I had no choice.

"This is Terry Orr," I said. "May I speak to Mabry?"

"No, you certainly may not," the woman squawked.

"Excuse—"

"You, sir, are nothing but trouble."

"I'm sorry. Who am I—"

"How dare you bring your problems into this house?"

She said "this house." Not "my house."

Mother or mother-in-law?

I said, "Do you think—"

I heard a hand cover the mouthpiece, and then I heard only bits of a muffled squabble, and finally Reynolds came on.

"Terry?"

"How'd it go?"

"Fine," he said, "fine. I caught him crying during the night, but I think he's all right now. Still a little scared, but all right."

"You think I can talk to him."

Reynolds said yes. "He's at the table with Henry. Hold on."

As I waited, I watched a group of senior citizens hobble off an Atlantic City–bound bus and head toward the rest rooms, ignoring the costly fast food and saving their appetites to rip into the free breakfast buffet at Bally's.

"Mr. Orr?"

"How are you, Allie?"

"I'm fine, I guess," he said. "Mr. Reynolds is nice, and so are his kids."

"That's good," I told him. I heard what he didn't say: The women wanted him out of the house.

"When do you think—"

"Not yet, Allie," I said.

He sighed. "OK."

"Allie, I need your help."

He listened, and then he told me what I needed to know.

"Anyway, I think so," he added.

"That's good enough for me."

I asked him to put Reynolds back on the line.

"Mabry, I know I've got you in deep with your family—"

He said, "Don't worry about it. This boy can use a friend."

Some 50 miles from Harlem, and I could feel the sincerity of his remark.

"Where are you?" he asked.

I told him. "This thing is coming to a head," I added. "Last night, they made a move on Buddy McPorter. Took him, beat his friend bad."

"This is fact?"

"There's at least one witness," I said. Christine hadn't seen Brabender at work, but Politano had.

"You tell Addison?"

"He knows." By now, Sharon had called him.

"So you didn't tell him."

"Mabry, don't bring him into this yet," I said. "If you do, the kid's going back to the old man—"

"And we don't want that," he replied. "All right."

I was glad to hear him say "we." I needed somebody at my back, especially now.

I told him I'd be in touch, and I headed toward the rental car, passing the scavenger birds and the toddling seniors. Pulpo's gun rattled in my coat pocket.

Allie told me his mother took refuge in her work, and he said that if she was out this morning, he'd guess it'd either be at Sandy Hook Bay or the Twin Lights on the mainland. She liked the quiet on an early Sunday morning, he said, the peacefulness;

and she took her time when she worked. "She doesn't hurry," Allie said, and I envisioned his mom in a heavy yet stylish coat, camera up on a tripod, as she waited for the light to play on the structures she was shooting, unaware that her friend Buddy McPorter was close to the same fate his father had suffered.

Could there be any doubt now that it was Brabender who had tossed John McPorter onto the fence?

I decided to take Route 36 and try Sandy Hook. With the sun coming up above the Atlantic, and the thin clouds overhead dotted with turquoise, rose and pink, it seemed like the kind of day a photographer would head for the water, despite the chilling temperatures.

After crossing the Navesink River, I went north onto Sandy Hook on a narrow two-lane road and kept looking to the east, toward the ocean, to spot the lighthouse Allie had mentioned. I passed several beaches, a sign for something called Spermaceti Cove and an empty visitors' center, and then a deserted military base.

Fort Hancock, according to my lessons at St. Matt's, had been established in 1895 by the U.S. Army to protect New York Harbor's shipping channels, and the granite walls that once hid 12-inch-caliber gun batteries still stood on the property, though the guns were gone. On the right side of the road, facing the silver bay to the west, was an abandoned row of Colonial Revival houses of yellow brick with green dormers, green trimming, white pilasters and white columns. The sturdy houses, no doubt set aside for officers who had worked at the base, were neat and well kept. I counted 18 houses in all, and no doubt there were more to the rear, closer to the ocean side. A ghost town, I thought, but ready for reoccupation, if the need arises. Twelve-inch-caliber guns with a 20-mile range aren't worth much in the 21st century, but a place that could house 12,000 military men, women, their families and civilian workers a short ride from downtown Manhattan might be invaluable. Otherwise, the Army might've sold these houses: At Silver Haven prices, they could've gotten a million for each.

They were probably better off in the hands of the National Park Service. The likes of Harlan Powell would have razed them rather than find good use for such well-built and serviceable old homes.

I followed the road as it bent to the east and approached the granite bunkers near the old ordnance proving grounds. As I wondered briefly if any unexploded shells sat under the blacktop, or mines under the sand, I drove toward a gravel parking lot behind the sign that said North Beach, and I saw two old-fashioned station wagons, a beat-up vintage Woody and a new black Land Rover, and no silver BMW like the one I'd watched Alexandra Powell drive some 24 hours earlier.

I decided to press on. Black sand led to the

beach, and I had trouble walking it in my running shoes as I wriggled around rising dunes, shrub thickets and prickly vegetation immune to the winter frost. As the sand turned to an earthlike brown, it became easier to traverse, as if it lay atop a concrete pathway; and after a few more yards, I reached the same pearl-colored sand that covered most Jersey shorelines. As I went up the incline, I heard the roar of the ocean, the caw of the seagulls.

The long, narrow beach was deserted, except for a few fishermen who had their lines out beyond the breakers, their poles nestled into cradles dug deep in the sand. Two of the men were going at it alone, watching their lines for a snap or tug, staring out at the water from behind fur-lined hoods, pails and tackle boxes at their sides. Another man, older, stooped at the shoulders, had a young companion, perhaps a granddaughter, and she poured coffee from a thermos. Steam rose from the plastic cup into the crisp, salty air.

I started south toward a shuttered observation deck, and I looked at the driftwood and countless clamshells that dotted the sand. By the water's edge, tiny, stout birds scurried on little legs, pecking at unseen food, dodging the splash of the waves, pressing on as if impervious to the attacks of the bigger birds. In the distance, the sun had pushed above the horizon, sending a streak of gold light across the gray water.

The wooden stairs to the observation deck were

just ahead. I left the sand for a concrete walkway and, passing icicles on shower heads, rest rooms, I took the stairs, staying close to the inside rail as I made the turn at the first landing.

She had her camera on a tripod, the tripod was up on a six-sided table, and the camera's long lens was facing north, toward the water, toward Staten Island, Brooklyn, lower Manhattan, and she hadn't noticed that I'd arrived. She wore a heavy pale-green parka, a thick white turtleneck sweater, dark-brown slacks, fur-lined boots. Her sunglasses were perched atop a dark-brown knit cap.

She sat on one of the benches that were affixed to the battleship-gray table, and she held in her gloved hand a trigger at the end of a line that ran up to the camera.

To the west, almost directly above her head, was the Sandy Hook lighthouse.

"Seems to me you ought to put a lighthouse on the edge of the water," I said as I approached her. "But what do I know?"

The wind from the west ruffled my hair, stung my cheeks.

"It used to be," she replied. "Erosion, shifting sand, time . . . Everything changes."

I took my hands out of my pockets. "I've got Allie."

She looked up at me, more alarmed than pleased. "Is he with you? Here?"

"You want him back?"

"What is that supposed to mean?" she asked, her voice crisp with severity.

"It means what it means," I replied. "You want him back?"

"Of course I want him. That is an absolutely stupid remark. How—"

"It's going to cost you the envelopes," I said. "All of them."

She drew back. "Are you blackmailing me?"

"Buddy took them from his father's safe, stashed them in his locker at the juice bar, and gave them to you on the day of his father's funeral. Now I want them. It's my turn."

"I asked you if you were blackmailing me."

"I'm offering you a trade. Give me the envelopes and you get your son."

Anger rose to redden her face.

"You can keep the $471," I added.

"Do you have any sense of the trouble you're in?" she said, glaring at me. "If I tell my husband what you're proposing, he will deal with you. Do you understand me?"

She let go of the shutter line, stood.

"Do you understand what I'm saying?" she repeated.

"I think it's more likely he'd deal with you," I said. "Once he learns that it was you who took the stuff from his trunk, once he learns you'd rather let him think Allie had what you took, and that Allie, not Buddy, stole from the old man—"

"Oh, you know nothing," she said angrily, bitterly. "Nothing."

"I know you're the kind of woman who'd rather expose her son to the streets of New York than give up her scheme to destroy her husband."

She looked at me and, finding no words to defend herself, tried to slap me.

I blocked the blow, held onto her wrist.

I said, "Did you really think whatever you were going to get from Harlan was worth more than the life of your son?"

I shoved her and she tumbled against the bench, grabbed the tabletop to keep from falling.

"You're damned lucky your boy is more resilient than you think. Leaving him on those streets with less than four dollars—"

"He had his credit card, and all the cash—"

"Your husband cut the flow," I said, as she came away from the bench. "Your boy was exposed."

She stared at me.

"I don't give a rat's ass for you or your husband," I added. "You're giving me the goddamned envelopes, and then I'll look up that son of a bitch myself."

We stood in silence, defying each other. I could've told her she was wasting her time trying to chill me. After the beating I'd taken from Brabender, the attack on the parkway, the threat to Sharon, the death of McPorter, the terror in Allie's eyes, my resolve wasn't about to waver. I had no losses to cut, no need for an alternate plan; I wasn't going to bail because I didn't like the way it was playing. Now that Allie was safe, I was going to get Powell and Brabender, for what they did to the old man and what they tried to do to me, and that was all of it. I'd had enough.

"By the way, if you're waiting to hear from Buddy, you won't. Brabender's got him."

She stiffened. "Buddy's in danger, and you're here?" she asked, her voice rising.

"I don't give a shit about Buddy," I told her. "He's part of your scheme."

"You don't—"

"Think he's given you up yet?" I asked. "Maybe. I've seen Brabender's work . . ."

"No," she said sharply, "no, I don't believe you."

"Of course you do. Christ."

She stared at me, and she was thinking, and when she realized what I said was fact, she said, "He'll kill him. You know he'll kill him."

"Oh, yeah. He'll kill him dead."

I watched as she stepped away, began to pace.

"Buddy won't say anything," she said to the sand, the frigid air.

"Doesn't matter," I replied. "It's over."

"Buddy loves me."

"So I heard. What did you promise him? When you walked away from Harlan, you'd go with him?"

"I don't suppose you'd believe I do love him," she said.

"Are you kidding? You love somebody but you?"

As I stepped back, the sand shifting under my

shoes, I noticed that Alex Powell's battered leather camera bag rested under the table. When I opened it, I saw a manila envelope atop the lens, film canisters.

"Go ahead," she said, as if resigned.

I lifted the envelope and, removing my gloves, undid the clasp.

It contained a contact sheet of black-and-white photos as well as several prints from the roll.

Harlan Powell in a vast, crowded parking lot, talking to a man in a dark, conservative suit. Fit and ramrod-stiff, the man wore sunglasses and, with his precise hair and club tie, he looked like the embodiment of law enforcement. Powell seemed diminished in his presence.

"Do you know this man?" I asked, as I looked at the next shot in the series: the man slipping an envelope into his jacket pocket.

She said, "His name? No, of course not. But he's one of them."

"One of who?"

"The Commission," she replied as she went up on the tabletop. "You know."

"The Securities and Exchange Commission?"

"Of course," she said calmly.

"Where was this?" I asked.

"The Cherry Hill Mall. It's where they meet."

"You followed him?" Down by Philadelphia, Cherry Hill had to be at least 80 miles from Silver Haven.

She nodded. "Countless times."

I noticed there were no photos of the SEC agent giving anything to Powell. All the action was one-way.

I asked, "What does it mean?"

She was looking through the camera's viewfinder toward the Verrazano-Narrows Bridge, which seemed to vanish slowly, then reappear, in the hovering mist.

"He's not the man everybody thinks he is," she said.

She came down from the tabletop, reached into her bag and withdrew a small pink chamois to wipe off the lens.

"But he's not looking for these, is he?"

"No, he doesn't know about those," she replied as she climbed back up to where she had been. With a slow, circular motion, she repeatedly swept the pink rag around the lens.

"I need the rest," I said.

"The rest I can't give you," she replied. "I can't."

"Even if it means someday your son might face what happened to John McPorter, and what may have happened to Buddy?"

She peered into the viewfinder, then came around and looked at the lens. She seemed satisfied.

"Lady, what are you doing?" I said, bracing myself against a sudden gust of wind. "We're talking about your son."

She came off the table. "You said so yourself. It's over."

The pink rag went back into the leather bag.

"I don't think Harlan will hurt Allie. No, I don't believe so . . . And Lou won't do anything unless Harlan tells him to."

"Too late for that," I replied. "Allie's already been hurt. He's scared, and he's got nowhere to go. Except his work, and he's too young to be living that way."

She said, "You'll take what I've given you to Sharon, and you'll bring Allie to me."

I stared at the photos. Her husband didn't know about them, but Alex considered them important enough to carry with her, though not important enough to conceal.

"Your husband is in violation of his plea agreement, isn't he?"

"That's no secret," she said. "He violates it every day. Lou is a convicted felon."

"So you don't want your husband in jail . . ."

"I want him out of my life, out of Allie's life."

She looked past me, toward the seagulls hanging upon the breakers, toward the sun as it floated above the horizon. And then she climbed back onto the tabletop, looked into the camera and held down the trigger, snapping photos, one after another, in rapid succession.

I looked at the bridge in the distance. It was gone.

I waited, listening to the click of the shutter, the crash of the waves, the groaning wood. Finally, she came off the tabletop.

"What do you have on him?" I said. "Besides knowing he's in contact with the SEC."

It had to be something that would drive him away, that would force him to leave the cushy setup he had in Silver Haven—the big house, the plush cars, the country-club life, the people who thought he'd gotten over on the government.

"Your husband's working for the SEC, isn't he? He's a mole."

"A mole. The word doesn't quite describe him," she said, anger seeping through her sudden flippancy. "Doesn't quite describe his arrogance, his threats toward Allie and me. His trysts, his women. His lifestyle.

"A mole," she added, shaking her head. "It sounds so benign . . ."

"Not in the sense that he's on the inside, rolling over on his friends. That's not benign at—"

"Harlan doesn't have friends," she replied. "Golf partners. Sex partners. Drinking buddies. Admirers, gofers. People who fear him. But no friends."

"And the SEC got him to wear a wire," I said.

She looked hard at me. "Harlan is a coarse, ill-mannered, thoroughly reprehensible thug who made his fortune, and now he thinks he owns the world and can do with it what he chooses."

"He wore a wire," I said. "That's what you have on him. You know who he's turned in."

"And if they knew," she said, "it would destroy them. And him. Especially him."

"You keep that secret and he lets you walk with the kind of money you need. At least that was your plan until Allie told his father about Buddy and the safe."

"And it still might've worked if Lou didn't— The police must know he killed poor John."

I didn't hear her. It was coming to me fast now, and I saw it: What she took from Harlan's car had to be tangible evidence of his activities, not merely photos that suggested what he might be up to.

What she took from the car: tapes.

No, the SEC would have those.

His notes.

A diary. A record of his activities.

Something he could use against the Commission if they turned their back on him.

Something that had a little more than the tapes showed.

"I want my son," she said.

"Give."

"Don't be confused by—"

"Give and you get Allie."

She paused thoughtfully, and then, as she stood on the bench, ready to go back to the tabletop, she said, "Lou drives him to Mass. Harlan. Nine o'clock."

She gave me the name of a church in Silver Haven.

I went to the parking lot, and I looked at her Land Rover, the dull sun reflecting off its flawless shine, and I was thinking.

And when I approached the vehicle, I saw that what I'd thought might be right: What it was she had, she had to keep with her. And not dangling out of her camera bag.

I went up on the back bumper, looked over the spare tire and into the cargo hold, and I saw it had been rigged with a locker of sorts, the kind that photographers use for equipment, lens, camera casings and the like. And I saw that the locker had been scratched, damaged, but its hasp was new, and so was the lock.

Powell had been there, or Brabender, a week ago, maybe more. They thought she'd moved the material—material that fit in manila envelopes—from Powell's car to her Land Rover.

They probably went through her BMW too.

She was confident they weren't coming back, at least not today: She'd left the Yale lock undone.

The doors were locked.

I walked over to the Buick I'd rented, popped the trunk and dug out the crowbar for the jack.

It took only two shots to break the back window.

The alarm started screeching after the first blow.

I climbed on the back bumper and, reaching between the jagged glass on the frame, threw off the lock, opened the locker.

Only one lens, and a brick of Ilford film, sat in the cradles of gray foam. I tossed them to the backseat, lifted the foam.

Two envelopes. One flat, the other plump with documents.

I had no time to open them: A few of the fisherman were running up the black sand toward the lot.

I jumped into the Buick, ripped out of the lot, and flew past the gun batteries, the glittering bay, the buildings on Officers' Row.

No one was on my tail when I got back on 36 heading south.

Silver Haven was maybe seven miles from the southern tip of Sandy Hook, and there was no open drawbridge to hang me up.

CHAPTER 13

J on Craw sat in his shiny patrol car, with
its purple piping and shotgun rack, on the west
side of Tanager Street, outside St. Sebastian's,
Silver Haven's Gothic-style stone church. He wasn't
looking for me; or if he was, he didn't bring much
pride to the assignment. From where I stood, on
Menhaden Lane at the side entrance to the church,
I could see that he was reading the sports pages
of the Asbury Park Press. I figured it was his job
to direct traffic when Mass ended and the congre-
gation started across Tanager, or when the cars
emptied the lot behind the church. Low stress,
but a high-profile task; see and be seen. Otherwise,
he might've dumped it on Maura Maki or one of
his other officers.

I'd parked the Buick a block west of the church's
ample lot.

I opened the first envelope, the thinner of the
two.

Negatives, and when I held them up to the light
I could see two women, and they were naked,
kissing, groping in some, and I couldn't tell if it
was Sharon and Alexandra, though I'd bet that

big fat tree near the end of the roll was still on the campus of Wellesley College.

The next envelope held what it was all about: Powell's handwritten notes for the past year, dates, names, locations, names of the SEC agents he met with, additional information on the neighbors and friends he'd spied on, personal data that didn't come out for the wire.

The amount of money the Commission paid him. Expense money, it was called.

Didn't cost Harlan Powell $2,000 to set up a meeting with a Freeholder Kirkenbauer at the Salt Creek Grille in Rumson, unless he ordered an '84 Montrachet.

I dug into the third envelope, the one I'd taken from Alex's camera bag, got out of the Buick, walked up and down three orderly rows of late-model cars, vans and SUVs until I found Powell's white Mercedes, and I took one of the photos of Powell and his SEC handler, and stuck it face-down under the driver's-side windshield wiper.

I went back to the Buick, slid into the front seat, and I waited, tucking my hands under my arms to stay warm.

When Mass ended, Brabender came out via the St. Sebastian's side door and headed toward the parking lot, while Powell went to have his public grip-and-grin with the priest, maybe nod-wink at Sheriff Craw.

Brabender. He should've been halfway to Guadalajara now, racing from his crimes, ready to slip into a new identity, disappear for a decade or two. But no, not him. He's either too stupid to understand that his boss's pact with the SEC hadn't given him license to kill John McPorter, try to kill me and take off with Buddy. Or maybe he'd caught Powell's arrogance as if it were a communicable disease.

Meanwhile, Powell's setup was perfect. In Brabender, he had the ideal fall guy—an ex-con who somehow believed that his boss wouldn't cut him loose when trouble called, just because he'd put the goon on salary, let him drive the Mercedes, drink his liquor, maybe share the local lap dancers. Christ, Powell probably told him they were friends.

When Brabender gets called in by Addison for the two McPorters, Powell will throw up his hands, open his eyes wide and, declaring ignorance and innocence in the same breath, claim he had no idea what Brabender was up to. None; who? Me? "There is no way on God's green earth that I would ever . . ."

He's not about to hang himself, at least not intentionally.

Brabender was a thug, an oaf, a weak man, a murderer. Eight to five says he also grew up in a run-down town, looked up to sharp-angle guys like Powell and was happy as hell to find a job waiting for him when he skulked out of South Woods. A born patsy, and one way or another, he'd pay.

But Powell had to answer for it too. As it was

now, he'd be able to put a mile between himself and his old pal. Powell was going to run to his SEC buddies and plead for help. If he'd been an effective mole, they'd probably give it to him. They'd scold him—"You should've come to us in the beginning, Harlan"—but if he convinced them he had nothing to do with McPorter's murder and whatever had happened to Buddy, they'd shield him to keep him in the field.

And Brabender would be on his own.

Now, in his black trench coat, white shirt and rust-colored tie, Brabender lumbered up the slight incline outside St. Sebastian's, surrounded by men and women in their Sunday best as they ambled toward their cars. Cleansed, they chatted amicably, women in their 30s speaking with their friends, men straggling behind and asking after the kids, talking football, work, career. Brabender spoke to no one, and as he entered the lot he withdrew a key from his pocket.

Halfway to the vehicle, he pressed a button and the Mercedes's lights flickered, its horn made a short, identifying bleat.

And then, after seeing only its white back, Brabender absently grabbed at the photo, as if it were an inconsequential flier for a new car wash, thin-crust pizza, an available nanny.

Then he turned it over.

A dull expression coated his face as he saw his Powell with his SEC Joe.

But he didn't panic. He opened the car door,

leaned in, carefully placed the photo in the glove box, and then he eased into the driver's seat.

He backed the Mercedes out, careful to dodge the playful kids, the parishioners who continued their conversations, milling by the back bumpers of their cars despite the temperature, the tepid rays of the mid-morning sun.

As he brought the squat vehicle around a row of cars, I started up the Buick's engine.

Powell got into the white car at Tanager and I followed, letting a sea-green Lexus slip in between us. It wasn't until they were halfway to Shining Ridge Road that Brabender reached over, popped the box and gave Powell the photo.

Seconds later, Powell slammed the meat of his hand against the dashboard, and then he did it again.

Brabender kept his eye on the road.

A ranting Powell tore the photo in half, no doubt swearing at his wife.

I thought, Now there is a man who enjoyed the illusion of being in control.

They went to Powell's house, and if they expected to confront Alex, they were out of luck. If she knew what was good for her, she was driving her Land Rover with its shattered window to Centre Street for a conciliatory get-together with her friend, a no-nonsense interview with an NYPD lieutenant and, if all went well, a reunion with her son.

To stay out of the range of Powell's security cameras, I parked behind a snow mound on Balustrade, the nearest side street to his lavish pale-blue Colonial, and I wondered if Powell would send Brabender hurrying over to Sandy Hook or the Twin Lights site to find Alex, or whether he and his muscle would lay low, expecting her to return at any moment from her morning shoot. Or maybe they'd come out with Buddy in tow, his eyes blackened, hands tied behind his back as he shivered in the frigid air. Or maybe they'd hang back, strategize over cups of fresh-ground coffee drawn by his maid, and sweet rolls, omelets.

Suddenly, I was reminded that I hadn't eaten since the few mussels I'd had last night with Julie.

She was on her way to her parents' now.

She kept inviting me to join her, but I said no, inventing reasons when I had none.

It was a good thing, what I had with Julie. Enjoyable, easy, comfortable.

What am I talking about? "Enjoyable, easy, comfortable": sounds like bad ad copy for a moped. Dinner at Pizza Hut.

What I had with Julie was great.

I admit that. Why wouldn't I?

But to talk about a future when—

Powell emerged, wearing his canary-yellow sweater, a black shirt with two buttons open at the collar, and black slacks, no topcoat, and he had a supple golf glove folded in his hand.

Brabender carried two clubs, a driver and a pitching wedge, and he held open, and then closed, the passenger's-side door for his boss. The clubs went on the backseat, laid gently, tenderly.

As Brabender kicked over the engine, the gates to Powell's property opened slowly, and they started to shudder to a close when he made a left onto salt-streaked Shining Ridge. I waited, pulled out and fell in behind the Mercedes.

We kept moving on Shining Ridge, crossing under bare branches, icicles on telephone lines, and Powell was hectoring the big man, his head bobbing repeatedly as he boiled in anger. Brabender had two hands on the wheel—white knuckles, no doubt—and he was taking it from Powell.

Somehow, I didn't think Powell was chastising him for the way he'd handled the old man and Buddy, the hardworking, grift-minded son.

He wanted his diary back.

He was reminding Brabender that all of this was about his diary, his notes. His status, money.

But if he was smart, he wasn't blurting everything that was on his mind. He wasn't saying, "Nobody told you to kill Mac. And what the hell were you thinking when you fucked with Buddy?" Not yet.

Neither of them knew Politano was alive, and they knew nothing about Christine.

If they did, if they knew there was a living witness to Buddy's kidnapping, they'd be zipping to nearby Allaire Airport to take a private jet to the British

West Indies or some other country without an extradition treaty with the U.S.

But no. Instead, they were pulling into the parking lot of the Silver Haven Golf Center.

Sun reflected off the tinted glass on the façade of the posh, three-story building, and a young man in a purple Silver Haven High sweatshirt and purple stocking cap was sweeping and resalting the front steps that led up to its entrance. Powell blew by him without a word, deflecting his toady greeting.

Brabender stayed in the car. Oily vapors escaped from the tailpipe.

By 11 a.m., a dozen or so cars were in the lot, and I finally had a chance to step out of the Buick, when a fat-ass Suburban pulled next to me and three young guys done up to look like golfers popped out, carrying identical Callaway Big Berthas. I glanced at Brabender, who, with his back to me, was blithely running a purple chamois across the front end of the Mercedes, and I stepped behind the three preppies. Brabender didn't turn away from his task.

The man behind the counter, a sixty-something with an off-season suntan, greeted the three by name, swiped the bar codes on their ID cards across the reader and sent them on their way.

"OK if I play a bucket or two?" I asked.

"No problem, young man," he said cheerfully. "Only we charge by the half-hour. Members get preference, but we've got plenty of room today. Plenty."

I gave him $25, took a receipt and I went past the pro shop and vending machines to the glass entry that led to the three-tier driving range, grateful that the Silver Haven Golf Center didn't post guards with metal detectors at its doors.

I was outdoors again. The driving range faced a long stretch of snow-speckled grass surrounded by thick pines and, in case Paul Bunyan turned up, high netting some 400 yards away. Golf balls flew from tees above me and to my right, and the boy who had been sweeping the steps earlier now followed me with two buckets of balls.

"How many tee stations you got here?" I asked him.

He put down the buckets, looked at the red marks the handles left in his palms. "Eighty."

"All heated?"

He nodded.

"And security cameras?"

"Yep." He was a good-looking kid, about Bella's age, with sandy hair. But he hadn't learned how to charm an extra dollar out of the clientele. He wasn't thinking about anything but getting away from me, a stranger wearing wrinkled jeans and 14 stitches in his dome.

"What, you guys sit around and laugh at the mistakes we make?"

"On the security monitors?" He frowned, shook his head. "Nobody looks at that."

"The insurance guys made you do it?"

"I don't know. Ask my grandfather."

"He run the place?"

"Owns it," he said, and lifted the buckets.

I told him to put me in the middle.

Hot waves from the overhead heaters felt good on my head, ears. I put my hands up by the orange coils and left them there until the feeling returned, until the blood reached the tips of my fingers.

Powell wasn't on the first level, though the three guys who'd come in when I did were, and they made serious faces before each mighty blow and then stood there and admired their shot as if it was the greatest anybody had ever made. No one seemed to notice me, the only golfer wearing a denim coat.

Carrying a driver I'd pulled from the public bin, I went upstairs and found five more guys, spaced far apart. They drove the ball into the distance, watching it rise, then fall harmlessly to the grass and snow some 20 feet below, before they centered another ball on the tee.

I went to the third level and found two young golfers, teenagers, working diligently, watching each other's form, commenting with gravity, sincerity.

No sign of Powell and his yellow sweater.

I turned to head back to the stairwell. And I saw Brabender.

He'd taken off his trench coat and tie, and he was barreling at me.

"Where's Buddy?" I shouted, as I stood my ground.

His expression didn't change. He was about 20 yards away.

"You do him like you did the old man?"

He kept coming.

"You dumb piece of shit," I barked.

He raised his arms, held out his hands to grab me.

I hit him with the golf club on the side of the head.

He stopped, staggered.

I threw the broken shaft off the balcony, and I charged at him, setting him up with a straight left to the nose, and catching him with a hard, chopping right cross to the point of his chin.

I've starched the son of a bitch, I thought. He's going down.

He shook his head, squared himself and threw a long right that missed by inches.

I came under him and, sliding to his left flank, brought a right hook to his kidneys, then another.

He was grimacing as he turned around.

He stepped back to measure me.

He dug under his jacket, and I figured he was going for the brass knuckles, the ones he used to drop me the first time I saw him.

Instead, he came up with a gun, a nine-millimeter that seemed to disappear in his big hand.

As he fired, I dove to my left, sprawling behind the wooden divider between the two tee stations, and I pulled the Smith & Wesson.

Brabender burst into the space, arm extended, his gun pointing at me.

I fired, and the round caught him square on the right shoulder.

His arm dropped instantly to his side and his gun slid from his fingers.

He looked at me, looked at his shoulder and lunged at me.

I rolled around the plastic turf, kicked him hard in the side of the knee. As he stumbled, I got my feet under me, spun and shoved him from behind.

He flew off the balcony and I heard him land with a thud on the icy turf two stories below.

I didn't wait. I got up, dashed past the empty stations to the stairwell, and headed down to the first floor.

Powell was sitting on a black leather sofa in a lounge next to the locker room. Three other men were with him, one on the sofa, two others on matching chairs.

They were guys his age, comfortable with their prosperity, by the looks of their clothes, their healthy glow, toothy grins. They didn't mind listening to stories told by a man who'd sold out his friends, cheated on his wife, berated his son, sanctioned murder.

They thought he was a guy who could help them earn a few extra dollars, show them how to work the system.

Powell said to one of the men, "Wally, the point is—"

"Get up," I said.

He had a bottle of vitamin-enriched water in his hand and it fell, dropping to the beige carpet.

The other men snapped back, startled, frightened, confused.

"I said get up."

I had the gun pointed at the center of his smug face.

He stood.

"Over here."

"You don't know what you're doing, Orr," he said as he wriggled past the black Lucite table, the golf magazines.

"Turn around."

He did, slowly, and he held up his hand.

"Lock your fingers behind your head."

One of the guys, 40ish with a beer gut under his argyle sweater-vest, pink shirt, turned toward the door.

"No," I said, "you're going to want to see this."

I shifted the gun to my left hand and then pressed the muzzle under Powell's jaw.

Then I ran my hand across his chest, then from shoulder to shoulder.

"You're not wearing a wire today, Harlan?"

"You're crazy," he spit.

I spun him around and I pushed the gun against his forehead.

"What was that?"

He looked up at me, thought about saying it again. But he kept quiet.

"Put your hands in your pocket," I told him. "Deep."

He did.

I moved the gun to my right hand.

The three men were anchored to their chairs.

I said, "Your pal here is working for the SEC. And he's been recording your conversations."

The two guys in the chairs stared at each other in confusion.

The round man on the sofa looked like he was going to faint, and he started to shake.

"Think about how many of your friends have been called in by the Commission," I told them. "Think about when they'll be coming for you."

Powell said, "Don't listen to—"

I smacked on the top of his head with the gun butt and he hissed in pain.

"See," I told him, "you're not invincible."

"We'll see," he uttered.

I waved the piece in his face. "Let's move."

He shuffled toward the door.

"Instead of calling the cops," I said to the three guys, "get out your cells and contact your lawyers." Looking at the pale man with the diamonds on his sweater, I said, "I'm guessing at least one of you is fucked."

I jabbed the gun between Powell's shoulder blades and told him to move.

Blood dribbled onto the back of his collar.

Tell me where Buddy is, or I'll strap you to the bumper," I said, steam rising from my mouth.

"You'll never get away—"

"Buddy," I repeated.

He looked at me. "How the fuck would I know where Buddy is?"

"'Cause you told Brabender to snatch him."

"Wait. You're telling me Lou— Lou did what?"

I knew he'd go that way. He's going to sell out the world before he takes another fall.

I drove the muzzle into his ribs. "Get behind the wheel, chump."

"Chump?" He gave me a crooked grin.

I shoved him toward the Buick's open door. "In."

He stared at me with as much defiance as he could muster. And then he climbed inside.

"Take off your belt," I said as I slammed the door.

I got in behind him, and I told him to hand me the leather strap.

When he did, I broke off the pin, looped the belt through the gold buckle, slid it around his neck and I yanked it hard.

Powell coughed, shook his head violently.

When his face went red, I released the strap.

"What is *wrong* with you?" he cried, sputtering.

"I don't know how I got to be who I am," I replied.

"What?" He looked at me in the rearview as I dropped the ignition key on the passenger's seat.

"Drive," I said.

"You got to be—"

"Take me to where you think Buddy is."

"I don't know—"

I hit him again with the gun butt, and then I grabbed at the leather strap.

"OK, OK," he said, as he groped for the key.

A moment later, the engine kicked over with a roar.

CHAPTER 14

Rendered cooperative by the belt around his neck, Powell bounced the Buick into the Exxon station on Route 36 and put it at the side of the bay, away from the pumps and away from the highway. Across the narrow street, a drab, aluminum-sided mother-and-daughter was the lone sentinel. Thus far, the blinds hadn't moved.

"I don't know if I'm right," he said, as he cut the engine, offered me the key. "But I know Lou—"

"No speeches," I said as I opened the back door. "If he's here, he's here. And you'd better hope he's alive."

I let go of the belt and stepped into the cold air. Powell joined me.

"Sign says it's closed," I told him. "Break the—"

"Wait," he said. "They keep a key in the john."

"Let's get it."

Surrounded by the scent of detergent and decay in the grimy bathroom, Powell went to the tall garbage bin, which overflowed with discarded paper towels, and turned its rounded head onto the soiled tiles. A key was taped to the rusted bottom.

"Let's go," I said.

"Orr, listen to me—"

Lifting the Smith & Wesson out of my pocket was enough to shut him down.

We stepped back into the sunlight, went along the side of the building to the front door.

"Make it snappy," I told him.

A few cars had passed the station since we'd pulled in. Sooner or later, someone was going to stop by to fill up.

We went into the office where I'd first met Ezra Torkelsen. His downscale girlie magazine still lay on the old wooden desk. Red pistachio shells were scattered on the grimy linoleum.

"In the back," I said.

We entered the bay, which, beneath the disarray, was tooled for engine repairs and body work. Before us, Brabender's Darth Vader SUV rested high on the lift, and on the floor below was the front bumper that had tapped me into the death spin on the parkway. Two rolling tool chests, their drawers open and contents disheveled, stood at odd angles behind the chassis, and a sander, and a shielded light on a long orange cord was hooked to a slot in one of the rotors, just below where the Torkelsens would patch and paint the scar in the front panel, change out the cracked plastic sheath that protected the headlight.

I stepped under the Cadillac, reached up and touched the lamp. Warm, but not hot; it had been off for a while, though not overnight.

"Somebody left in a hurry," I said. My voice echoed in the confined space.

Despite the sunlight through the rectangular windows high on the back and side walls, the bay was dark and foreboding, and I knew I had little time to meander.

"Where would he put him?"

"I don't know— I've never been—"

I pushed him from behind toward a door at the left side of the bay, toward the barrels that had rumbled across the floor when Brabender took it to Ezra a few days ago.

"Open it," I said softly.

"Orr, what are you—"

I put the nozzle of gun against his spine. "Keep your mouth shut and open the fuckin' door," I whispered.

As he reached for the knob, I stepped back, raised the gun.

If someone came through that door, they'd run into Powell first, giving me time to fire.

There was no one but Buddy in the room, and Buddy was dead.

Dried blood coated his nostrils and his upper lip, his eyes were swollen shut, but, as he lay in his boxer shorts, old Everlast T-shirt, crumpled amid the dried mops, the battered street brooms, dented buckets, solvents, Borax and liquid soaps, it was impossible to tell what had killed him, even after I'd pulled the string on the bare light bulb. His limbs were at awkward angles, and his head lolled onto his chest.

"I had nothing to do with this," Powell said.

"Want to bet a set of brass knuckles broke that nose, blackened his eyes?" I said as I took out my cell.

I had Luther's number on speed dial.

"Back to the car," I said, as I worked the phone with my thumb. "Fast."

Easy on the gas," I told him.

"I'm shaking, Orr," he said. "Almost pissed my pants, goddamn it. I don't know if can drive—"

I raised the gun as if I was going to dent him again.

He shut up, tried to look pitiful in the rearview mirror.

I said, "I guess you've figured out by now that nobody's fucking around."

"Orr, I had nothing to do with that. I'm not bullshitting you."

"Except maybe to tell him to handle it," I said, "and lend him a ride to go to Buddy's and back."

Powell was getting it. He'd finally begun to understand that this thing could end with more than a fine, a slap on the wrist. He could wind up in a federal penitentiary. Or dead.

"You do what I say and you live," I told him,

as I slipped the belt loop around his head, neck. "You don't and you join Buddy."

"Orr, you've got to believe me."

"Go," I told him.

He took us out of the station, headed us north.

"You speed, I shoot you," I said. "You run a red, I shoot you. Flash the high beams, I shoot you. Jerk the wheel . . ." I put the gun against his temple. "You got it now?"

"I got it."

"And if you think I won't pop you because you're doing sixty on a highway, think again," I said. "I'll yank this belt and your foot will jump off the gas."

He looked at me in the rearview.

"And then I'll shoot you."

I knew they'd be looking for us on the parkway, the turnpike, and at the tunnels. So I had him drive west to Route 9, then took 440 on to Staten Island.

I was heading us toward the Gowanus Expressway, waiting for a break in the flow, when he started to scream.

I parked the Buick by a hydrant on Baxter Street, which was packed tight, bumper to fender, fender to bumper, even on a Sunday afternoon.

Over in Columbus Park, not far from where I'd

met Allie yesterday afternoon, men in shorts played soccer, ignoring the cold, racing furiously across the cracked concrete, shouting in Spanish.

The sun had moved west. It was over the Hudson now.

I opened the trunk. "Let's go," I told Powell.

He was in fetal position, his hands tied behind his back with his belt, and he was shivering.

I didn't bother to wave the gun.

The last time I buried a man in a trunk it was about 75 degrees warmer than today, and he was only in it for 20 minutes or so.

Powell went in over by the Bay Ridge Channel, where the wind blew in torrents, threatening to rip the clothes off our bodies.

I wasn't going to listen to him scream for another second, even if it meant he'd popsicle before we reached the D.A.'s.

But he continued to holler even as he bounced against the spare in the trunk.

I'd bet *A Prairie Home Companion* has never been played so loud.

Shadows from the edge of the Criminal Court Building ran across the rear of the car.

"I'm bleeding," he said. His voice was an ugly rasp from shouting, and then from trying in vain to shout over the blasting radio.

The only time I turned it down was when I made for the Williamsburg Bridge to Manhattan, and I called Sharon.

Powell put down one butter-soft loafer, then

another, and after I undid the belt, he tried to get the crease to return to his slacks.

Then he put his hand on the back of his head, then brought it back to show me the blood.

"I hope you need fourteen stitches," I said, as I shut the trunk. "More. A hundred and fourteen."

"Fourteen—"

"Did you think I was going to forget Brabender ran me off the parkway?"

He made a face to show his confusion, his concern. Wait: Now he's indignant, as if such violence offended his sense of propriety. "He ran you—"

"Did you think I was going to forget John McPorter?"

"Now, wait a minute. I—"

I held up my hand. "Spare me."

"I really don't know what you're so upset about," he said, as he tried to regain his customary dodgy poise. "In the end, what's all this to you?"

"You're about to find out."

He dusted off his sweater, careful to keep the blood away from yellow cashmere.

"There must be some sort of accommodation we can reach," he said. "I was thinking, and like I said, a man in a racket like yours—"

I looked at him. "You know, I should've dumped your ass in Bed-Stuy, you—"

"Hey, hey," he said, "hey. Let me talk here. Negotiate. Come on, let's see if we can do business. See if there's a way out."

"All right," I said. "How much will you give me for the photos of you and your SEC handler?"

He swept the front of his slacks. "You have more of them?"

"How much for your diary?"

He didn't reply.

I smacked his forehead with the heel of my hand. "And how much for your son, you worm? Were you ever going to ask me about him?"

Despite his anxiety, indignation flashed across his face. "Don't string me along, Orr. We're trying to be men here—"

"It's over, Powell. Done. *You're* done. So drop it. Drop it now."

I shoved him aside, reached into the passenger's-side door, and withdrew three envelopes from under the front seat.

"Here," I said, as I slammed the door, "what you killed McPorter for, and Buddy, and tried to kill me. The story of you, big man. The story of you, and it fits in a handful of envelopes."

He watched as I came toward him.

He said, "You know, you're going to be in trouble with the SEC."

"Think they'll take a hard look at my mutual funds?"

"You know what I'm talking about, Orr."

"Yeah, and to clear my ass, I'm supposed to walk you to their Broadway office, hand you over to your godfather. He brings you to Homicide, you roll over on Brabender and walk away."

He played with his sleeves, making sure only the edge of the black cuffs showed beyond the sweater's sleeves. "It's the smart thing to do," he nodded.

I stepped closer to him and let him feel my breath on his face.

"When I'm done with you, you'll be lucky if they let you out of solitary," I said. "And if they do, I'll give the name and address of the penitentiary you're in to everyone you flipped for the SEC. You'll need a swivel for your head to watch your ass."

"Bullshit," he said. "Who's going to help you tell your story?"

"Allie."

He laughed. "Allie? My son won't roll over on me."

"You're saying he doesn't take after you?"

"My son loves me," he said defiantly.

"Your son is afraid of you, and that's not love. In fact, that's a prelude to hate."

He thought about it, ran his hand through his thick hair, bit his lip. "No," he said finally, "you can't make me for it. For any of it."

"We'll see," I told him.

I put my hand on his shoulder, spun him and pushed him toward Centre Street.

We walked in the cold shadows to the sounds of the game across the lane.

I was surprised to find Julie waiting for me in the south lobby.

She looked at Powell, looked up at me, and she was all business. Less than 30 seconds later, two uniformed court officers took Powell off my hands, leading him away.

The Silver Haven weasel knew the drill, and as he went down the gray hallway, he held his hands behind his butt as if he'd been cuffed. Drops of dried blood speckled the back of his yellow sweater.

I told her I was surprised to see her.

"I've been here all day," she said. "Sharon scared the daylights out of me. She paged me this morning while I was in church."

Which explained why she wasn't wearing the kind of neat, casual attire she usually wore for Sunday Mass and dinner at her parents', and instead was in a gray tweed business suit.

She said, "There's a problem, Terry."

I nodded. I shrugged.

"You'd better come upstairs."

"I've got to make a call," I told her. "Two calls."

"Your daughter's fine," she said. "I spoke to her 20 minutes ago. She's going shopping with Daniel and Wendy, and then they're going to see Dennis at the Pump."

"OK. But I've got another call to make," I said. "Is Alex Powell upstairs?"

Julie said no. "Or if she is, I haven't seen her."

I handed her the three manila envelopes.

"Could you give those to Sharon for me?"

"These are?"

"You'd better ask her." I knew Julie well enough

to trust she wouldn't open them without Sharon's approval.

"I'm going outside," I said.

"I'll come with you."

"No, you don't have your coat and—"

"You won't be long, will—"

I leaned close to her and said, "Jule, what I'm about to do, you can't be part of. Please."

"Terry . . . ?"

"It's best if you stay here."

I went outside and dialed Reynolds's number. After I finished, I returned to Baxter and put the Smith & Wesson down beneath the spare tire.

Snow mounds at the curb were black with soot.

CHAPTER 15

I entered her office to find Executive A.D.A. Sharon Knight standing by the window onto lower Manhattan, holding a strip of negatives, then another, up to the light.

"Can you make them out?" I said.

She shook her head, tossed them on top of the three manila envelopes on her desk.

"Neither could I," I said as I sat next to Julie, next to Sharon's messy table of overstuffed accordion folders, half-used legal pads, old issues of the *New York Law Journal,* a Westlaw book or two. I added my coat to the pile.

Sharon had pushed up the sleeves of her black turtleneck, taken off the charcoal-gray sweater-vest that matched her skirt.

I waited until she eased into the chair behind the desk. But before I could speak, she leaned forward and began to rub her hands together.

"Do you have any idea of the problems you've caused for me?" she said.

"Yes," I replied, "but I had no choice."

"You shot a man, Terry."

I could swear I heard Julie gasp.

Sharon looked at her, looked at me as she fingered the black pearl that lay on her heavy bosom.

"You were working for me and you shot a man."

"I wasn't working for you," I said. "You asked me to find Allie and I did. End of assignment. You made that very clear, and so did Lieutenant Addison. I went to Silver Haven on my own to confront Brabender and bring in Powell."

"And you think that's all there is to it?"

"Sure," I replied. "Didn't I call you this morning to tell you about Allie?"

"Yes, but you were more than a little vague, Terry. You wouldn't tell me where he was, for instance."

"Is that right? I should've. But I knew I was off the clock."

Sharon looked at Julie. Julie looked at me.

"I had no choice," I repeated. "Brabender shot at me."

"And Powell? You brought him here."

"Remind me to tell you how the police operate in Silver Haven."

She lifted the stout envelope, then passed it to Julie. "Have you read these diaries?"

"Only to verify what they were."

As Julie began to scan the handwritten documents, Sharon said, "This is going to put me in an awkward position with the Securities and Exchange Commission."

I pointed toward Broadway, toward the Woolworth Building where the SEC had its regional office. "Somehow I think those guys will appreciate it when you help protect one of their agents from having his photo in the *Times*." Or the *Asbury Park Press*.

Julie flipped a page. "He gave the SEC seven or eight cases, and he consistently told them he could do more. Told them there was more going on than they knew."

"Which may be so," Sharon replied. "It'll be interesting to see how the Commission reacts to having one of their moles pulled."

"Er, does either of you care that we're talking about a guy who's complicit in two deaths? I mean, this *is* the Homicide bureau, isn't it?"

Julie stopped reading, handed the pages and the envelope to her boss, gave me the world's most patronizing smile.

As Sharon tucked the pages into the envelope, she asked me to explain it in simplest terms, A to B to C.

Julie turned in her chair to look at me

"Alex had it with Harlan," I began. "She took those diaries from his car and added them to the photos she'd taken down in Cherry Hill, and she had Buddy put them in John McPorter's safe. Allie saw Buddy do it and told Harlan. Eventually—or sooner than that—Harlan confronted Alex, who then told Buddy to get the stuff out of the safe. When old man McPorter told Allie that the stuff was missing, Allie figured his father would think he had taken it."

"So Allie ran away," Julie said.

"And when I went to Silver Haven to look for Allie, Powell probably thought I believed his son had the stuff too."

"Which you did," Sharon said as she sat back.

"Powell decided he wanted Allie found, so he sent Brabender to John McPorter and the Torkelsens after Elixa Oostenbrugge."

"The girl with the tattoos?" Julie asked.

I nodded.

"As for me, the Sheriff tried to scare me off, but Powell and Brabender wanted something permanent."

I pointed to the Band-Aid on my forehead with my now swollen dislocated finger, which was doing all right until I punched Brabender.

"With Politano shielding him, Buddy did a good job of staying out of sight—Allie's disappearance bought him a few extra days' grace from suspicion—but I figure Brabender saw him with Alex at the funeral. He went after Buddy thinking he still had the stuff, or at least knew where it was."

Julie said, "Buddy should've just turned it over to the police."

Sharon replied, saying, "I'm sure Alex wouldn't let him."

"There's some sort of love angle here," I said. "We'll have to ask Politano, but I gather Alex told Buddy that when she took off, he could come with her. The yutz."

"Terry, the man's dead," Julie said, chastising me.

"He conspired to put Allie on the street. He may be a victim, but he checked himself into the game."

"And my dear old friend Alex came to me to help legitimize her story," Sharon said. "She claimed to believe the envelopes—and that damned $471—was with her boy. If I helped her look for him, and the goods, it would fortify her claim that she knew nothing."

"Yeah, but sooner or later she was going to play that hand," I added. "Until Allie took off— accidentally, by the way. Before he knew McPorter was dead, he was living it up in Secaucus in a 14-year-old's bachelor pad—and until Brabender started killing people, it was a pretty good plan."

Julie looked at me. She seemed to recoil.

"I didn't say it was a moral plan, an admirable plan," I said. "It was clever. I mean, she had that son of a bitch by the— Well, you know what I mean."

They both nodded.

"I ought to tell you, Sharon, that your friend deserves Harlan Powell. They were born for each other."

She said, "I prefer to think he wore her down."

I shrugged. She knew better, but maybe those photos stirred up an old sentiment or two.

"Meanwhile," said Julie, "John McPorter was killed over information he did not have. A pity."

Sharon stood, as if to chase us from her office. "What about the boy?"

I'd let my eyes wander slowly from Sharon to the envelope to the gothic crown on the Woolworth Building, the downtown skyline, silent sentries in the Sunday afternoon sun.

I said, "He may be here already."

"Want me to check?" Julie asked.

Sharon nodded as I stood.

When we were alone, Sharon said, "You were on pure adrenaline."

"Actually, I'm running on fumes," I said. "I haven't slept or eaten much. Must be the high blood pressure that kept me going."

She came around the desk. "You're going to have to answer for Brabender."

"I imagine that might be so," I said.

"What you should've done is stay home, Terry. Once you found the boy, you should've stayed home."

"I told you, Sharon—"

"That he wouldn't be safe until you found the envelopes. I know. But only the fact that you brought Powell here tells me you didn't go to Silver Haven to kill both of them."

"Are you serious?"

"Terry, I told you the second time we met that your temper is going to do you in."

I asked, "What did I do the first time?"

"Stared out the window, said 'Marina' to no

313

one in particular, didn't touch your lunch."

I remember that. Addison was there; the Blini Hut on Nassau. He thought Sharon could find busy-work for me at 100 Centre Street, keep my mind occupied.

The second time Sharon and I met was after I'd tried to kick my way into a homeless shelter in the East Village, thinking Weisz was inside. I told blue to call Addison, who asked Sharon to expedite my release. She made it like it never happened.

Bella never found out. At least I don't think she did.

"Wasn't my temper this time, Sharon," I said. "You'll know why when you see the boy."

She tapped me on the arm, smiled. "Yes, but you knew you were going back there before you met him."

She walked toward the office door. I grabbed my coat and followed her.

"Hold tight, Terry," she said as she stood by the open door. "Let's see how it goes."

As I stepped into the corridor, passing Ginny Gonzalez's deserted work station, I heard Sharon call to me.

"And thanks," she said. "Thanks very much."

Mabry Reynolds, not Allie Powell, was sitting in Julie's cubicle. His dark khaki slacks wore a military-crisp crease, and his thin black sweater fit like it

314

had been sprayed on his taut, rippled frame. His coat rested neatly on his lap.

He unfurled it as he stood and hung it over his left arm. As I shook his hand, I noticed Julie had the photo of the two of us that Bella had taken. There we were, happy in a gold frame: at the South Street Seaport, smiling, laughing, my arm on Julie's shoulder as she leaned into me, hand on my stomach, with the Brooklyn Bridge behind us, the July sun directly above us, at ease in each other's embrace.

"You've met," I said. "Good. She give you any trouble?"

Reynolds smiled awkwardly, with an appealing, and unexpected, shyness. "Hardly."

"How did it go?" I asked him.

"No problem," he replied. "He's quiet."

"And scared."

He absently ran his hand over his shaved head. "And scared."

He said good-bye to Julie, who stood to shake his hand. "Nice meeting you, Mabry."

"And you," he replied.

I told her I'd return after I walked Reynolds to the elevator.

"Sharon Knight see you?" I asked him as we made our way down the corridor, passing one unoccupied cubicle after another. Lights were out, copy machines silent, phones didn't ring. On this side of the building, justice rested.

"No."

"You know Sharon?"

"She's visited Everett Langhorne," he replied. "At the school."

Made sense. In her bid for Congress, she could use the help of one of the city's most notable educators, especially one who communicated with scores of former students and parents from a core constituency.

"She's a keeper," I said, as I held back the door and Reynolds passed by.

The policeman on Sunday guard duty had more on the ball than did Officer Casey, and he turned from the playoff game on his mini-TV to insist Reynolds sign out.

"You leaving, Mr. Orr?" he asked.

"No," I told Officer Dupree, who, with that question, became the first man who occupied that seat who'd ever remembered my name. "I'm going back in to see Miss Giada."

The plump black man said, "Sweet girl, that Miss Giada."

As I pressed the elevator button, Reynolds said, "This is good work, Terry, don't you think?"

"I'm not sure," I said. "I mean, it feels right now, with the kid OK and his father in deep with the law."

"I like it," he said. "I'm thinking of asking you to call on me again."

I looked at him. "You like the work, Mabry, so maybe you'll be calling on me."

"I just might," he said. "I just might."

As the elevator arrived, I shook his hand again. "I mean it," I said. "If I can help, let me know."

Reynolds nodded as he backed into the elevator.

"Hey," I said, as I put my hand against the rubber rail, "are we square on this?"

Reynolds smiled. "I still say that kid don't eat much."

He hit the button for the lobby. As I stepped back, Reynolds nodded again. The door sealed shut.

Julie had her tweed jacket on the back of her seat as she reviewed a court transcript, Westlaw reporter open and dotted with yellow Post-it notes. Her gold crucifix dangled below her open collar.

"Have you seen the boy?"

She said she had; briefly, in the conference room. "He asked for you," she added, as she shut the law book.

I sat where Reynolds had been, rubbed my ear, still ringing from Powell's screams. "So, you OK with all this?"

She tapped her calligraphy pen on the reporter. For some reason, she always used wide-tipped calligraphy pens to make notes. I'd never asked why.

"Your recap didn't quite explain it all to me," she replied. "But I can't deny I have an odd sensation of pride, even though your methods are a little . . . primitive."

"I—"

"But you did it. It's done," she said, rattling the pen. "So what are you going to do now?"

"Right now? I'm starving, to be honest with you. I'm thinking of heading to Katz's for matzo-ball soup to warm up. Then pastrami on rye, a knish. Dr. Brown's cream soda. After that . . . who knows? You?"

"After I see Sharon, I'm off to my parents'."

I said, "This late? Is everything all right?"

"Fine. Sal's upset, but—"

"The struggling architect."

She smiled. "I'm surprised you remembered."

"Dominick, Bruno and Salvatore," I said, naming her brothers. "Dominick's married to Lorraine, Bruno to Angela. Sal is single."

"Now, if you'd only meet them . . ."

I said, "Let's go talk to Allie."

Before I could leave the chair, she reached out and took my left hand, and she ran her thumb across my sore knuckles. "Gabriella said something interesting to me today. She said I should call her Bella. What do you think that means?"

That my daughter is engineering my life again, or trying to. "Beats me."

"And she told me to be patient with you," she continued. "That you're trying."

"Christ." I stood. "That's it. I'm history."

She turned to her books, closed them, put the pen in a cup with its mates, pencils, markers.

"What are you doing later?" I asked.

"See, not only do you not talk, you don't listen . . ."

"I meant after."

"Home," she said, "then to bed. I'm in court in the morning."

"Do we have time for a phone call?"

"I'll think about— Yes, of course. I'm kidding. Yes. Don't pout."

I leaned down and kissed her cheek. She put her hand on the back of my neck and held me.

"Tell me you love me, you big dope," she said softly.

I ran my hand across the side of her face, and I caressed her chin, her neck, and I stepped back and I looked at her, and my heart ached.

She filled the silence. "At least say you'll come to my parents' house next Sunday."

"We'll see," I said.

"Progress," she muttered.

I started toward the corridor, and we walked along, side by side, our hands not quite touching.

"Terry, do you mind if I call her Bella?"

"It's up to you. And her," I replied.

"Where does it come from? I mean, I know it means 'beautiful' in Italian . . ."

I said, "Davy couldn't pronounce 'Gabriella.' It came out as 'Bella.' Marina thought it was perfect. Me too."

She nodded thoughtfully. "Every time you say your daughter's name you think of your wife and son . . ."

I hesitated. "Jule, what I think . . . You know, that is the big . . . I don't know. The big something."

"'The big something'? How articulate."

I opened the conference-room door to find Allie alone, his head resting on the back of his hands, his palms flat on the table. A Diet Coke sat near his elbow, and law books stared down at him.

Such a lonely boy, I thought, and with no one to turn to. One parent threatening to take him down, the other remaining silent in the face of his pain.

Julie and I both stood in the door frame, leaning in.

"She's not coming," Allie said, as he sat up, folded his hands together as if to pray.

He'd been crying.

"No, she's coming," I said. "Maybe she's running late . . ."

Julie stepped into the room, put her hand on the back of his pink shirt.

I noticed it had been cleaned, pressed.

"She won't come," he said. "My father will be waiting, if she does."

Julie looked at me. We both realized no one had told Allie what had happened—to his father, to Buddy.

"I'll talk to him, Terry," she said. "This needs to be on the record."

I leaned in, offered Allie my right hand.

Instead of shaking it, he took it with his left, held on to it.

"Maybe I could go with you," he said, the hope in his voice surrendering to reality.

"I'm a phone call away." It was the best I could do.

I let go of his hand, squeezed his shoulder.

"What's going to happen to me?" he asked, looking at me, up at Julie.

You're going to have to find your own way, I thought. You're going to have to try to forget what's gone on, and you're going to fill that hole in your heart with your art, your designs, and maybe someday somebody will love you for what you've become.

"I don't know, Allie. I wish I did."

"Terry . . ." Julie's expression told me it was time to go.

I rapped a knuckle on the frame, nodded good-bye and went toward the reception area and Officer Dupree. Down the elevators, through the south lobby, along Centre to Houston. Past the sagging tenements of the Lower East Side, collar turned up against the whistling wind, the gray shadows, idle thoughts, the weight, the past.

CHAPTER 16

Beagle came to see me only when I'd opened the refrigerator for a bottle of sparkling water to wash down the acetaminophen.

"Nothing for you," I said, with my hair still wet from the long, long hot shower. "No meatballs, no stuffed pork chop, no leftover caponata, no nothing. All right?"

All wrinkles and oversized ears, she turned, waddled back to the sofa.

I went downstairs, buried the gun in a cardboard box amid the copies of *Slippery Dick,* and I hid the clip in the rafters, brushing aside sticky cobwebs, antique dust.

As I passed the heavy bag, I nudged it, apologized for abandoning it, and I showed it the knuckles on my hands, raised and raw, courtesy of Brabender's cement chin.

Back upstairs, I wondered about loose ends. The only one that came to mind was a call to Addison. But I figured he'd already spoken to Sharon, Politano and maybe Christine, if not Powell, and now it'd be better for me to listen to how he saw it than to tell him what I knew. In the past five years, not a week had gone by without Luther Addison dropping in on me, or at least calling. I knew I'd hear from him no later than tomorrow.

For what I intended to do this evening, I needed nothing—no keys, wallet, ID—so I zipped up my black hoodie and started for the front door.

Then I stopped, went to the refrigerator, broke off a piece of fontina and tossed it in Beagle's bowl.

I hustled over to Hudson, aided by the brisk wind off the river, and trotted along the quiet street to the Pump. At a front table, two young men, one with a U-shaped stud in his eyebrow, were bickering over something—the contents of a letter, it seemed—but they were in D's place and they were drinking tea, and I figured things were looking up.

In back, Bella and Daniel perched on the edge of my daughter's yellow recamier, and D was between them, sitting cross-legged on the oatmeal-colored floor. Daniel's sister Wendy stood behind the sofa, behind her boss, and all four of them were staring at Bella's laptop.

My daughter looked like she wanted to yank out her pigtails. She was making click-click noises with her teeth.

Diddio stared at the computer screen, his expression vacant, stultified.

"Mr. Orr," said Daniel, "you have arrived at the perfect time."

He had his baseball cap on backward.

"She's going to kill him, isn't she?"

"Oh, yes," Daniel Wu replied.

"Hello, Wendy."

She smiled and bowed ever so slightly. In her red, embroidered V-neck blouse and snug black slacks, her shining black hair hanging down her back, Wendy looked particularly beautiful this evening. I would've thought men would drop in on the Pump just to see her, though there was no shortage of pretty, petite Chinese women in lower Manhattan. But if Wendy, who was quiet enough to seem secretive, had half her brother's wit and a quarter of his charm, she'd outshine them all.

"Dad," Bella moaned. "Help me here."

"What is it?"

"He doesn't understand. He *won't* understand."

Daniel took a bite of Mrs. Maoli's pumpkin biscotti, wiped the crumbs off his sweatshirt.

D looked up at me. "I think they're insulting me."

"It is not about you, Dennis. Please. It's about this place. The *future* of this place. Arrrgh!"

Bella snatched her fedora off his head, returned it to her own. Her pigtails and their multicolored ribbons still lay on her shoulders, the straps of her overalls.

"What?" I asked.

"Dad, sit," Bella said, tapping the screaming-yellow seat.

I came around the table, slid by Daniel and his

sneakers, which were off his chubby feet, and sat between him and my daughter. Diddio pushed up, then back, using my legs as armrests.

I looked at the laptop. Filling the screen was the phrase: leo's dream.

"What is this?"

"It's a marketing plan," Bella said. "To save Leo's."

Daniel said, proudly, "We did it."

Tip-Top, their secret project. "And you made a PowerPoint presentation."

"It's mandatory," Daniel chimed.

"Let's see it," I said.

Bella hit the ENTER button.

By now, the couple who were seated at the front of the room had joined us, and I was studying the plan for the second time. When it was over, they nodded knowingly, and the man without the eye stud, with the perfect salt-and-pepper goatee, looked at me and, pointing at the screen, said, "This is thoroughly sensible. It's your idea?"

I pushed my thumbs toward Bella and Daniel.

"What are you guys, fourteen years old?"

Daniel said, "Fif—"

"Yes," Bella barked, who knew younger was better in the savant department. "Fourteen."

The man smiled, "Well, I run the Jardin de Soleil marketing team at Escada, and, honey, we could use both of you."

Bella beamed.

"I love the look of the place," the other man said, as he scanned the room. "But what does it have to do with *tea?* Cher's boudoir, maybe. But *tea?*"

"What do you think, D?" I asked as the two men went back to their table.

"She wants me to start from scratch."

"Mr. Diddio," Wendy said quietly, directly, "I think what they are telling us is that you make the very best tea under the worst circumstances."

I turned around to look at her. Her cheeks were red: That sentence was a virtual outburst from the demure 19-year-old.

Bella and Daniel had divided their presentation in thirds: History, Health and Highway to Success. The first part more or less told D that he needed to reflect the traditional working-class and artisan roots of TriBeCa, without alienating the young marrieds who had leveraged everything but their children to afford their million-dollar, 1,000-square-foot apartments.

"The furniture goes," Bella said.

"Put an ad in *The Advocate,*" I added.

"That's the spirit, Mr. Orr," Daniel cheered.

The second told him that if he wanted to appeal to people who could just as easily get a cardboard cup of Lipton across the street at Zolly's for 75 cents, he needed to sell the health benefits of "the tea experience"—especially the link between the consumption of tea and a reduced risk of cardiovascular events and certain cancers. Bella tossed off the phrase "flavonoid antioxidants" like it was part of everyday speech.

"People will pay more for something if they think it's good for them," she said. "Even if it's not."

"You must tell people that they must sit and sip their tea," Daniel said. He made his voice as basso profundo as he could. "Relax," he crooned, rippling the air with his stout fingers. "Relax."

The third section was the action plan. "Lunchtime is a problem, Dad. Tea is out, apparently. The Europeans want espresso after their meal, and the Americans want to seem European. They only agree on the biscotti, which we'll have to commercialize."

Commercialize?

"Maybe we could put in a conference table," she said, looking around, "where people could continue their meetings. Or study their blueprints. What they bought at the shops, blouses, shirts, jeans and stuff. Or change diapers. You know."

"Yes, lunch *is* a problem," Daniel said. "But a diaper table . . . I don't know."

"We'll toss it around," Bella nodded.

For the nighttime, it was back to basics: "What's your brand, Dennis?" Bella asked. "Ultimately, it's about music."

As the slides rolled by, Bella said, "Do the unplugged thing, Dennis. Ask Cock Michaels to perform, and some of his friends. *Your* friends; get

Keith to bring in Mick. Have Sheila play the cello. You can pay her a few bucks and let her rehearse in here."

Our neighbor Sheila Yannick, who D dated now and then, practiced 12 hours a day, maybe more.

"I don't want problems with the union, man."

Bella ignored him. "And bring back the jukebox!"

"Yes," Daniel said, hoisting a finger in the air.

"The jukebox," I heard myself say.

When Leo ran the Tilt, people from throughout the five boroughs came to see what Diddio had programmed that day, choosing from the several thousand CDs he had. In the neighborhood, people who hadn't read a word Diddio wrote about rock knew he was the guy behind the great selection.

"But I see you don't like my name," I said. "The Tea Water Pump."

"Dad, when we say that we have to return to the historical roots of the neighborhood, we don't mean the 1700s," Bella said. "'Leo's' is a good name."

"T, everything we did, they want us to get rid of," D moaned.

The room screamed *A Clockwork Orange* styled by Isaac Mizrahi. "I think we got carried away trying to change things."

"Sometimes," Daniel said, "you just have to tweak. That's all."

"Just think of it," Bella said. "Dark walls, subtle lights, club chairs, tables with candles, photos of old TriBeCa, a little stage with a couple of mikes and a stool, a single spotlight—even if nobody's playing that night, it looks cool—the jukebox, people drinking tea, feeling all sorts of superior 'cause they think they're healthy."

"It'll be like a Greenwich Village coffeehouse in the early '60s," I said.

"Except it's tea and it's healthy and it's the 21st century and here's Dennis Diddio, the music man, and people think maybe Thurston Moore's going to play, or Lou Reed. Tori Amos."

"We need a piano," D said.

"There you go!" Bella said, as she slapped her hat back onto his head.

"You can keep the plants," Daniel said.

"Keep the plants," D said, as he used my legs to lift himself off the floor.

As he walked toward his giant urns, his fragrant selection of loose tea leaves, Bella drew close to me and whispered, "Dad, you're down $30,000 here. Make him do what we say."

I turned to my right. "Daniel?"

"I rarely see the same person in here twice," he said with a sympathetic shrug.

From behind his station, D groaned, "The dream is over."

Bella walked me to the front door as Daniel packed up the laptop and Wendy bused the table where the two men had had their tea and quarrel.

"You are seriously underdressed. Again," she said.

She looked at me, from top to bottom—the black hoodie, the navy-blue sweatshirt beneath it, the blue jogging pants, my old sneakers—and she shook her head.

"I've got on long johns," I explained. "I do."

"And so you've been up since 3:30, doing nobody knows what, and you've decided to run. You need exercise? Now?"

"Bella, when you are going to stop managing me?"

"When you stop needing a manager."

I closed my eyes, I put my hand over my mouth. Of course, that was her answer. I would've said the same thing.

"You would've said the same thing," she smiled.

I gestured toward the back of the room, the yellow recamier, Daniel, on his knees, unplugging the laptop, the soles of his floppy white socks facing us.

"That's a good thing you did," I told her.

"This is another man who needs help," she replied.

"So let me ask you, Bella. What's it going to be: marketer or angel?"

"Writer," she replied. "Morrie thinks I'll get a $250,000 advance for *Mordecai Foxx*. He says he can get the manuscript optioned by Hollywood as soon as we sign the book deal. He's very clever, our Morrie." She stopped, put her hands in the pockets of her baggy jeans, swayed. "Yeah, he's good."

An adult crime thriller, set in New York in 1872, written by a 12-year-old, the daughter of a private investigator. I didn't need a PowerPoint presentation to tell me it was a concept that would sell.

Headlights swept across the frosted window, the glass in the door.

I asked her what time she'd be coming home.

She said, "Not too late. Maybe another hour. I've got Evil homework."

"You'll be here?"

"Dad, you didn't know where I was all day today and now—"

She stopped as I ran my hand across the top of her head, crossing the part in her brown hair, and I gently caressed her cheek, cupped her chin.

"I just wanted to tell you I'm proud of what you did, Bella. With D. You and Daniel." It was going to cost me at least another 30K, but what the hell. "You've got a good heart . . . When you're not obsessing about money."

"Let's see. Obsession," she mused. "Where did I learn about that?"

I told her I'd see her later, and I went out to Hudson to stretch, to get ready to run.

Three miles along West Street sounded about right.

"Watch out," she advised. "There's ice, and the traffic . . ."

★ ★ ★

331

High blood pressure? I don't believe it, no. Look at me: no sleep, tested, and yet I'm doing six-minute miles, two, three days after lying in a knocked-out heap at the side of the road. The hospital not once, twice. Look at me.

All right, seven minutes. Ripping up West Street, though.

I could've put it off until morning, early afternoon. Tomorrow morning, maybe, I could've taken the Broadway uptown, got out, stretched in the station, away from the dull, frigid sky, and run along Riverside Drive, past the Gothic towers of the Union Theological Seminary, Grant's Tomb, toward the George Washington Bridge and back, under frail, crooked branches yearning for warmth, statues of Kossuth, Tilden, Joan of Arc . . .

But sit in an empty house? Tonight? No.

Action. Go. Now.

You can't outwork me. Nobody is going to outwork me.

If I don't have it, I'm getting it. That's me.

"Orr, you're a good kid," said Phil Canarelli, coach of the Barnabas Bees, "and that's not good. It's not good. Once in a while, you've got to stick your elbow in their throat, the side of the head." Smacks me on the side of the head. "You set a pick, Orr, you want them to think they hit brick. You get a chance, you drive their balls up into their stomach. You hear me, boy?"

Coach had a habit. Sucked up phlegm, spit it

into his handkerchief. Smoked a pipe, gave him horrific breath. Shaved in the dark.

"I got you, Coach."

"Good," he said as he returned the handkerchief to his back pocket. "Now go lay out Tooley."

Tooley? We're teammates. "I can't lay out—"

"If you don't have it, Orr, you got to know how to get it. You hear me?"

Maybe I shouldn't run in black, dark blues. I just scared the bejesus out of that woman back there, the one walking the perky terrier, lost in thought, that yellow stocking cap, yellow mittens, hands-free phone, nobody to talk to, staring at the river.

"Asshole!"

Me?

Me?

Me.

High blood pressure? Naw. A faulty . . . What's it called? A spigmometer? No. Sphygmomanometer. Bingo. I'd like to put that on the Scrabble board.

Bella once played the word "xylem" off my "banal." Triple word score too. She was eight years old at the time. Or seven, maybe.

"Marina, no Italian words. Come on," I said. "I mean, *infelice*?"

"It means 'unhappy,'" Bella chirped.

★ ★ ★

What'd I say to her? Something like "You, I'll deal with later." As I stood alone in my bedroom, still stunned by what I had learned, I said, "Marina, I'll deal with you later." Something like that.

Yeah, I dealt with her. Great job. Thorough.

Dealt with her, never thought about her again.

"*Non sei tu,*" says she, the specter in my room, my head.

Not me? Then who?

Last summer, I saw a woman, who had been sunbathing as naked as Godiva, running frantically along one of those old piers over there, out on the Hudson, screaming that a rat was chasing her, two rats, three . . .

I was nothing before I met her. Could that have been so? If so, how did I attract her?

I mean, if I was nothing, why did she fall for me?

"You were meat on the side," Loretta said.

Oh, fuck you, Loretta.

If I was meat on the side, who was the man in her life?

Who was the something to my nothing?

Pop, I don't know what I did," I said.

We were putting boxes of old summer clothes

into the woodshed in the back of the cellar. Each tenant had a woodshed, all 14 in the building, padlocked, a few steps from the dented garbage cans, rusted lids, the scent of rotting food. Regina's clothes wouldn't fit next year, mine wouldn't, but the exercise was not without its function. Retrieving the clothes next spring would give my mother an opportunity to remind us how much of a financial burden we were, and how we didn't appreciate things.

Not Regina so much.

"Pop?"

The best I was going to get out of him was a shrug.

I had the plastic Christmas tree in my arms. I'd moved it, and the ornaments, the old tinsel, made room for the boxes.

"She should tell me at least what I did."

That was when the mouse appeared.

Ran right across my father's Florsheim.

He dropped a box. *"Christ, un topo! L'avete visto?"*

The first time I heard my father speak Italian.

I had no idea he could.

When I visited his barbershop, and Anthony and the other guys were chatting in Italian, laughing, my father replied only in English, if he joined in at all.

I used to sit on the terrazzo floor, look up at them. They were funny guys, full of life, Augie pushing the broom, all bug-eyed and roly-poly, him. Made the sandwiches, always made one for me. Olive oil, oregano, red peppers he made at home . . .

I came off West at Vestry and walked over to Washington to get the stitch out of my side, to catch my breath. Steam rose from the top of my head, from under my collar.

I brought up the hood to keep warm, tugged at the zipper, and I slowly made my way along the empty street, my sneakers slipping on rounded stones. Icicles hung from the trim on the façades, and a lone pigeon flew across the narrow street, finding a perch on a rusted rail jutting from red brick.

At Hubert, I went west to Laight, then continued south on Greenwich, under violet lights, and I heard the groan of an engine in the alley. Moments later, an old delivery truck emerged, tattered tarp on top, and I heard the grinding of gears as it lurched onto Beach, moving away.

Above me, the streaks of magenta clouds stretched across the somber, starless sky.

Shivering, though no longer winded, I came upon the corner of Harrison, across from my house, passing parking meters and snow piles, passing through stark light and into shadows at the edge of the building on the north side, and I felt him before I saw him, and then a flash of red rushed toward my eyes, and instinctively I ducked.

And Lou Brabender tumbled over me, flew over

me, and the big man landed with a thud on his back. His shirtfront was awash in blood.

I leapt at him, but Brabender got his hands up and he shoved me away. Despite the wound in his shoulder, and the blood loss, he was still eager, still formidable. His eyes were slits, and, teeth bared as if they were fangs, he radiated fury.

I rushed at him, and I landed on his stomach with my knee, and I got off a quick right to his face. But when I tried to grab his shirt, my hand slid on the bloody cloth, and I slipped, and I fell on top of him. He easily tossed me aside, and as I rolled to get to my feet, he grabbed at me, and I saw his right arm was almost useless.

As I stood, he spun on the cold ground and, with unexpected agility, he kicked my legs out from under me. I landed hard, felt a rattle in my ribs, felt as if the air had been sucked out of me.

Still on his back, Brabender groped in his left pocket, and I knew he was going for his gun.

I dove on him, held onto his left wrist where it protruded from the pocket of his open trench coat.

I punched at his right shoulder, at the open wound, and again, again, but he didn't surrender, and he struggled to get the gun out.

As we continued to grapple, I heard only our grunts, groans as we strained, and the sound of our shoes scraping the frigid sidewalk. Brabender swatted at me with his lame right hand, pawing at my head, the back of my shoulders, and then he got one of his feet under me, and with a bestial roar, he drove me away, and he brought the gun from his pocket.

Lying on his back, his elbows lifting his shoulders off the ground, he pointed the silver automatic at me, and as he struggled to his feet, he kept it fixed on the center of my body.

I inched to my left, toward the cobblestone street, away from the shadows.

He staggered as he tried to remain upright. "Where's Harlan?"

I thought I could dive between the parked cars to my left-hand side. Maybe the lights of The Red Curry on the other side of Greenwich would warp his vision, alter the shot.

"Where's Harlan?" he blared.

"In custody," I said, "and the D.A.'s got the diary."

He swallowed hard, grimacing, unable to mask his pain.

His blood dripped from my clenched fists.

"You should've bought it on the parkway," he said.

"It's over," I told him, as I inched toward the cars. "Make it easier on yourself."

He coughed and then he drew himself up.

"Pray," he said, as he peered down the barrel of the gun.

I heard a shot, and I felt nothing.

I looked at Brabender, who stared at me with hollow eyes, his left arm still extended.

Then I heard a shout, coming from behind: "Right there." Then again. "Hold it. Right there."

Brabender wobbled and his arm sank to his side.

I bolted forward and I grabbed his throat, his gun hand. But he didn't resist.

He fell, the weight of his body wrenching him away from my grip as he collapsed to the concrete.

As I went for Brabender's gun, I turned and saw Rey Twist, standing on the passenger's side of Addison's car, his service revolver drawn.

He looked at me, and he told me to stand back.

As Addison emerged from the black car, Twist hustled toward me.

Then he insisted I give him the fallen man's gun.

Addison knelt over Brabender.

Twist slipped the gun from my quivering hand.

I took a long, slow breath and walked over to Twist, who was using the car radio to call for EMT help and maybe a couple of blue-and-whites from the First. I waited until he was done.

He stepped onto the cold cobblestone.

"Thanks," I said.

He nodded as he reached up to loosen his tie, unbutton his collar.

"How did you know?"

"Didn't," he replied. "Lieutenant said he needed to talk to you."

"My good luck."

"Knowing him is your good luck," he said as he walked away.

I leaned against the car, felt the engine's heat.

It wasn't long before the cry of the emergency medical wagon stole the silence, and whirling red and white lights appeared as the siren's wail grew louder. I saw Addison gesture for his young sergeant to point the techs toward Brabender's prone form.

My neighbors were peering out the front doors of their Federal-era homes, and windows were opening in the apartment building above the Thai restaurant.

I left the car, followed Twist onto Greenwich, and waited as the driver came to the scoop in the curb and cut the sound. The EMT team grabbed their equipment from the rear bay and dashed to their task.

"Listen," I said to Twist, "my daughter is with some friends a couple blocks from here. Do you mind if I go tell her I'm all right?"

"Better check with the lieutenant," he said.

Addison stood near the front of his black car, using his cell phone. I could hear his radio squawk as I drew near.

Standing by the open driver's-side door, I waited until he finished his call, peering behind me at Brabender, who now lay on his side on the frozen slab of concrete, the wind ruffling his blood-soaked shirt, his black coat.

Addison came around the back of the car,

stepping through the gray cloud that rose from its muffler.

"I've got to go to Bella," I said as he passed me.

The EMT team hoisted Brabender onto a gurney.

"Go," Addison said, "and get right back."

CHAPTER 17

Four hours later, with Bella upstairs in her bedroom, Beagle asleep in the living room, and Addison was talking about Brabender, amazed that the son of a bitch had fallen two stories with a bullet in his shoulder, got up and drove from Silver Haven to TriBeCa, parked Powell's white Mercedes on West Street, his blood pooling on the leather upholstery.

"They say he'll recover, despite the two slugs," he added.

"That's good," I said softly.

Powell was right when he said the D.A. couldn't make him for John McPorter, or Buddy, or the assault on Politano or me. They needed Brabender alive, and they needed him to roll over like The Surgeon's driver had.

Addison turned down my offer of iced tea, and he ignored the pignoli cookies I'd put out.

"What's your take on Brabender?" I asked.

"We hold on to what we have," he replied evenly. "For Powell, it's his millions, his status. For Brabender, the same thing, but a different scale.

Money, status. Some kind of friendship that makes sense to an ex-con."

"That, and he's a psychopath."

Addison said, "Elizabeth Harteveld tell you that?"

I didn't reply. I wasn't sure he was joking.

"How's Allie?" I asked. "I heard Sharon blistered his mother's ears when she finally showed."

"I don't think a lecture is going to change her ways."

"Maybe not," I said as he stood. "But—"

"Now I need the gun, Terry. The one you shot him with down at the driving range."

I went downstairs, pulled the string, tossed aside unopened copies of my book, dug out the Smith & Wesson. When I came back up, Addison was standing in the alcove, looking at the Gargano cliffs.

I handed the piece to him.

"I'm going to draw papers for you, Terry," he said, as he put the gun in the pocket of his black suit jacket. "You've had this gun for a while, and you're licensed. Understand me? But let's be clear: This is for Sharon's sake, not yours. You with a gun is like a baby with a hand grenade."

"Gun might've saved my life," I said. I reached up, clicked off the light above Marina's painting.

"Gun didn't do a thing, Terry. Rey's gun saved you. Rey—a pro. Rey—trained. Rey—focused. You—" He shook his head.

"Where'd I get it?" I asked, as we returned to the kitchen table. "The Smith and Wesson nine."

"Any chance Mabry Reynolds fixed it for you?"

I ignored the question. "No, I mean, for when you bring back the papers—"

"You hooked up with Reynolds on Saturday night," he said, pressing on.

"He called you."

He said no. "Not Reynolds. That's not his code."

"But . . ."

"You walked down Madison to 124th, then stood on the balcony, talking to Reynolds," he said. "And then he brings the kid to church and, after that, to Oscar's for brunch."

"Oscar's?"

He nodded. "I'd say ten people saw you, and maybe ten times that many saw Allie Powell."

I wondered just how many people up in Harlem believed they had to tell Addison I'd been around.

"He had waffles with fried chicken," Addison added, "and tried the grits."

"So why didn't you grab him?" I asked.

"Because Reynolds would keep him safe. I knew that," he replied. "The kid was safe with him."

"And if you didn't have him, you didn't have to turn him over to his parents," I said. "Did you talk to Congresswoman Knight about that?"

"Not until late this afternoon," he said, forgetting for a moment that it was well past midnight.

"So where are we?"

He said, "It looks like Powell is going to get cut

loose by the SEC, and Brabender and Powell can fight it out over who takes the fall for the McPorters. Craw forgets about you."

"Why would he do that?"

"So the SEC forgets about him," he said. "Powell rolled over on him too. Nothing major, but violative."

"So they'll let him skate?"

"If it's necessary," he replied. "They're not interested in Craw and his $5,500 gain."

I said, "Why do I think you had something to do with Craw easing off on what happened at the golf center?"

He didn't reply.

I reached across the table and retrieved his hat, passed it to him.

"Tell Twist I said thanks."

"You can tell him yourself," he replied. "He's outside."

"Christ, Luther, you could've brought the guy in—"

"He doesn't need to know about the gun, Terry," he said, tapping his pocket. "Nobody needs to know."

I grabbed my coat from behind the laundry-room door. It'd go over my T-shirt when I went out to make right with Twist.

"Luther, you can't be comfortable doing this," I said.

"The gun? The greater good, Terry."

"Sharon in Washington . . ."

"The greater good. Let it go at that."

He opened the door, pushed it against the bracing wind.

Fresh from her morning shower, Bella was sitting on the steps, baby-pink bare feet on the hardwood. Her strawberry shampoo reached up, assaulted me.

I skidded on the slush. "What?"

"We need to talk."

Her too, I thought. Luther's mini-lecture, disapproving gaze, kept me from the 18 hours of sleep I'd planned.

Beagle waited until I removed her leash, then she waddled off toward her sofa, choosing the warmth of the living room over a post-walk treat.

"About?"

I touched her cheek with the back of my fingers.

"Yow. What the— Your hands are *cold*. Yow."

"You are now alert," I said as I took off my coat.

"I *was* alert."

She had her damp hair done up with a big yellow clip that matched her old ratty robe.

My denim coat went back behind the laundry-room door. "I repeat. About?"

"About Marcus."

"Oh."

"You really want to meet him?"

I went across the kitchen to run the hot water. "If you'd like. I don't want to make a big soap opera out of it. Whatever you'd like."

"I'll bring him to the Pump."

"When?"

"I don't know."

"Bella—" I told myself to shut up; no sense stirring the prickly teen. "No, that's good. That's fine. What's best for you."

I turned to wash my hands, drop a Pop-Tart in the toaster for my daughter.

"I'm going to work out with him tonight," she said.

I cut the water flow, turned. "Tonight? I thought we—"

"Dad, it helps both of us," she said, protesting. "Me and him."

I looked at her. She was coiled, ready to strike.

"No, you're right. Better for both of you," I said. "Makes sense."

She frowned in confusion. "Really?"

"Sure. But if he needs a big man to bang around . . ."

She removed the clip from her hair, shook her head, sent a spray of water across the room. Christ, her hair was longer than I'd realized.

"I was thinking you should join one of those Wall Street teams," she said, as she tossed the clip onto the table next to the folded copy of this morning's *Times.*

"I don't know—"

"Make some new friends."

She sat at the table, opened the paper, went for the Arts page.

I could smell the pastry warming in the toaster, smell the sugar beginning to melt.

"What were you and Lieutenant Addison woofing about last night?"

I lifted a pignoli cookie, took a bite.

"Was it the gun you put in the basement on Saturday?"

"Bella, what are you doing, going through—"

"I brought down my hamper for Mrs. Maoli and I saw you'd moved the boxes," she said, her eyes still fixed on the story she'd begun to read. The headline promised the return of My Bloody Valentine, whatever that was. "I didn't touch it."

I said, "If you want, I can explain."

"Not necessary," she said, flipping the pages until she found the jump. "I always figured you used Leo's gun. That's what you guys do. Play with guns."

I looked at her, watched her reading the paper, looked at her pretty face, her furrowed brow under her mop of moist hair, looked at the young woman at the table.

"Oh, goodie!" she shouted. "They're playing at Irving Plaza on Thursday. Dennis can get us tickets. Yeah!" She clapped her hands, beamed. "*Très* cool."

When I could think of nothing to say, I went over to the sink, grabbed a dish towel and tossed it across the room. It landed directly on top of the gray snow I'd dragged in.

"Very impressive," Bella said, looking down at the striped towel.

"Not that I was trying to," I said. "Impress, that is."

"Oh no," Bella replied, as she reached for a cookie. "Not you."

EPILOGUE

I sat in the green leather club chair, the tips of my sneakers on the red-and-cream Persian rug, and I told my story, which sort of came out the way I wanted it to: Powell and Brabender in the background, the Julie thing out front.

"Terry, if you recall," Elizabeth Harteveld said, "we've actually touched on this issue several times. Your laissez-faire attitude—"

"That's too harsh," I said, interrupting a sip from the bottled water I'd brought with me. "It suggests apathy, which is not the case."

"Agreed," she said calmly, "yes. You are not apathetic to Miss Giada, at least not intentionally so."

I returned the bottle to the table, placing it among the plant's leaves.

I'd called Harteveld the morning after I'd shot Brabender and dragged Powell back from Silver Haven, and she'd said she would see me. The first opening she had was for four days later, at 3:00 p.m. I took it, and spent the intervening time sleeping, letting my headaches vanish, the gash on my forehead heal, congratulating myself for not bickering with Bella in more than 100 hours, finishing Neiman's *Evil in Modern Thought* and sneaking over to the Film Forum to see a new print of Olmi's *Il Posto*. I had lunch with a busy Julie at the Seaport, took the Buick back to Hoboken, and then I rode the ferry back to the north cove, staring at the breaking ice in the churning water, then looking north to the George Washington Bridge as the sun danced on its silver towers.

And I took a call from Saleha. Jade eyes, brown skin, robust figure; from Afghanistan.

As for the rest of the time . . .

"Shall I continue?" Harteveld asked.

"Laissez-faire," I said.

She balanced a blue folder on her knee. Her lab coat, as always, was flawless—white, lightly starched—and her bifocals hung on a gold chain that lay on the lapels of the coat, her pale-blue turtleneck.

"Earlier, you said you feel it's unnecessary to express your feelings to Julie—"

"I don't know if I said exactly that, Elizabeth, but go on."

She crossed her legs at the ankles. "In fact, you said she expects you to say things that ought to be clear to her by your actions."

"Right," I said. "I mean, I'm not the kind of guy to go running around saying 'I love you' all over the place. Is that so unusual?"

"I couldn't say," Harteveld replied. "Do you think it is?"

"I don't know," I said, "but it seems kind of redundant. You know, I'm there, I'm attentive, and we enjoy ourselves." I felt myself shrug. "I guess I don't get it. I mean, I know some people need the words, but Julie's smart, she's aware . . . I don't get it."

"In your family, your mother, father and sister, did you articulate your feelings?"

"Not really, no. Unless my mother and sister were telling me what a loser I was."

"And your father?"

"My father would go days without speaking," I said. "I told you that before."

"Yes, you did. But I wondered if you meant it figuratively . . ."

"My father made the Mona Lisa seem chatty."

She smiled. "So you rarely expressed your emotions . . ."

"Positive emotions? Well, if by 'rarely' you mean 'never' . . ."

She nodded. Not in agreement, but as a sign that she was listening, digesting what I'd said. Or at least writing it down.

"But I enjoy being with her," I said. "I really do. I'd miss the hell out of her. Julie's special."

"Yes, but do you love her?"

"Elizabeth . . ."

She looked at me.

"I don't know a damned thing about love," I said. "That's clear, isn't it?"

"Is it?"

"Absolutely."

She said, "Terry, your feelings for Julie run deep, and I believe they are quite sincere."

"So, is that love?"

"One might say yes," she replied.

"All right."

"And yet you can't tell her."

"Elizabeth," I said, "not yet. You know? Not yet."

"Did you have any difficulty articulating your feelings with your wife?" Harteveld asked.

"No, and look what it got me." I leaned forward, putting my forearms on the thighs of my jeans. "I tell someone I love her and . . ."

I looked at the rose flecks in the rug, at the glossy parquet that surrounded it, at Harteveld's brown pumps.

"Are you suggesting causality, Terry?"

"No," I said, as I looked up at her. "Of course not."

I kept quiet for what seemed like several minutes.

"It's a heavy thing," I said finally. "The suggestion of, you know, some deep commitment, and I'm not ready. I'm not, and she knows it."

"She does?"

"Oh, yes. But she believes I'll grow. Improve. You know. And maybe she's right. Maybe I have a way to go before . . . Well, whatever."

She said, "Perhaps it's nothing more than she's looking for a gesture—a concession, if you will—that demonstrates your willingness to understand her perspective."

"I—"

She held up her slender hand, the gold pen.

"Or I would suggest Julie may believe those three words are a key to unlocking your natural reticence. I think it's worth exploring."

"So you think that the way I express myself indicates that I'm thinking about myself rather than her," I said, as I reached for the bottled water.

"Not necessarily. But I think it isn't out of the question that you can find a means of expression that is mutually satisfying," Harteveld replied.

I twisted the cap, removed it.

"I think it's a risk worth taking," she added.

She opened the folder again, scribbled on a sheet of yellow paper, the gold pen flitting across the page. When she finished she looked at me, smiled.

I spent the entire trip on the phone and, though none of my fellow passengers in the dining car on the Amtrak train to Philadelphia seemed to mind, I had the feeling I'd pressed the limits of civility.

"Too much?" I said to young woman behind the snack bar, as I slipped back into my navy-blue suit jacket and stepped toward the exit.

"We get all kinds," she replied as she continued to wipe the counter.

As the train wheezed into the 30th Street Station, people behind me were quickly wrapping up their phone conversations, putting away their laptops, grabbing their trench coats from the overhead racks. The rolling business lounge was about to empty. And then it would refill with a new collection of suits, this batch on their way to D.C.

I put a $5 bill in the plastic tip cup.

The Philadelphia sky was overcast, and the angular steel-and-glass buildings that surrounded the train station seemed dour and lifeless without the sun. A late-February storm had blanketed the East Coast from Boston to Baltimore with eight more inches of snow. Now, three weeks later, soiled heaps and mounds still clung to concrete columns, the sides of buildings. Salt stained the streets outside the train station.

I found a cab and asked the driver how long it'd take us to get to the courthouse at Sixth and Walnut.

"Ten," he said. He was a huge man, and the steering wheel pressed against his ample stomach.

"I'll need you for at least an hour," I said, as I redid the top button of my Oxford, tugged my yellow-and-navy club tie until it was tight against the collar.

He held out his hand, palm toward the gray sky.

I slipped him a $50 bill, and jumped into the cushy backseat.

I looked at my watch, and I told him I wanted to start at the courthouse, as close to the queue of limos as he could manage, and then circle Washington Square as best we could before rolling down Walnut Street.

Grunting his consent, he pulled the cab away from the curb, waving his arm at oncoming traffic instead of tapping the blinker.

He drove with his hands on the bottom half of the wheel, his arms pressed against his gut.

The limos were double-parked on Walnut Street in Center City, where businessmen, lawyers and politicians patronized some of the finest restaurants in the country, and the cabbie took his time as we cruised the 1500 block. I'd spoken to the reservations desks at ten of the restaurants, in some cases twice, first double-checking under the name Harold Finsterwald, once the city's premier criminal attorney, then under his name. I knew he'd spend the recess in one of these upscale places: While on call for The Surgeon's trial, he had Alfred Prendergast or one of his deputies take him to the MarkJoseph Steakhouse or the Bridge Café for his lunches, and Danube for the dinner on the night in between. Wine included, I doubted he'd had a meal that cost less than $200 while on retainer.

The 78-year-old Finsterwald was defending Millicent Chasen, the daughter-in-law of old Philadelphia money who was accused of trying to poison the woman with whom her husband had enjoyed a 12-year affair. Most of the evidence, according to *The Philadelphia Inquirer*'s Web site, was circumstantial, including the victim's testimony—which had to be delivered in writing because the injuries had destroyed her throat and vocal cords. The exception was Mrs. Chasen's fingerprints on the can of Drāno found in the trash that had been carted to the landfill from the Chasens' neighborhood. A sizable quantity of Drāno granules were found in the victim's jar of Brioschi, which bore a partial print from the defendant.

But Herbert Küsters said fingerprints were unreliable.

He once said that about five minutes before he smacked Julie across her lovely face.

Küsters was facing Finsterwald and, as I entered Le Bec-Fin, they were just about finished with their appetizers. The young blonde to Küsters's right was toying with a green salad with apricots, while the two men had enjoyed soup—their spoons sat in the gold-rimmed bowls. Finsterwald talked; Küsters and the blonde listened, and the sour-faced German seemed only mildly amused by the ancient attorney's anecdote.

Behind Küsters, golden fabric graced the walls above a banquette, and the clatter of silverware on china and genial conversation floated across the room, as did a sense of propriety, of Parisian-style luxury. Every table was taken, and few gold-embroidered seats were empty. Red wine flowed, and the guests relaxed.

I slipped in behind two men in dark suits, regulars

apparently, who were led to their seats by a pretty Frenchwoman, serious yet gracious, and I moved toward Finsterwald's table.

Küsters glanced at me and returned his gaze to the attorney, who continued his tale.

The seat directly in front of me was empty.

The blonde stared up at me, and she put her fork on the side of her plate.

"Yes?" she said, politely.

I drew back my right hand and, with as much force as I could muster, I brought my open palm across Küsters's left cheek.

The crack thundered throughout the restaurant.

Küsters spilled out of the chair and tumbled onto the pale-gold carpeting. His bread plate, knife and a crusty dinner roll fell on him.

The gasp I'd heard was replaced by a sudden silence.

As I stood over Küsters, glaring at him, breathing hard through my nose, Finsterwald reached and grabbed my right arm. I lifted my hand, and gently shook off the little gray-haired man.

"You know what that's for, don't you?" I said.

Küsters looked up at me, and he blinked.

A red welt was forming on the side of his face. Blood trickled onto his lip.

Finsterwald started to speak, but I nudged him away, grabbing his frail arm so he wouldn't fall.

As I adjusted my suit jacket, I said to him, "I'm walking away."

The lawyer was confused, and he looked at Küsters, at his blond deputy, then at me.

I said, "He'll tell you all about it."

I turned, passed the spiral staircase that led to the mezzanine, and went for the door.

No one tried to stop me.

The cabbie was waiting for me outside the restaurant. He was parked in front of a black stretch limo and behind a gleaming black sedan.

I jumped in, wriggled the tie down to half-mast, unbuttoned the collar.

"Back to the train station," I told him. "I'm going home."

He hung his arm out the window, waved it, and we eased into traffic and drove on.

After Terry and Diddio bickered briefly while working to prepare the Tilt for its conversion to the Tea Water Pump, Terry asked his former college roommate to "put on some music . . . cheer me up. Like you do." Here's what Diddio selected, songs that appeared on a CD he later burned for Bella that he called **Share** the Joy:

"Whistle While You Work"	NRBQ
"Flim"	Aphex Twin
"Theme from Ernest Borgnine"	Squarepusher
"Serpent's Dance"	Tauschen Sie
"Where's Johny Sabatino?"	Dzihan and Kamien
"Tended"	Viktor Krauss
"Sidewalk Blues"	The Dirty Dozen Jazz Band
"Jive at Five"	Count Basie
"Hound Dog"	Big Mama Thornton
"Wang Dang Doodle"	Koko Taylor
"Seeing Is Believing"	Bobby King and Terry Evans
"Get Rhythm"	Ry Cooder
"96 Tears"	Garland Jeffreys
"One Step Beyond"	Madness
"Bond with Bongos"	Sex Mob
"Jump Monk"	Charles Mingus
"Pockets on Fire "	Anna Ryder
"Whenever"	Beth Orton
"Two of Us"	Michael Penn and Aimee Mann